TESTIMONY

PAULA MARTINAC

PALM BEACH COUNTY

For queer teachers and students, past and present.

From the file of Dr. Virginia Rider

Excerpt from the Testimony of Miss Lee-Anne Blakeney,
sophomore, Baines College for Women,
to the Committee on Values and Moral Standards

Interview conducted by Arthur Burnside, Esq.,
Chief Counsel, Baines College for Women

Arthur Burnside: Were there any other instances that you recall Dr. Rider making you feel uncomfortable?

Lee-Anne Blakeney: Sometimes she touches your arm when she's talking to you, or maybe she puts a hand on your back. Other girls have mentioned it, too.

AB: When she does, is it different than, say, what a mother or aunt might do?

LB: A little, maybe.

AB: More like what a man might do?

LB: I guess.

AB: Tell me, did you notice this about the professor before the accusations against her came out? Could you speak up instead of shrugging?

LB: I may have, I'm not sure. But I did notice she was different. All the girls have. There's just never a man in her life, and she's pretty, you know?

PART I

Fall 1960

Chapter One

Gen

At just after nine o'clock, humidity licked the early September air. On the first floor of Waylon Hall, Gen Rider unlocked her office, a narrow space sealed like a tomb since classes ended in May. The air inside smothered her, and she recoiled.

Flies dive-bombed the screen as she lifted the heavy sash of the window that faced the verdant quad. The blue blades of her desk fan made a comforting swish but offered no relief, scattering dust motes and pushing around thick, stale air.

Gen undid the top two buttons of her linen blouse, which she'd ironed so meticulously the night before but that already showed every wrinkle and trickle of sweat. Her nylons itched, her brassiere pinched, and from the corners of her eyes she could see her dark pageboy frizzing. By 10 a.m., when her class on Civil War and Reconstruction commenced, her third-floor classroom in the old brick building would be an oven.

The noise of a car motor distracted her from trying to review her lecture notes, and she raised her venetian blind a few inches for a better view. The flashing red light belonged to one of the town's police cruisers, not campus security.

A strapping officer Gen had seen in town and a slender one who looked like he could have been the other's son slid out of the front seats and slammed their doors. Where they were headed wasn't immediately obvious. Their heads swiveled between Waylon and Timmons, home to the college art and theater departments. Squinting in the sun to read the building names, the older man motioned toward Timmons, and the two mounted the steps to the front door, leaving Gen's line of vision.

Fenton, she thought, and a bubble of fear caught in her throat.

She had spoken to him just a few days earlier, when she phoned to see if he was back from his Manhattan sojourn. He had spent most of his summer break subletting a tiny flat in Greenwich Village and "drinking up the culture," as he put it, and he was still ebullient. In a breathless rush, he had catalogued the names of the Broadway plays he'd attended, most of which she'd never heard of. When he came to the end of his list, her friend apologized for babbling and asked how her trip to the beach had gone. Gen couldn't form the words to tell him about the breakup with Carolyn, the lonely summer stuck in town, so she said, "Lots of news. I'll stop by the theater and tell you all about it."

Fenton had surely had other experiences in New York as well. He considered himself an adventurer, and he'd been looking forward to all the city had to offer to "fellas like me." Although he never talked specifics, Gen knew that during the school year Fenton drove to bars in different parts of the state. There was an outdoor area in Richmond called "The Block," where a man could meet up with other men for sexual encounters, but Fenton claimed he preferred the bars. Gen worried his adventures might someday catch him up, but her friend assured her he was always careful and had never come close to arrest.

"I don't use my real name," he said. "Everybody knows me as Fred."

Now Gen's eyes fixed on the squad car as she gulped in heavy air. She glanced from the window to her notes and back again, over and over, expecting to see Fenton escorted from the building in handcuffs.

But just before it was time to leave for class, the policemen emerged from Timmons by themselves. They each carried a cardboard box to their car and drove away without turning on their flasher.

Gen's heart slowed to a normal beat.

In her first class, she faced a roomful of wilting girls who fanned themselves dramatically with sheets of notebook paper. Most of the students at Baines College for Women hailed from well-to-do families and likely had artificially cooled homes they'd left reluctantly. It was also possible that reviewing the course content had heated them up.

"This is not the Civil War you know from *Gone with the Wind*," Gen had said as preface. "We won't talk about the Lost Cause of the Confederacy except to try to puncture that myth."

The class wasn't new to the history department's catalog, but Gen had completely revamped it since she had taught it two semesters earlier. She had held off introducing the revised version as well as a brand-new "History of the South" that closely examined Jim Crow until she secured tenure. Her mentor, Ruby Woods, a full professor in English, had advised the caution.

"I know you think it's your mission to teach our girls about the South's shortcomings," Ruby had said, "but why don't you hold off? A white woman researching Negro history already draws attention, so your teaching needs to be beyond reproach."

Gen outlined the semester's schedule for the girls and gave an overview of the reading material, some of it written by Negro scholars like W.E.B. Du Bois. The titles *The Souls of Black Folk* and *From Slavery to Freedom* made a few students shift uncomfortably in their seats, and a girl in a full skirt with daisy appliqués raised her hand tentatively.

Gen recognized her as Lee-Anne Blakeney, a history major who let everyone know her mother, an alumna, was a prominent donor to the college. Although she had been one of Gen's brightest students in a survey class, Lee-Anne tended to undercut her own intellectual abilities with a lot of Southern belle-style eyelash fluttering.

"Was it really so much about slavery, professor? In seventh

7

grade we learned that was a myth, that the war was more about states' rights." Lee-Anne fingered a lock of her strawberry blond hair.

Gen knew about the school textbooks authorized by the Virginia General Assembly, which also put forth lies about the "bonds of affection" between slaves and masters.

"Well, Miss Blakeney, give me the semester and we'll see if we can't dis—supplement what you learned as children."

She'd almost said "dislodge what you learned" but thought better of it. At the word "children," Margaret Sutter, another history major who always sat in front, chuckled quietly, and Lee-Anne shot an annoyed glance in her direction.

"What I think you'll come to see," Gen continued, "is that you can't understand the war *without* a thorough discussion of slavery."

Lee-Anne let her wavy hair fall over her eyes as she earnestly scribbled into her notebook.

Before she dismissed them, Gen ended with a note about her expectations. "This is an intellectually rigorous class, girls. Those of you who've studied with me before know I demand full commitment. You'll be expected to participate." The warning was aimed at students inclined to drop a class that seemed too demanding or too focused on issues they didn't want to bother about, like the plight of Negroes.

Back in her office, Gen left her door open in hopes of a cross breeze. There wasn't time in her schedule to check on Fenton, so she hunched over her notes for her next class, making last-minute adjustments. A familiar voice cut through her thoughts.

"Hello, you."

"You're back!"

Ruby Woods and her husband, Darrell, made it a practice to escape to their cabin in the West Virginia mountains for the summer. Now Gen's friend and mentor stood in the open doorway, burdened with a load of mail and books. The English Department was situated upstairs on the second floor, and during the school year Ruby made a habit of dropping by Gen's office a few times a week to check in.

"You have a good couple of months?"

"Not particularly. I meant to finish my chapter on Ovington's meeting with Du Bois, but—"

Gen stopped short. Ruby had voiced concerns about her research on the founding of the NAACP more than once, worrying that Gen's department would view it as too radical to recommend she get tenure. But Gen had squeaked by anyway, securing tenure in the spring, and she wasn't sure if Ruby would continue to raise warning flags.

She didn't. After a pause, she said, "Writer's block?"

Gen shrugged. "Something like that."

"Did you at least have some fun?" Ruby cocked her head. "I don't see that tan you usually come back with."

"No fun either, sad to say." Gen shuffled some papers so she wouldn't have to look directly at Ruby.

"Too bad. After your tenure triumph, you deserved a few months to recoup. You know what they say about all work and no play."

Gen shifted the conversation deftly back to Ruby. "You're one to talk. I bet you left Darrell on his own to fish while you finished one article and started another."

Ruby's sly smile suggested Gen had hit the mark. "Well, how about these two workhorses have a quick lunch after our twelve o'clocks and catch each other up?"

Gen hesitated. Catching up with Ruby brought complications. Her mentor had watched out for her, advised on her academic career, surrounded her with support. Still, for all Ruby knew, Gen was just a determined career woman who eschewed romantic relationships, and Carolyn was a similarly unmarried colleague whom Gen traveled with. Ruby never remarked on Gen's frequent trips to Richmond, where Carolyn lived. "Research at the State Library," Gen claimed, to explain them away. Ruby had no idea that the other tale Gen had spun, about a fiancé who died on Utah Beach, had been concocted to shut down speculation about her private life.

If Ruby started asking too many questions about why her

9

summer had fizzled, Gen might cry outright and divulge things she didn't mean to. All summer long, there'd been no one to spill her grief to. Most of her friends had been part of Carolyn's circle. No matter how many fun evenings they'd shared with Gen over the years, the women had retreated to the shadows of her now-former life. The pain of it all still bubbled inside Gen like stew on a slow simmer.

So, as much as she craved company and conversation, Gen begged off from Ruby's invitation, saying she was swamped. "How about early next week?" she suggested, knowing that the raincheck might slip from Ruby's busy mind. "I'll call you."

Ruby gave Gen a skeptical sideways look. "That sounds fine. We'd probably just spend it talking about Mark, anyway."

"Mark?"

Ruby's face turned grave. "Patton. You didn't hear? It was the lead story in the morning paper."

"I skipped breakfast." The *Springboro Gazette* was folded in her briefcase, to be perused at lunch.

Gen knew the college art gallery director casually, through Fenton. Mark had been at Baines a few years. She'd fallen into a conversation about modern art with him at a cocktail party at Fenton's apartment—the place was so small they were squeezed in next to each other—but that was probably last fall. She suspected he and Fenton had had a "thing," her friend's word for love affairs, by the easy way they joked and touched each other's arms.

"He was arrested in the park." Ruby coughed discreetly. "With . . . another man. A Negro."

"Oh! Poor Mark."

"He's been fired, of course."

"A police car was at Timmons this morning," Gen said. "Do you think that's related?"

Ruby had been hovering in the doorway, but now she stepped into the office and closed the door behind her, resting her books on the corner of Gen's desk. She took a dramatic breath. "It's likely. Apparently, they raided his apartment and confiscated . . .

personal material. They must have come to look in his office, too. There's some sort of police investigation being launched."

Gen's stomach burned as if someone had struck a match in it. "It's all so sordid. Mark always seemed like a lovely man. A confirmed bachelor, for sure, but his private life should be his own, shouldn't it? I would have never suspected something like *this*. I hope—"

Ruby let her sentence drop off, but Gen guessed she was hoping something about their mutual friend, Fenton. The administration tolerated its effete theater director because he knew how to style wigs and apply theatrical makeup, and was a student favorite. His productions drew audiences from Roanoke and Staunton, raising revenue for the college. But all that would mean nothing if he was caught in a public scandal.

Ruby picked up her books. "Well, I'm sorry to start the day on such a sour note. I hope the rest of it is cheerier for us both."

After her second class, Gen called Fenton in the theater, but he was skittish and said he couldn't talk. First-day pandemonium, he claimed. He was the lone drama teacher at the college, who also cast and directed all the school plays, managing students from both Baines and its brother college, Davis and Lee. Gen waited until she was packed up to head home, then dropped in at the theater to gauge for herself how her friend was holding up under the weight of the news about Mark.

She tagged along behind him through the theater wings as he took inventory of props that might suit for the fall production of *Charley's Aunt*. He'd lost some weight since she'd last seen him. Slender to begin with, now his jacket hung off him loosely, like a teenager who had borrowed his father's clothes.

"Hon, you don't want to be seen with me right now." He glanced around, as if spies might be hiding in the scenery and props. "It's not safe."

The fear she had felt when Ruby told her about Mark resurfaced as a catch in her throat. "Are you and Mark . . . involved?"

Fenton continued to inspect the props, making notes on his check list, but she saw a flicker of pain in his hazel eyes. "No names, please." After a pause, he continued, "It's been over for a while."

She waited, but he didn't elaborate.

"Well, what say you come for barbecue on Saturday? We'll try to forget what's happening and have a gay old time."

He winced at the word *gay* but allowed, "I did miss barbecue up north. Count me in."

"You could bring me flowers," she suggested. "Everybody will think we finally fell in love."

"What they'll think is you finally lost your mind. Given up all hope of finding a *normal* man."

She lowered her voice. "Little do they know I only like *abnormal* men like you."

He put down a china vase he'd been assessing and turned toward her with a pinched look. "Gen, you realize how serious this is."

"I know."

"They caught five men. They won't stop there." Fenton forced his trembling hand into his jacket pocket. "I had a nightmare about Mark last night. I told him *so* many times how risky his behavior was, parks and tearooms and such, but did he listen? And it turns out he was doing it with a Negro behind Big Beau, for God's sake!"

She flinched at the dismissive mention of Mark's Negro lover. She never took Fenton for a bigot, but he was so upset, this wasn't the time to press the issue. The town's venerable shrine to the Confederate dead featured the names of local soldiers engraved along its base, plus the battles they served in. It took its nickname from the bronze statue mounted on the pedestal of an officer on a prancing horse—almost as majestic as Robert E. Lee on Monument Avenue in Richmond. Before Gen was born, the Daughters of the Confederacy had raised the funds to honor Colonel Wylie Beauregard Thoms of the 10th Virginia Cavalry, who lost his life in the Battle of the Wilderness. Many of his descendants still lived in the Springboro area, including the History Department's Henry Thoms.

"So you never—"

"No! I always play it safe."

She wasn't sure how "safe" it could be, frequenting bars in Richmond, but she couldn't point that out with Fenton so distraught.

"Sometimes I think gay girls have it easier," he said. "You don't *have* to meet up in bathrooms where the person in the next stall might be an undercover cop."

Gen bristled. "Yeah, women have it so easy, being invisible to each other! Or we might risk everything coming on to a colleague who turns out to be horrified by our very existence. Or some girl we teach could get angry about her grade and—"

"Touché." Fenton sighed and scratched something off in his notes. "Thank God you've got Carolyn. That must be a comfort."

She blurted out the barest facts of the breakup while they perched on uncomfortable, wrought iron chairs with tags that read, "Earnest/Spr 59"—props from an Oscar Wilde production that had drawn huge crowds.

"I truly don't know what to say." Fenton rubbed the palm of her hand in a soothing way. "Except that I never much liked her."

Gen stiffened. "You barely knew her."

"That's right, she never *deigned* to come to you, always making you travel to her. Selfish and self-centered, if you ask me."

"It was my choice," Gen said. "Richmond was safer for us than a town where everybody knows everybody's business."

"Still, I saw her maybe twice in what—five years?"

"Six. Which gave you plenty of time to let me know what you really thought, *friend*."

"I couldn't tell you the truth. You were so much in love."

Gen let go of the anger that had flared in her. Many times, she'd kept her opinions close to the vest with friends, too.

"Love," she said with a shrug. "That's something I won't be rushing back into."

Their heads swerved at the sound of light footsteps coming

from the direction of the stage. Fenton dropped her hand, his eyes widening, and leapt to his feet. Gen was surprised to see one of her students emerge from the shadows, clutching what looked like a script.

"Oh, I'm sorry, Mr. Page! Dr. Rider! Did I get the audition time wrong?"

Fenton fished out his gold pocket watch. "I'd say so. We won't start until at least four-thirty."

"Sorry. It's my first time going out for school play."

"Well, you're welcome to take a seat in the orchestra, Miss—"

"Margaret Sutter. I think I'll just come back later." Margaret mumbled another apology and slunk out the way she had entered.

Fenton clicked his tongue. Gen wasn't sure what bothered her fastidious friend more, the girl's earliness or the fact that she'd come backstage uninvited.

"Margaret's one of my advisees," Gen said. "Always comes to office hours. She's a good egg, but she can get underfoot."

Fenton's face registered annoyance. "I don't like them skulking around. Eavesdropping, even. What were we talking about when she showed up?"

Gen raised her eyebrows. "I believe you were telling me how very much you disliked Carolyn."

His cheeks colored. "I'm sorry, hon, I shouldn't have—"

"I'm teasing, Fenton. Feel free to hate Carolyn as much as you want." She cast a look at her wristwatch as she stood to leave. "Anyway, I don't think the girl could have heard much. Maybe she saw you holding my hand and will tell everyone we're a couple."

He expelled his relief with a burst of laughter. "Ah, yes, but a couple of what?"

Gen arrived home after a long day of teaching and didn't bother to kick her shoes off before fixing a frosty gin and tonic. Talking and engaging for so many hours had both worn her out and energized her. She wouldn't soon forget how her students' eyes blinked double-time as they flipped the pages of her syllabi. She guessed some would drop the class before the next meeting, intimidated by the long reading and assignment list. Her ideal would be a tight group of history majors engaged with the material.

When she was finally in her armchair, feet up, G&T in hand, she took the still-unread morning paper from her briefcase and read the story about Mark with its headline designed to titillate: "POLICE ROUND UP LOCAL HOMOSEXUALS." The subhead implicated the college: "Arrested Men Include Baines Instructor."

Gen didn't recognize any of the names except Mark's. One man was picked up in the public restroom of Town Hall, unwittingly exposing himself to an undercover officer. Cops found two other men in a parked car in an alley behind a bar. But Mark's arrest near Big Beau with a Negro named James Combs received the most attention as a "desecration of our historic monument," according to the mayor.

Gen realized she wanted nothing more than to tell Carolyn everything that had happened, both at school and in town. Sharing their days had been a routine, and Gen had the long-distance phone bills to prove it.

Her eyes drifted to the telephone bench. She didn't mean to, but she found herself calling the operator in Towson, Maryland. "Carolyn Weeden, please. I don't know the street." There were three Weedens in the town, but only one with the first initial *C.*

Gen's fingers brushed the receiver. She picked it up again, took a long breath, and dialed Carolyn's number. Before the second ring, she hung up.

She kept thinking about the number as she cracked an egg for dinner and finished her second drink, then picked at her scrambled egg while standing at the counter.

After rinsing her plate, she dialed a second time.

"Hello?" It wasn't Carolyn's voice, but it sounded familiar. "Is anyone there?"

Gen dropped the receiver into the cradle with a *thunk*.

She'd had her suspicions about how quickly Carolyn had gotten the job at Goucher College and why she'd accepted a three-year lecturer contract with no hope of tenure. The call seemed to confirm her worst fears. There was someone else, a woman whose voice Gen thought she recognized but hoped she didn't. She flopped onto the seat of the telephone bench and wallowed in images from a shared past she had mistaken for happy.

Gen had met Carolyn at the annual conference of the Southern Historical Association in 1954. By then, Gen had toiled as a lowly lecturer at Baines for ten years—hired during the war when male faculty were scarce—and had just been promoted to assistant professor. SHA included many Northern-trained scholars among its members, some of whom were friends from the graduate program at Ohio State, and it seemed like the right fit. The organization's conference in Columbia, South Carolina, counted among its speakers some of the most progressive historians of the time. They weren't much older than Gen, but their work left her starstruck.

When Gen arrived, she had found the Hotel Columbia swarming with men. She gravitated quickly to the first woman she found—Carolyn, a lecturer at a women's college in Richmond.

"I've counted five skirts so far," Carolyn had quipped. "You bring it up to six." They moved together like conjoined twins, spending much of the weekend laughing over cocktails about the men who asked where their husbands taught.

Carolyn had shared Gen's passion for socially conscious history, but there was an undercurrent of something else running between them, too. No romance bloomed at the conference, but they exchanged plenty of deep, searching looks. Back in their respective towns, their letters and phone calls crescendoed with suggested passion: "When will I see you again? Has it really just been a few weeks?" and "I don't think I can wait until next

November to see those eyes!" Within days of receiving a note signed "Missing you so much it hurts—C," Gen had crossed the state and climbed into Carolyn's bed.

Now the pain of Carolyn's departure lodged in her chest, festering into resentment. She and Carolyn were supposed to be a team—for life. How could Carolyn betray her? And how would Gen ever find someone new, when meeting Carolyn had been serendipity?

Her self-pity finally tired her, and she pulled herself up from the bench and dried her eyes. *I am fine on my own*, she thought. She didn't need love right now. Instead, she could concentrate on building her friendships. She picked up the phone a third time, but this time she dialed Ruby to set a date for lunch.

Chapter Two

Gen

A handful of students lingered behind after Gen's Civil War class, surrounding her desk. She was accustomed to this post-class "ring around the rosie," as Ruby jokingly dubbed it. Students rarely showed up for her established office hours, choosing instead to pepper her with questions about assignments and readings as she packed up her own notes and books to vacate the classroom for the next professor.

Margaret Sutter hovered to the side of the room until the other girls had left. She said she had a thesis statement for her theme paper and wondered if Gen would take a look at it, even though office hours were over for the week.

"Your first paper's not due till midterm, Margaret," Gen said warily. "Wouldn't you like to wait and see what all your options are?"

The girl bit her top lip. "I like to start my papers as soon as possible," Margaret explained, "in case I run into problems. I have a lot on my plate this term."

You're an A student, Gen thought but didn't say. She didn't want to trivialize the girl's earnest approach to her studies, which Gen recognized from her own college days.

With Margaret in tow, Gen moved into the hallway, where Lee-Anne Blakeney was whispering with Susanna Carr, who was also in the class. Given Lee-Anne's reservations about studying slavery in such depth, Gen had hoped the girl would drop, but she appeared to be soldiering on. Lee-Anne caught Gen's eye and chirped, "See you next time, professor!" but her eyes settled on Margaret and not her teacher.

Gen nodded to Lee-Anne while she continued talking to Margaret. "Walk me back to my office?"

Margaret's face lit at the invitation, and they descended to the first floor in tandem.

What Gen's office lacked in size, it made up for in coziness. She had installed an Oriental rug from her parents' house and two lamps so she didn't have to read by fluorescent light. With the help of the janitor, she'd covered every inch of the walls with framed photos of forest trails, waterfalls, and sandy beaches—all from trips she'd taken with Carolyn, all carefully curated so her lover never appeared in any of them.

From the corner of her eye, Gen noticed Margaret assessing the collection.

"I've probably said this before but your photos are beautiful," Margaret commented as she sat waiting for Gen to organize her books and papers.

"Thanks. I took most of them."

"Gosh, really? I'd love to know how to take pictures as good as these. You must have a terrific camera. I still have a stupid Brownie I got for my twelfth birthday."

"I do have a very good camera." The Leica counted among her prized possessions, an extravagant Christmas present from Carolyn their first full year together.

"How did you learn to use it?"

"A patient friend taught me." Carolyn sprang to mind again, the unhurried way she'd guided Gen's hands on the camera body. Gen rolled her shoulders to dispel the memory. "Now, Margaret, tell me about your idea."

Margaret drew a typed sheet from a folder for Gen. "I get nervous sometimes when I have to talk, tongue-tied almost. So I wrote it down."

"You do very well speaking in class, though."

Margaret shrugged. "I have to force myself. Some of the girls here are, well, snobby and judgmental about all sorts of things, like when they think you're talking too much or too loud."

Gen had witnessed the behavior in her classes, occasional flashes of annoyance from girls who deemed forcefulness and inquisitiveness too "male." In high school, Gen and Laurette Sparks had helped each other develop public voices to match any man's in strength. They practiced in Gen's bedroom, projecting speeches to the far corners of the room. "Did you say something?" became their private joke when one of them resorted to a wispy voice.

Margaret's face flushed as she continued, "But you . . . you make it easier to speak up, Dr. Rider."

Gen always advised her students to rid themselves of their "Aunt Pittypat" voices, the reference to the skittish character from *Gone with the Wind* always filling the classroom with giggles. Most of them ignored her recommendation, though. "Boys don't like girls with loud voices," she'd heard more than once, but a smattering of students, like Margaret, heeded her advice.

"Well, let's get to this thesis statement, shall we?" Gen said to cover her embarrassment at the compliment.

She bent over Margaret's typed sheet, her pen following the words. Each semester, she waited for the student who sparkled with new insights, but Margaret's idea was as unpolished as an old shoe. Gen sat back in her chair and laid her glasses across the sheet of paper.

"The battle of Antietam is certainly a solid choice," she said. "You're interested in military maneuvers, I take it?"

Confusion flitted across Margaret's face. "Isn't that what the Civil War is? Battles and such?"

"It can be, of course. But there are plenty of other topics that might interest you as we progress through the semester. Social or economic or even cultural topics. No need to tie yourself down so early, even if it's a busy semester."

Margaret nodded. "I have so many extracurricular activities, though," she pointed out. "The history honors society, for one. I'd love to submit something for the national conference. And you saw me at the theater, trying out for the school play? I got a callback." She blushed again.

"Well, that's wonderful, Margaret. I'll keep my fingers crossed for you."

"Thanks, but being in a play can be pretty time-consuming. I'm not sure why I did it. I thought maybe I'd make some friends." Margaret's hands twisted in her lap, and Gen felt a pang of sympathy. College had been a lonely experience for her, too, commuting from her parents' house every day and never having much in common with girls who treated it like finishing school.

"Making friends can be hard," Gen acknowledged. "You just need to find your tribe."

Margaret sighed. "The problem is, I don't know who my tribe is."

This seemed like a longer conversation, one that would force Gen into the role of counselor rather than professor. She aimed to keep a professional distance. "Be friendly, not a friend," was her motto.

Gen deftly steered the conversation to a more professional track. "Give it time, Margaret. You're doing the right things to meet people. Now, about your paper. It might be easier going with a topic you're really engaged with. For example, if you're interested in photography, I could see you focusing on Matthew Brady's work or on war photographs in general. It was the first war documented so thoroughly in photos."

She stood and located a volume on one of her shelves: *The Civil War Through the Camera*. Another present from Carolyn. Gen opened the cover to make sure the endpaper didn't bear a private inscription meant for her eyes only, but there was just her floral-printed book plate with the words "This Book Belongs To" and her name in swirling black ink.

21

"I don't think our library has this, but you're welcome to borrow my copy."

"Oh, my gosh! Thank you, Dr. Rider."

"It was a gift, so please don't spill anything on it. I'll make a note that I lent it to you."

"I'll guard it with my life."

"No need to die for it," Gen said with a smile.

"This is just so—" Margaret shook her head repeatedly, fumbling for words to capture her emotion. She had told Gen on another occasion that she aspired to be a college professor—"like you, at a girls' school just like this one"—so maybe she felt she'd been admitted to a private club.

Gen handed the typed sheet back to Margaret without any markings on it, but the girl refused it and made no move to leave. Instead, Margaret settled in her chair like she was readying for an extended gab session with a friend. "Oh, you can toss that," she said. "I can't believe I came up with such a silly topic when there's so much else to talk about. Could you tell me more about Matthew Brady, Dr. Rider?"

Gen stood to end the meeting, running a hand down the side of her slim skirt to smooth it. "Now, I can't do your work for you, Margaret. That's for you to research. I do hope you enjoy the book."

Margaret stared at her in surprise for a moment, then gathered up her books and left with an apology for taking too much of her time.

A brown paper lunch bag tied with satiny pink ribbon nestled in her department mailbox late that afternoon. No tag, no note. Inside was a small stash of Hershey's kisses, already starting to soften in the heat.

The secretary told Gen she didn't know how the bag got there. "So many people in and out," the young woman said over the clack of her typewriter keys. "Could have been anyone."

It wasn't the first time a Baines girl had given Gen candy or another token of affection, but crushes had been more frequent when she was a young instructor closer to her students in age. Now forty-two with strands of gray in her hair and tortoise-shell reading glasses, Gen assumed her students all viewed her as a dour old lady.

And the suggestion behind a gift of "kisses" unnerved her slightly. She was still staring at the bag with a mix of confusion and concern when her colleague Henry Thoms passed directly behind her to fetch his own mail from the box below hers. He was so close she caught a whiff of his Old Spice.

"Secret admirer?" he asked.

Gen noted the hint of sarcasm in his patrician voice, the way "secret" sounded almost dirty. Thoms was not a fan of hers and may very well have voted against her tenure. She would never know for sure as those votes were confidential, but she had once overheard him tut-tutting to the chairman. "All that Negro nonsense. As if there weren't more worthy subjects for research. Really, it tarnishes the department." Although she hadn't heard her name on Thoms's tongue, no one else in the department qualified as a scholar of "Negro nonsense."

Gen extended the bag toward Thoms. She reckoned teasing was the best way to deal with her nemesis, the highest-ranking history faculty member after the chairman. "Perhaps these kisses were meant for you, Henry. I've gotten your mail by mistake before. Help yourself."

Thoms smiled and reached into the bag. "Perhaps just one." He unwrapped the foil and plopped the sweet into his mouth.

She was about to leave but Thoms engaged her again. "Heard you're assigning that Woodward book this term, Virginia. The Jim Crow one." He never used her nickname, insisting that her given name was so much more fitting and elegant.

Gen winced at his perfunctory reference to a distinguished text. "I am indeed," she replied, though she wondered how he knew. She hadn't discussed her syllabus with anyone in the department, so news about her required reading must have reached Thoms from a student—another unsettling thought. "It's definitive on the decades after Reconstruction."

Thoms shrugged. "The jury's still out on that," he said, wiping traces of the soft chocolate from his mouth with his handkerchief. "I've a mind to write a review of his new one. Southern history as a *burden*, indeed."

She pursed her lips, holding her thoughts in. Did he also know that *she* planned to write a review? Thoms enjoyed provoking her, but she refused to take the bait. "Another kiss for the road, Henry?"

He waved off the offer. "Wouldn't want Mrs. Thoms to smell it on my breath."

"Well, you give her my very best."

Gen escaped with her mail and the bag of kisses before Thoms could get in another combative word. She intended to save the candy for Halloween, but instead she ate the chocolate drops one by one throughout the weekend.

Chapter Three

Fenton

In summer and early fall, Fenton's flat reminded him of a tree-house. The rooms huddled on the top floor of a stately old home, and leafy willow oak branches brushed the windows, shielding him from the rest of the world. He'd become accustomed to thinking of his space as a haven from prying eyes.

Until Mark Patton was arrested and the Springboro mayor announced a crackdown on "vice." The police had raided Mark's apartment and office and carted off whatever they fancied they needed to prove their case against him. Mark's landlord had changed the locks, leaving him sleeping on a friend's couch after he made bail. He called to ask Fenton if he could stay a night or two with him. "Till I can get something more permanent." What worried Fenton was that the "permanent" place might be state prison.

"It's awfully cramped up here, old chap, as you know." His compact apartment was a combination living room-bedroom with a double hot plate for meals and a bathroom the size of a closet. During their four-month affair, he and Mark had spent most of their evenings at Mark's roomier one-bedroom. "And my couch is so hideously uncomfortable; well, you can barely call it a couch at all."

A sigh traveled from Mark's end of the line. "You don't need to make up excuses, Fen. I've heard them all, and I get it. The thing is, I'm not allowed to leave town and nobody wants to associate with me. I implicated the friends who posted bail for me just by getting in touch with them. I'd be better off back in the town jail."

"Don't say that. No one's better off in that hole." Guilt hit Fenton like a punch in the gut, and he considered relenting. If he snuck Mark up the back stairs late at night, maybe. Or would Gen take him in for a night? She had a spare room with a comfy sofa bed, but Mark and Gen knew each other only casually, and it was a lot to ask.

After an awkward pause in which Fenton didn't offer anything, Mark's tone switched to resigned. "I do need to tell you something. And not on the phone."

Mark suggested they meet in the town library, and Fenton hesitated. Two years earlier, toying with the possibility of changing what he called his "habits," he'd had a handful of chaste dates with the children's librarian, a World War II widow about Gen's age. He abruptly stopped calling her when he realized the folly of it and had avoided the library ever since. But the children's room sat at the back of the library, and he reasoned he could hurry to another floor without the woman spotting him.

Fenton proposed a spot in the stacks on the third floor, past the dustiest genealogical materials that no one but the town historian ever consulted. In another time, he and Mark would have hugged each other upon meeting up. Now Fenton kept his arms at his sides, as did Mark, like strangers who just happened to arrive in the deserted stacks at the same moment.

Mark's face looked gray, and circles ringed his eyes. He swiped his hand across his face. "I know I look like shit."

"You've been through a lot."

Mark came to the point in a whisper. "Listen, Fen, the police took a lot of stuff from my apartment. Some things that might affect guys like you. I thought you should know."

Fenton's mind raced through the possibilities. Mark had

amassed a stunning collection of beefcake photo magazines with names like *Physique Pictorial* and *Tomorrow's Man*. He had spent a small fortune on the literature, buying it on trips to New York and Greece, and he shared it liberally with friends.

Did Mark ever take photos of him? Not that he recalled. They never wrote each other notes or letters. No need, as they worked in the same building and could steal moments between classes to arrange assignations.

"I don't see how your collection could affect me—"

A shuffling noise made Mark's eyes dart over Fenton's head. Fenton automatically grabbed the nearest tome from a shelf and opened it. The words blurred in front of him. From the corner of his eye, he saw the ancient town historian making his way to his usual carrel without even registering their presence.

Mark grabbed Fenton's arm and pulled him further into the stacks, his voice a hush. "The magazines won't damn anyone but me. I'm talking about my diaries."

Fenton's hands went cold. He had forgotten Mark catalogued his love affairs like museum artifacts.

"I used code names. You're Georgia, for your home state." Mark reddened. "But—well, I may have written about the time we had the quickie in the men's dressing room at the theater."

Fenton's stomach lurched. He remembered the incident well. He had stayed behind after all the students left a performance of *The Importance of Being Earnest*. The young actors and actresses were never careful about props, and Fenton liked to keep everything neat. Mark had attended the show and followed him backstage. They fumbled their way to the dressing room, where Mark suggested he wear the top hat that was lying out, casually discarded by the student who played one of the leads.

"God, Mark! You *may* have? Did you or didn't you?"

"I'm sorry, Fen. I did."

"Why would you do that?"

Mark's mood shifted from contrition to annoyance. "Well, why do you think? It was thrilling. One of my more memorable encounters on campus."

For Fenton, the dressing room incident was a one-off, and he wondered how many "encounters" Mark had enjoyed in academic buildings. Fenton cleared his throat to cover his frustration that Mark had put the small homosexual community at Baines at such high risk.

"Well, I trust you didn't write about our *encounter* at any length."

Mark's shrug didn't reassure. "How was I to know my diaries would land in the Springboro Police Department someday?"

"You're a homosexual, for God's sake," Fenton hissed. "Your private life is up for grabs."

Fenton's thoughts drifted to his own personal possessions. He didn't keep diaries, but he had a stash of books under the bed, as well as an envelope stuffed with sentimental letters from a man who had started as a friend and mentor but metamorphosed into more.

"Are you sure the police can just take your things like that? Is it even legal?"

"That's the sixty-four-thousand-dollar question. I wish I knew the answer. Hopefully, I'll find a lawyer who does."

Fenton watched Mark's hand reach over and come to rest on his jacket sleeve. He'd been a tender lover, although they never fell in love. He knew Mark hadn't meant him harm, but he could be harmed just the same.

"I wouldn't worry. I did give you a woman's name after all."

"It's a little late not to worry."

Mark's recklessness was the main reason Fenton had ended their affair after a few months. Neither expected or wanted an exclusive relationship, but when Mark had sex with other men, he stayed in town instead of traveling to Richmond or beyond, like Fenton did. No matter how discreet Fenton was, he could be dragged into Mark's pursuit of thrills.

"What were you thinking?" Fenton continued. "At Big Beau of all places!" A white man having sex with a Negro exacerbated the situation, but he stopped short of pointing out the obvious.

Mark blew out a long breath and skirted the question. "Anyhoo," Mark said, "I should let you go. I just wanted you to be on your toes, given our history."

"Right," Fenton said.

"You'll probably be fine. Hey, I'm not sure cops can even read." Mark's attempted levity fell flat.

Fenton hastened back to his office with a tightness in his chest. He tried to rub it away with his fist but couldn't. When he passed a couple of students, they greeted him with wide eyes, as if he were beating his breast.

Maybe the police wouldn't catch on at first; maybe the woman's name would throw them off. But they might eventually figure out that no one would have access to the locked men's dressing room but the theater director.

On stage, Fenton took his accustomed seat at the head of the long folding table with his script in hand. Now that *Charley's Aunt* was cast he'd assembled the players for a table read. His productions were always a mix of talent from Baines and the men's college, Davis and Lee, which didn't have its own drama department.

Reading the first pages went as choppily as he expected. He squirmed at their appalling British accents but didn't correct them. The Shakespeare man in the English Department would volunteer as vocal coach, as he had in past productions.

As Act One progressed, the cast grew more accustomed to their roles and the read fell into an easier rhythm—until Andrew, one of the male leads, stumbled over the part where his character talked about wearing a woman's costume for a stage role.

"What are you playing?" the student in the role of Jack cued him.

"A lady—an old lady— and I'm going to try on the things before—" Andrew stopped mid-line, his eyes popping.

Fenton tapped his pencil. "What is it, Andrew?"

29

"I don't have to *wear* lady's clothes onstage, do I?"

He'd worked with Andrew in other comedies, including *The Importance of Being Earnest*. The young man had got the role of Babbs because he exhibited a strong sense of comic timing and an ability to handle pratfalls with ease.

"Of course you do. It's a major plot point that Babbs impersonates Charley's aunt. How could you miss that?"

Andrew blinked rapidly. "I'm sorry, sir. I guess I haven't read the whole play yet."

Students around the table chuckled. Fenton hissed for them to be quiet, then turned what he hoped was a calm face toward the young actor. "Andrew, old chap, you won't actually *look* like a lady. You'll look silly. It's high farce, not *Romeo and Juliet*. Here, read the stage directions. 'He still walks, talks and moves like a man, and never attempts to act the woman.'"

"Yes, sir. I just don't know how I—" Andrew's voice grew fainter and fainter.

"Cross-dressing on stage enjoys a long tradition, Andrew. And as you know, because we have more male roles than female in this production, we have a girl playing Barrett." Fenton nodded toward Margaret Sutter, the history major who had surprised Gen and him backstage the first week of classes. She sat directly to his right—a chair students often hesitated to take. "Margaret seems to have no objection to dressing in men's clothes to be our Barrett."

The girl's face colored bright crimson, and her eyes fell to the table. When he heard a few more titters down the row, Fenton regretted singling her out.

"So, Andrew, can we move on now?"

Andrew whispered something to the boy to his left. His friend, cast as Charley, offered an explanation. "A girl dressing up is different, sir. Andy's worried about playing a … a fruit."

Fenton's hands tightened on his armrests. "I won't tolerate such language, Jim. And how you've reached that conclusion about Babbs is beyond me. He's in love with Ela Delahay. Have you never seen the movie with Jack Benny?"

Blank faces stared back at him, and Fenton felt his age. The movie had been released back in the early '40's, when he was in high school and these students were in diapers.

"The part is played for laughs," Fenton continued. "You'll do splendidly, Andrew, and get several curtain calls, I'm sure."

Andrew looked unconvinced. "But Mr. Page, I mean, the mayor and the police are hunting down fr— homosexuals."

"Babbs is *not* a h-homosexual!" Fenton tripped over the word, his childhood stutter getting the best of him. He wasn't sure he'd ever said it aloud like that, in front of so many people.

Slow down, he told himself.

"So you're too young to have seen the movie version. How about *Some Like It Hot?* You've seen that?" Heads bobbed in recognition, even Andrew's and Jim's. "Well, I defy you to tell me that wasn't a funny movie. If stars like Jack Lemmon and Tony Curtis can wear women's clothing in the service of plot, I'm guessing a student actor can, too."

A hush engulfed the stage.

"If anyone wants to drop out, I can't stop you. But if you do— well, those of you with theatrical ambitions? In New York or Hollywood, you won't have the luxury of turning down parts." He glared directly at Andrew, whom he knew intended to try his luck at acting after college.

Fenton stood up, buttoning his jacket as if ready to leave and then unbuttoning it. When he dabbed away his sweat with his hanky, his fingers grazed his neck, which was alarmingly hot to the touch. A faint hum echoed in his ears. He needed to sit down again but froze in place.

Margaret's clear voice pierced the noise in his brain. "Sir, why don't we take five?" A few students at the table coughed, but she persisted. "I'm sorry, isn't that what directors say?"

The sensible suggestion made it possible to think, and the hum receded. Margaret would have been a good stage manager, better than the girl he'd chosen.

"Yes. Yes, it is, Margaret, thank you. Actually, we'll take ten. That means ten minutes. Walk around, stretch, get a cookie from the tray. Decide if you want to remain in the play. If you aren't sure you'll return after the break, please leave your script at your place for your understudy."

Fenton escaped to his office under the stage. From his top desk drawer, he fished out his Pall Malls and lighter. He pictured the half-full pint of Jim Beam in the bottom drawer, but he left that in place. As he puffed, the smoke circled him like a hug.

When he returned to the stage, he took silent inventory of the actors and actresses. To his amazement, they were all in place, scripts open.

"All right, then," he said, with the warmest smile he could summon, "let's pick up where we left off."

Chapter Four

Ruby

Every academic year since V-J Day, Ruby had noted the increasing number of male faculty replacing women who either retired or left to start families. She founded her women's faculty group in response to the disturbing trend. The women who remained at Baines found it harder and harder to secure tenure and promotion. When someone did, like Gen, it was cause for celebration.

They met once a month in Ruby's living room, a light-drenched space created by tearing down a wall that had separated two smaller, stuffier rooms. Twenty years back, she and Darrell had rescued the Queen Anne house from hard times and, room by room, restored it to glory. Across the street, the Blakeneys' house matched theirs in every exterior detail but its crisp yellow color, like spring forsythias; Ruby preferred their plain white. A nineteenth-century logging baron had built the twin houses for his daughters, and more than sixty years later, everyone in town still referred to them as "The Two Sisters." Not that Ruby felt very sisterly toward Amanda Blakeney.

On the buffet Darrell had arranged a plate of tollhouse cookies, a coffee urn, and cups. He'd put out a bottle of champagne to toast Gen's promotion. As usual, Gen was the first to arrive. Years back, she had overcome her embarrassment at being early. She never came empty-handed. The Mason jar in her hands overflowed with dahlias, their blooms as big as saucers.

"I copied from Fenton," she explained. "He brought some to dinner a couple of weeks ago, and I thought they were a wonder. He said they were the last of the season, but I found some today at the florist's."

Ruby winked. "Thank God for men like Fenton."

The rest of the group straggled in. Juliet May, assistant professor of French, plopped down next to Gen on the sofa. She was a bright, career-minded woman, the kind Ruby liked to mentor. As Gen had before her, Juliet was taking all the right steps in her Baines career, including presiding as resident adviser over Cavendish House—prime real estate on campus. Along with two other antebellum residences dating from the earliest days of Baines, Cavendish sat up on a hill, judging the other dorms.

When everyone was settled with their refreshments, Ruby called them to order and centered discussion on Juliet's tenure application in Modern Languages. Juliet passed out mimeographed copies of her CV, so the women who had been through the tenure process could offer critique and advice.

As Ruby scanned it, one point caught her attention. "Why does it say your stint at Cavendish only goes to May?" she asked.

"Because this will be my last year living there," Juliet replied. "I need to have a private life. Away from campus."

Ruby couldn't believe she had to state the obvious. "But you're going up for tenure. It's not the time to give up a major service commitment, especially not for an excuse like privacy." She glanced around the circle of faces. "Am I right?"

Frances Palmer, from Biology, nodded vigorously. Almost Ruby's age, she'd never married but had set up housekeeping with another spinster on the outskirts of town. "I second that," Frances said. "You can enjoy your privacy *after* tenure."

Juliet cast her eyes from one to the other in the circle. "It's hard for single women. Harder than you might realize."

Ruby glanced instinctively at Juliet's left hand, which, as always, wore a stunning sapphire and diamond ring. She assumed Juliet had a fiancé somewhere, or that maybe, like Gen, she'd lost her man to war.

Juliet turned abruptly toward Gen, who was taking a sip of coffee. "What do you think, Gen?"

Gen returned her cup to its saucer with a tiny clink. "I might have to agree with Ruby and Frances on this," she said. "It will look bad to give up the post, no matter how much you want to. I had to sacrifice things when I was going up for tenure so I'd look like a team player. My promotion came with a cost, for sure." Gen leaned toward Juliet, and Ruby thought she heard her say, "We'll talk more later."

Ruby suspected Gen's "cost" meant giving up membership in the local NAACP. On Ruby's advice, Gen had begrudgingly stopped paying dues and attending meetings when she got a shot at promotion.

Juliet took in a measured breath before she spoke. "I'll leave the subject with this," she said. "You can't maintain any privacy when you not only teach your students but also live with them. I bet most of you can't even imagine it. Why, when you're married—like you, Ruby, and most of you—you go home at night to your husbands and families and enjoy breathing room. I can tell you, that's a privilege."

Ruby shifted in her seat. She was unaccustomed to being contradicted, especially by an assistant professor just launching her career. With almost three decades of teaching and multiple terms on the Tenure and Privilege Committee, she understood the workings of Baines backward and forward.

In the awkward pause that followed Juliet's statement, Darrell entered the room with a second plate of cookies. Ruby's husband had taken up cooking after his retirement from law when she pointed out it was unfair for him to expect her to get dinner on the table after she'd worked a full day and he hadn't. After some initial grousing, Darrell gave in and found he enjoyed the creative outlet. Recently, he had moved on to baking.

When he realized he'd stepped into an awkward discussion,

Darrell apologized and withdrew quickly. "I wasn't even here, ladies!" he said with a little bow.

"Better be careful, Ruby," Vanessa, a music professor, said with a giggle. "You don't want your man turning into Fenton Page."

Silence descended on the room again, and Ruby's face tightened. "That kind of talk is uncalled for, Vanessa. Especially with what happened to Mark."

The mood of the gathering shifted at Mark's name, and Ruby turned them back to Juliet's CV. "Well, Juliet, you've heard our advice. Whether or not you take it is up to you. What other comments do we have for our young professor?"

There was just a smattering of remarks after that, and the meeting ended earlier than planned. Most of the women claimed they still had papers to grade or class prep to do. Gen, too, deposited her coffee cup on the buffet and prepared to leave, although she often stayed after the others had gone.

Ruby caught Gen by the elbow and whispered, "Have you seen Fenton?"

"I have. I'll have to tell you about it later. I owe him a call."

Ruby nodded approval. She worried about Fenton and a colleague in English, John Hiram. Of course the women's group could never discuss the topic openly, but the threat facing some of their male colleagues hovered in the shadows.

"Please tell him to call me. We'll have lunch soon."

Although she wasn't sure what compelled her, Ruby watched from the front window as Gen ambled down her walkway with Juliet. The two had a brief, serious-looking exchange on the sidewalk. Then Gen got into her car, Juliet mounted her blue Schwinn, and they headed in different directions.

Ruby's morning was off to a hurried start, and she didn't have time to chat with Amanda Blakeney. Yet there she was, scrambling across the Blakeneys' front lawn, then across the street, then up Ruby's walkway to the porch. *Does she watch for me to leave?*

Ruby wondered. The woman was fond of bringing Ruby's short-comings to her attention—and always, for some reason, in the morning. One of Amanda's pet peeves was her neighbor's failure to draw up her venetian blinds evenly. "It gives a house a disheveled look, don't you think?"

When she wasn't complaining about blinds, Amanda might enlist Ruby to signing petitions. The most recent, just last week, had been an effort to get the street converted to one way.

"The cars just seem to roar through here these days," Amanda had said, brandishing her clipboard. "The boys from D and L have found the quickest route to our Baines girls! Honestly, I'm just waiting for somebody to be run over."

Ruby had signed obediently, even though she'd never noticed the alleged roaring. Over the decades, she had learned about keeping the peace with her neighbors and flattering them when-ever possible, especially Amanda.

This morning, Amanda wanted something else. "Ruby, a word?" she called out.

"I'm so sorry, Amanda, I'm late for a meeting." Ruby fumbled in her pocketbook for her car keys. She managed to flash a smile. "I wanted to walk today, it's so glorious, but I don't have time."

"Just a minute?"

Ruby nodded. As much as the woman rankled her, she could spare her a minute. In some ways, Amanda was a model neighbor, bringing soup when Ruby was ill and a casserole when Darrell's mother died, keeping an eye on the house when she and Darrell went to their cabin in the mountains. She'd even presented a graduation check to each of their three sons.

Amanda met her at the curb, where Ruby's car was parked. "You're so knowledgeable," her neighbor said, "and I wonder what you've heard about the investigation of the unfortunate Mr. Patton."

Ruby reached past her neighbor for the door handle of the Bel Air. "Oh, I'm sure I don't know any more than you, Amanda. Just what I read in the *Gazette*."

"It's just, I've heard a rumor that the police are broadening their investigation into . . . you know, these vice matters." Amanda frowned, unable or unwilling to elaborate. "I heard they might even talk to other Baines faculty."

"Where did you hear that?"

Amanda winced at the sharpness of Ruby's tone.

"Irene Carr mentioned it at our bridge game. She wondered about the theater director and someone in your department?" When Ruby didn't respond, Amanda added, "Irene can be an awful gossip, though, stirring up trouble for no reason."

And the pot calls the kettle black, Ruby thought.

"I don't know her well," Ruby said, which was technically true. She knew Mrs. Carr mostly as Gen's next-door neighbor. Gen had complained more than once that Irene Carr commented on her comings and goings in an unnerving way.

"I wondered if there was even a hint of truth to it."

"I'm sure I don't know." Ruby struggled to keep a casual tone.

"It's all so unsavory, isn't it? I do hope Baines can escape a bigger scandal."

"If I hear anything, Amanda, I will let you know."

"I see you had your women's group last night," Amanda added as Ruby settled herself behind the steering wheel. She was probably in her mid-forties but acted like an ancient biddy, keeping close tabs on everyone else.

"I did indeed. See you later, Amanda."

Ruby closed the door with a definitive slam and waved through the glass. She sped off down the street toward campus. Amanda would probably complain to someone that she roared.

Chapter Five

Gen

First came the Hershey's kisses in her department mailbox. The following week Gen found a box of creme-filled Girl Scout cookies propped against the door of her office. Someone likely had a kid sister who hadn't unloaded all her boxes during the cookie season.

Gen knew she was likely to devour the cookies in short order if she took them home, as she had the candy kisses. She had developed a craving for sweets after the breakup with Carolyn, and she alternately binged on chocolate ice cream and Tom Collinses to mask her pain. The failed attempt resulted only in tighter waistbands on her fall wardrobe.

Now, Gen dutifully placed the cookies in the department office for everyone to enjoy, not saving even one for herself. The treats vanished by the end of the day, and she spotted the history chairman helping himself to two vanillas.

She would have forgotten the gifts in time, chalked them up to some girl's innocent gesture of regard. Maybe Margaret Sutter was quietly repaying her for the loan of the Civil War book.

The situation turned less childlike when a package appeared on her porch, wrapped in brown paper. Inside was a lurid pulp novel, *Girls' Dormitory*, its spine cracked and cover tattered.

Two summers back, Carolyn had picked up the novel at a drugstore and read it in one sitting during their Rehoboth trip. She had pronounced it "a delightful dose of trash" and urged it on Gen. The cover, with three girls in various states of undress, sparked Gen's interest, but the description of a college dormitory housemother who "initiated" students made it seem too salacious to bother with. Gen had tossed it aside for *Doctor Zhivago*, which she'd been saving for vacation.

She knew Carolyn hadn't mailed the novel; the package had been placed on her porch with care. Whoever wrapped it tied it up with the same pink ribbon as the candy kisses she'd received at school.

Gen's skin crawled at the thought that her "admirer" knew where she lived. Granted, Springboro was a compact town where people recognized each other by sight, if not by name, and she was the only Rider in the local directory. Still . . .

Worse, *Girls' Dormitory* was about a lesbian predator at a girls' school—a creepy message, for sure, but possibly an ominous warning.

The novel's housemother plot brought back a memory. In her second year at Baines, the dean at the time asked Gen to be a dormitory housemother. "We rely on our single ladies without families for these positions," the dean had said. "It will look good on your CV if you ever go up for promotion."

The dean mentioned no end date for the appointment, which had made Gen nervous to accept. She wasn't dating anyone at the time, but that didn't mean she wanted to become a nun. With the advice of a friend at another college, a woman she'd dated in graduate school, Gen finessed her refusal—an excuse about a long-term lease. She'd never told anyone at Baines about the housemother offer, not even Ruby. *Girls' Dormitory* landed too close, an eerie coincidence.

And that turned her thoughts to Juliet, who wanted desperately to give up her housemother position. In the five years Juliet had taught at Baines, she and Gen had met for coffee only a couple of times. After the women's meeting, Juliet had followed her out of Ruby's and asked if they could talk more about what applying for tenure had cost her. Gen agreed readily. Since securing tenure she was expected to mentor others, and she found Juliet affable. In the busy early weeks, though, neither of them had followed up. Now the incident with the book gave Gen an immediate reason to place the call.

Gen located Juliet's number easily in the phone book. Juliet agreed to meet on Saturday, suggesting breakfast at the town diner, but Gen set her sights farther afield—someplace where she never encountered anyone from Springboro. That morning, she drove east until she reached the sign: "Barrington, Virginia—Founded 1768—Pop. 10,602." It was a safe spot where she sometimes met Carolyn, midway between their two lives. Carolyn liked to fantasize that the "02" at the end signified a couple of spinsters who had met as nurses in Korea and set up housekeeping together when they returned.

Lace curtains draped the windows of Barrington Tea Shoppe, presided over by a war bride who had followed her American husband from England after VE Day. The cozy spot served finger sandwiches, pastries, and pots of tea, mostly to tourists snaking their way toward the Blue Ridge Parkway and points west.

Juliet had already procured a table facing the square. With her back turned toward the door, Gen almost didn't recognize her. At school and at Ruby's meetings, Juliet usually wore her blond hair in a bun at the nape of her neck, a professional look that accentuated her slender neck. For the weekend, though, she'd arranged it in a French braid that extended past her shoulder blades. The hairstyle and her cotton slacks and madras blouse gave her a girlish air. Gen wished she'd dressed more casually, too, instead of like she was heading to class.

As they deliberated over scones and tarts, Juliet said, "Thanks for reaching out, Gen. I've been so blue since Ruby's, I couldn't even bring myself to call you." She clutched her menu, her grip crinkling the sides of the vellum sheet.

Gen hadn't considered how disheartened her younger colleague might have been when the other female faculty downplayed her concerns—especially Ruby, so revered and yet so harsh when she disapproved. Gen's own reason for contacting Juliet faded into the background. "I should have called you sooner."

"It's a busy time."

"Not that busy." Gen fiddled with her napkin, unfolding and refolding it, ashamed that she hadn't offered Juliet more support. "I'm sorry I didn't speak up for you at the meeting. The truth is I'm a chicken."

Juliet snickered. "You don't fool me, Gen. A woman doesn't make it to tenure being a chicken."

Their pastries and pot of Earl Grey arrived, and Gen fell silent for a moment while the waitress served.

"Fact is, there was something I couldn't bring up in front of everyone. No one knows, not even Ruby—"

Juliet raised her eyebrows over her china cup, as if she expected a salacious reveal. "I thought Ruby knew everything."

Gen smiled at the assessment. "She likes you to think that, but I've managed to keep some things close to the vest. So you can't tell her, but here's the thing. My second year at Baines, the dean approached me about being a housemother at Paxton."

"No!"

"He implied I had no life at all, so I'd be perfect for it. There was no term limit either. It looked like I would just do it until I dropped dead or retired."

"That's the same line I got. How did you get out of it?"

"A friend helped me manufacture an excuse about signing a two-year lease I couldn't break. Apparently, the dean doesn't know a thing about leases. I was actually living in month-to-month rooms back then."

"I wish I'd had a friend like that four years ago." Juliet stared at the scone on her plate. "But I didn't know you, and Ruby told me to do whatever the dean asked if I hoped to get tenure some-day. So I said yes, but I had this sinking feeling about what could happen down the road."

Gen sipped her tea. "Maybe you could come up with an excuse

after the fact," she said. She glanced toward Juliet's left hand on the tablecloth, at the shiny jewel as blue as her eyes, surrounded by diamond chips. Juliet caught the shift of Gen's attention and spun the ring with her thumb.

"I don't have a fiancé. That would be the perfect excuse, wouldn't it? But there's no wedding in the offing, so folks at school will be on to me soon." Juliet moved her hand to her lap. "Family heirloom from Granny May. Keeps the men at bay. Nobody understands why a thirty-six-year-old woman wouldn't be married."

Gen had assumed Juliet was younger, and something loosened in her when she realized only six years separated them. "I'll see your fiancé and raise you one," she said softly, like a co-conspirator. "Everyone thinks *my* man died on Utah Beach."

Juliet's eyes popped, and it was clear she'd heard that tale about Gen, too. "You mean, he didn't?"

After a demure bite Gen explained. "I mean there was no fiancé. But that's our secret. Well, yours and mine and a few select people that don't include Ruby."

"Ha! She doesn't even know what she doesn't know," Juliet quipped. "So what *is* your story?"

Gen pressed the back of her hand to her forehead, feigning distress. "I've never recovered from the shock of getting the telegram. A bit callous, but it works."

"No, I mean, is there some private person you don't want Ruby to know about?"

Gen blinked quickly. The river of comfort had widened between them, and with the word "person" Juliet offered a way to jump in. But Gen needed more before she gave up all her secrets. "Not at the moment," she said. "Anyway, my story doesn't solve your problem, does it?"

Juliet peered at Gen as if weighing whether to press her further about her "private person," but she let the subject drop.

"You know, I think I may just roll the dice and give up the post," Juliet said. "I'm tired of girls knocking on my door at odd hours, and I'm dying to throw a raucous cocktail party. And I won't even mention *my* private life, which has been nonexistent for too long."

Gen made a quick segue into her own predicament. "I hate to tell you, but it isn't that much easier for single women living off-campus." She reached into her straw handbag, the one she had bought for beach trips with Carolyn, and fished out the copy of *Girls' Dormitory*. She passed it to Juliet under the table, afraid that the waitress or another customer might see the smutty cover art.

"I've been getting little gifts at school, candy and then a box of Girl Scout cookies. Crush-type things. But then I found this on my porch the other day."

With the book in her lap, Juliet scanned the front and back covers. "At *home*?"

"I want to think it's harmless, but it spooked me."

"Yeah, definitely creepy." Juliet handed it off under the table like radioactive material. "A sleazy dime store novel isn't something you give a crush. Any idea who knows where you live?"

Gen shrugged. "Anyone could look me up in the phone book. There's one student whose family lives next door, but she rooms at school and I never see her in the neighborhood."

"How about grudges?"

"Some girls don't like what I teach. They're so sure what they learned about Negroes in grammar school was the God's honest truth." When Juliet's face clouded with confusion, she explained, "My work's inspired by the movement for Negro rights. Right now, I'm studying the history of the NAACP."

"Ah." Her tone gave away neither approval nor disapproval. "But I don't see why that would lead to *this* particular book."

The statement felt like a fishing expedition, and Gen hoped she hadn't misjudged Juliet as a confidante. She quickly stuffed the book back in her bag.

"Have you told anyone?" Juliet asked.

"You."

Juliet bowed with a shy smile. "I'm honored you trusted me."

A prolonged silence followed in which Gen nibbled at the scone that now tasted like buttered cardboard, and Juliet took repeated sips of her Earl Grey.

"Well," Juliet said finally to break the spell, "aren't we the happy professors? Sometimes I really wonder what I was thinking to choose this life."

Gen started at the statement. She didn't recall choosing teaching, only that she had determined in childhood not to get married—even though at the time, she wasn't aware of her interest in other women. There were so few career options for girls. She quailed at the sight of blood, so nursing was out, and teaching became the default. In the summers when grammar school let out, Gen practiced her instructional skills by coercing her younger sister, Dottie, and other neighborhood children into reading and spelling exercises in their backyard. Dottie just wanted to swim and play, and she finally complained to their mother. Mama promptly ended the lessons and pronounced her older daughter "too pushy for your own good."

Gen and Juliet settled the bill and parted company with a promise of getting together again before too much time passed.

"Why haven't we been friends?" Juliet said.

"We can fix that now."

In the years with Carolyn, she'd put such store in a tight circle, one that didn't have room for new members. Now she felt lighter with one more person to confide in.

Chapter Six

Fenton

The cast for *Charley's Aunt* hadn't bailed on him, but Fenton lost his stage manager to vague "other commitments" just one week into rehearsals. He latched onto an idea he'd resorted to once in the past—co-stage managers, so there was always a spare. He summoned Margaret Sutter and Susanna Carr, who each had a minor part in the production, to ask if they'd be interested in doubling up.

"I have so much going on, Mr. Page," Margaret said. "You know, learning my lines, but also all my classes."

"How much work is it?" Susanna asked.

Fenton almost told the truth about the list of tasks, but he quickly pivoted to a sunnier version of the job. "Oh, it can be a lot of fun," he said. "You attend all the rehearsals, but the beauty of co-managers is you can split the dates and not have to show up as often. You prompt the cast if they drop their lines, and you record my blocking of scenes and help actors who forget. You boss people around. I did it in college and had a blast."

Margaret side-eyed Susanna, as if waiting for the other girl to volunteer first, but Susanna was feigning interest in the framed Broadway Playbills that lined Fenton's walls. Neither budged for several long moments.

And then his intercom buzzed.

Fenton punched the button. The secretary of the Art, Theater, and Music Departments said, "Call for you, Mr. Page."

"Could you take a message, Joan? I'm with students right now." He tossed the girls a smile.

"It's the police chief," Joan said without the customary chirp in her voice. "I told him you were busy, but he said it was important he talk to you right away."

Both students' eyes widened, and Fenton picked up the receiver. "One second, Joan. Girls, would you mind—?" He motioned toward the door, and Margaret and Susanna obliged.

"Fenton Page."

"Mr. Page, Chief Maynard with the Springboro Police. I'm wondering if you could stop into the department, say, today at three?"

Fenton's throat constricted, but he managed a polite refusal. "I'm afraid I'm teaching at three today, and then I have rehearsals for the school play that will last into the evening. Could you tell me what this is about?"

Fenton knew already. He had read the lead story in the morning paper three times: "RAIDS SPARK WIDER INVESTIGATION IN VICE ROUNDUP." His heart had picked up speed thinking the police might have already cracked Mark's diary code or that his former lover might have named names to lessen his own punishment.

The chief's voice was modulated and professional as he explained that they were casting a wide net in the vice investigation. There was no cause for alarm, he said. He used the term "person of interest" that Fenton had noted in the news story.

"I don't know what that means, person of interest," Fenton admitted.

"It means someone who might be able to provide us with more information that could help with our investigation."

"Investigation" reverberated in Fenton's ears. "Did someone suggest me?"

Maynard leisurely exhaled and dodged the question. "It'll take maybe thirty minutes."

Fenton paused as if checking a date book. "I can spare thirty minutes tomorrow at eleven-thirty."

"All right then, Mr. Page. We'll see you then."

"Chief," Fenton said before he hung up, "do I need a lawyer?"

"No, that's not necessary. You have a good day now."

The receiver missed the cradle and Fenton had to try again.

Through the frosted glass panel of his office door, Fenton spied one shadowy outline. Only Susanna Carr remained, waiting for him, her eyes still big and round.

"Margaret left?" He glanced around, disappointed. "Did she say she'd be back?"

"She might have said she had class. You know, we're not friends."

His heart was still pounding in his ears from the exchange with Chief Maynard. "You don't have to be friends with everyone you work with, Miss Carr."

Fenton rarely used last names, and the girl looked stricken. She stammered, "I wanted to tell you I'll do it by myself, the . . . the stage manager thing. I'd rather not have to do it with her. I can give up the Ela role. I don't care."

He had meandered into some student feud, probably about a boy. He wanted to scream at her, *Some of us have real problems!*

There was no time for petty intrigue or regret. Fenton accepted Susanna's offer to take over the job with effusive thanks and said he'd replace her in the cast with a student who had just missed making the final cut.

The room where the police officer led him smelled of coffee and cigarettes and made Fenton long for both, but the young man offered him nothing.

"Have a seat right here." The officer was clean-cut enough to be a Davis and Lee boy, but his "right here" came out more like "rat cheer." He motioned toward a table outfitted with a massive tape recorder. Two wooden chairs faced a metal one with dents in it, like it had been thrown a few times.

"Thank you, officer; you are most kind. All the good things I've heard about our local police force appear to be true." The officer scrunched his brow and left him on his own.

The longer he sat in the room, the tighter and more cramped it grew, like what he imagined a cell would be. Fenton would have no legal counsel with him today, but not because he hadn't tried. Darrell, Ruby's husband, was the only lawyer he knew, but he was a retired tax attorney.

"I'll have to dig around for some names," Darrell had said, as if attorneys who defended someone like Fenton burrowed underground. "Give me a day or two."

He had thought of calling the police station and trying to delay the interview, but Gen said she worried that would look bad, like the avoidance tactic it was. "Wear your navy three-piece," she'd advised. "Think about anything but Mark."

Fenton rarely wore the suit because the vest gripped him like a straitjacket, and now he tugged at it uncomfortably. He'd resisted wearing a lighter blue pocket handkerchief to match his tie and socks for fear that would make him look too debonair—too much of a fairy.

A lanky, silver-haired man bearing the name tag "A. MAYNARD" and carrying a file folder entered the room, followed by a shorter, less formidable officer. Fenton had pictured the police chief with a barrel chest, a jowly face and country drawl, but this man didn't fit the bill.

"Mr. Page, thank you for coming down to see us on such short notice." Maynard's voice exuded charm, as if Fenton had dropped in for a friendly visit. "I am Chief Maynard and this is Sergeant Hills."

Fenton recognized the name "Hills" from somewhere, maybe the *Gazette*. Or maybe Mark had mentioned him. He blinked quickly to dismiss Mark's face.

"Be warm and polite," Gen had counseled. "Whatever you do, don't let them see your peevish side." By that, he knew his friend meant the part of him that jumped to sarcasm when he was annoyed or angered.

When the men sat, Fenton reminded himself of his actor's training. "How can I help you, gentlemen?"

From habit, he started to cross his leg at the knee but noticed Hills observing his every movement. A voice played in his head—*Men don't sit like that.* His father would issue the admonishment right before he slapped him across the face so hard it left finger marks. Fenton planted both feet on the floor.

"We're hoping you might shed some light on an investigation we're starting up," Maynard said, opening his folder. With the file's contents upside down, Fenton couldn't make out any of the type, even if he squinted.

"Do you mind if we tape our conversation?" Maynard asked.

Fenton's eyes followed Hills's stubby index finger as it hit the record button on the reel-to-reel. He had to look away from the machine's turning, turning, turning, which threatened to mesmerize him.

For the record, Hills introduced himself and Maynard, gave the date and time, and then instructed Fenton to state his name, address, and occupation. When Fenton hesitated at first, Hills said, "Just a formality."

Maynard continued, "Now Mr. Page, you know about the arrests we had to make on Labor Day?"

Fenton nodded.

"For the tape, please, Mr. Page."

"Yes, I read about that in the paper."

"A colleague of yours at Baines, Mr. Mark Patton, was involved."

"I have many colleagues at Baines," Fenton said, but he immediately worried that sounded too confrontational. Plus, he couldn't outright deny knowing Mark. The lie could easily come back to harm him so he hurried to retract. "But of course, yes, I know Mr. Patton. Knew, I should say. He was let go a few weeks back."

"You're friends," Maynard said, glancing up from the file in front of him.

"We crossed paths, as you do when you work in the same building with someone. But he's not among my close friends."

Maynard held his eyes, his face expressionless, and Hills jumped into the fray. "Patton told us y'all liked to hang out at his place. Is that what 'crossed paths' means?"

Fenton opened his mouth but closed it while he considered his answer.

"I don't recall being in Mr. Patton's apartment," he said slowly so the *P*'s wouldn't trip him up. He'd drilled himself to correct his boyhood speech impediment, but it resurfaced whenever he was nervous or a shade less than truthful.

"Really?" Maynard pressed him. "Not ever?"

Fenton's lips formed a tight line, as if he were trying his best to dredge up a distant memory. "Wait a minute. Is his place over on Willow?"

"It is," Maynard said after consulting the file.

"You know, I think I may have been there once." Was that too little to admit to? "Twice at the very most. So many faculty members throw cocktail parties, and it's considered bad manners not to attend. I forgot Mark had several over the course of a few years."

"So you only went to parties there."

"Yes."

Maynard flipped some pages. "And do you recall what went on at these parties?"

The question threw Fenton for a moment, but he recovered without too much delay. "Honestly, no. Like I said, there've been a lot of parties, and they're a bit of a blur. I'm sure there was drinking. I've never met a faculty member who didn't like to imbibe." As intended, the light reply brought a smile to the chief's face.

"Anything else?" Hills chimed in.

Fenton was stymied. Could the interview be over so soon? "Anything else . . . about Mr. Patton?"

"About the parties you say you attended."

51

The addition of "you say" stood out, and Fenton cleared his throat—a trick he'd picked up when he needed to slow down and control his stutter.

"There was probably music, but that's just a guess."

"Any games?" Hills went on.

"I don't know what you mean. Like . . . charades?"

"Like looking at photographs, say. Magazines."

Fenton drew in a breath as he realized where this line of questioning was headed—Mark's impressive beefcake photos and physique magazine collection.

He could play dumb, ask what kind of photos and magazines, but that was too dangerous. Denial looked like the best route. "I don't remember activities like that," he said. "I don't know how well you know academics, gentlemen, but in my experience they tend to just drink and pontificate and then drink some more."

Hills snickered at that one, but Maynard acted as if he hadn't heard.

"Now at these parties, were there any women?"

Fenton blinked, possibly a few too many times. "I'm sure there were. I usually attend parties with . . . a female colleague. You know, a *close* friend."

Maynard made a note. Fenton took pride in catching himself before he blurted out Gen's name. He wondered if that had happened with Mark—an innocent interjection that gave away names.

During an extended pause, Maynard consulted more pages of the file. Fenton slipped his watch from his vest and glanced at the time.

"Handsome watch," Maynard said, startling him again. Fenton hadn't been aware he was looking at him.

"My granddaddy's," he replied, tucking it back into his pocket.

"You in a hurry, Mr. Page?" Hills asked.

"I have a meeting in forty minutes. The other thing we academics like to do is meet. And then have a meeting about the meeting." He enunciated each word slowly so the *M*'s didn't

52

catch up with him—tricky little bastards, just like the *P*'s. "I'm sorry my testimony hasn't been terribly helpful."

"Oh, no, it has, and I thank you for your time," Maynard said, slapping his folder closed and gesturing to Hills to switch off the recorder. "We may have some follow-up questions. Another day. Especially with regard to Mr. Patton's diary."

Fenton feigned indignity. "Well, I'd hardly know anything about a man's diary, would I? That's the height of p-private m-material!" He quivered at his own stammering, which he'd harnessed so well until that final lie.

"It is, isn't it?" Maynard said with a smile Fenton couldn't read.

Chapter Seven

Gen

"We'll start today with something that might feel off-topic," Gen announced to her Civil War class. "I like to draw connections between the past and present. Anyone heard the statement, 'Those who cannot remember the past are condemned to repeat it'?"

Margaret's hand was the only one that shot up. After glancing around, she lowered it quickly.

Gen wrote the names Nixon and Kennedy on the blackboard, then stepped aside. "So tell me, who watched the presidential debate last night?"

The rocky transition threw the girls off-balance. To Gen's surprise, only a handful of the twenty-four students raised their hands.

"You don't have any interest in the upcoming election?"

With a hint of pride, Lee-Anne Blakeney said, "Paxton House doesn't have a TV, professor."

The mention of the dorm Gen would have lived in if she'd accepted the housemother position all those years ago made her wince. She might still be trapped there, living with girls like Lee-Anne.

"Well, such an elegant dorm *must* have a radio," Gen said. "And I reckon most of you have transistors. I've seen you listening to them on campus, twisting your way across the quad."

The girls laughed. "The Twist" was the latest dance craze, so popular that even Gen and Fenton had tried it out in her backyard.

"You could have listened to the debate, at least. Really, girls, you need to show some interest in your future as well as in the past." Disappointment coursed through her. Gen ran down her notes as she realized she needed to salvage the first part of her class plan. "For those of you who did tune in, who can guess why I'm bringing up this current event when we're learning about a war that took place a hundred years ago?"

Susanna Carr, whose family lived next door to Gen, offered, "Because of Kennedy's opening statement?"

"Good, Susanna. What did he say?"

Susanna was stumped trying to recall the actual words, and Margaret chimed in. "He talked about Lincoln and the election of 1860. Something about Negroes still not being free?"

"Very good, Margaret. I jotted it down because it was so completely relevant to what we're studying today. And as an aside, I was forced to take a course in Gregg shorthand the summer I graduated from high school. My mother thought a girl having a career meant being a secretary." Gen smiled at the absurdity, but she knew some of these girls likely agreed with her mother.

"Senator Kennedy said, and these are his words, 'In the election of 1860, Abraham Lincoln said the question was whether this nation could exist half slave and half free. In the election of 1960, the question is whether the world will exist half slave or half free, whether it will move in the direction of freedom, in the direction of the road that we are taking, or whether it will move in the direction of slavery.'"

Lee-Anne's hand shot up. "But there's no slavery anymore."

"A fair point. But Kennedy went on to talk about Negroes not enjoying their full constitutional rights, how white children have a fairer shake in the country than black children, and he gave some startling statistics. For example, he noted that a Negro child has about one-half as much chance to get through high school as a white child."

"Is that really true, professor?" Susanna asked, when Gen called on her.

Gen started. "About high school? Yes, it is."

"But couldn't there be other reasons they don't make it through?" the girl added. "Like, maybe they don't try as hard?"

"Or maybe school's too hard for them?" Lee-Anne said.

Gen set down her notes. These two girls, peas in a pod, were prime examples of students she wanted to shake until she loosened their narrow beliefs about race. Yet, with their well-connected families, she couldn't afford to alienate them.

"There is a *legacy* of slavery that we carry with us today. Negroes may no longer be literally enslaved, but the legacy means they don't enjoy the same advantages in things like housing, jobs, and schooling. That is what Senator Kennedy was getting at with his statistics, and that is what I want you to remember as we learn about the Civil War and especially Reconstruction."

Her firm pronouncement silenced them, and then they all opened their textbooks as instructed. Gen wondered how long it would take for Susanna or Lee-Anne to let the class lesson slip to their parents or to Henry Thoms.

That week, Gen got a couple of hang-up calls at home—no one on the other end, just a dial tone. A likely prank, or someone who wanted to talk to her but couldn't bring themselves to once they'd dialed. She'd hung up on Carolyn's new number several times, so she was well aware the trick wasn't limited to children.

After her supper, Fenton phoned, asking to stop by. It didn't sound like he had a casual chat in mind. He explained his lack of sleep since the police had brought him in, his nagging fear that they'd show up at Timmons Hall for him or his belongings, as they had for Mark.

Then he arrived at the real reason for wanting to visit. The provost's office had summoned him for a meeting the following day, with no specific subject mentioned.

Gen gulped. Provost Lowndes Ramsey, just a rung below the president of the college in power, had been in his job only a year. She'd shaken his manicured hand at a welcome reception. As faculty members listened to his greeting, Fenton had remarked on the provost's trim build. "I wouldn't turn him out of bed," he'd whispered to Gen.

All that seemed ages ago now. Gen couldn't deny Fenton the company he needed, even though she'd just cracked the spine on *The Burden of Southern History* and wanted to spend the evening alone with it.

Fenton appeared at her doorstep in a wrinkled button-down shirt that looked like he'd dragged it from the laundry basket. Always so fastidious about his appearance, his dishevelment stood out. His mouth sagged in a way she hadn't noticed before.

"You look terrible," she couldn't help saying as she ushered him in.

"Thanks, hon."

She splashed Jim Beam into his glass without asking if he wanted it.

"Say, you didn't call and hang up on me, did you? About an hour before we actually talked?"

Fenton frowned, making the lines in his face more pronounced. "Why would I do that?"

"Sorry, of course you wouldn't. Probably a neighborhood kid."

Her friend belted back his drink while still standing up. Gen poured him another and watched as he polished that off, too. Fenton liked his bourbon, but he usually savored a glass or two over the course of a visit. As he placed the empty glass on Gen's liquor cabinet, his hand trembled.

"Have you had supper?" she asked.

"I had a stale donut from the diner. Does that count?"

Gen smiled and led him to the kitchen by the sleeve. She

flicked on the overhead as moonlight spilled through the window facing the Carrs' house.

"I already ate but let me fix you something real fast."

Aside from the barbecue recipe she served on special occasions, Gen had never bothered to learn to cook. When she was growing up, she resisted her mother's attempts to teach her daughters about "meals to please a man." Since leaving home, her most likely quick meals consisted of scrambled eggs or tuna fish salad. On weekends, she might attempt a recipe from Betty Crocker that she could eat all week, a casserole or spaghetti.

"How's leftover meat loaf sound?"

"Divine. Don't fuss, though. I'll eat it cold."

With its congealed tomato sauce, the meat loaf she plated for him looked unappetizing, but Fenton worked his way through it bite by bite.

"That was delicious. I didn't know I was hungry."

She'd brought the bottle of bourbon to the table, too, and he helped himself to a third round while she continued to nurse her first.

"I might regret eating, though," he added. "My stomach's not in the best state these days. Worried I have an ulcer again."

"You might let up on the booze."

Fenton let the third shot stand in his glass. He reached into his pants pocket and withdrew a piece of folded paper. He smoothed it open, showing a check for five hundred dollars with no name in the *Pay to the Order of* line.

Gen stared at the amount. "Hey, my meat loaf's good, but it's on the house."

He didn't crack a smile. "I want you to hold onto this," he instructed. "That's how much Mark said his bail came to. I don't want to be caught having to scrounge around and beg people for the money. I also don't want anybody having to write the check and implicate themselves. Especially not you."

Gen's pulse picked up speed. "Fenton, you're not going to jail." The statement rang hollow, said mostly to convince herself.

"I'd rather not pretend," he said. "If they arrest me, I'll need you to bring this to the station."

"But what if—" She restrained her thought: *What if the provost fires you? Won't you need this?*

As if reading her mind, Fenton said, "I have more put by." He motioned toward the check. "I cashed in some railroad stock my granddad left me. I was saving it for a rainy day, but it's starting to look pretty cloudy."

The bourbon burned its way down her throat. They finished their drinks at the same time, and she glanced over the stove at the yellow Bakelite clock that read 8:34.

She wondered how he had gotten himself to this point. Fenton hadn't divulged anything about the police interview, and she hadn't prodded him, as if not knowing the details could make it all go away. Yet here he was, asking her to make bail for him if necessary, and she deserved information.

She poured herself a second shot, shorter than the first. Drinking emboldened her, though she sometimes regretted what came out of her mouth. "So what happened, Fen? Did Mark give the police your name?"

"Don't know." His finger traced a mark on the cotton tablecloth, a phantom stain that hadn't come out in the wash.

"Didn't you ask?" She didn't mean it as a verbal slap, but it sounded that way, even to her.

"I was so flustered, hon, I was just trying to get it all over with. The police chief is a cool number, I'll tell you that. The way those two looked at me—" He shivered at the memory.

"Well, if Mark didn't give them your name, how would they have landed on you? Surely, just being a bachelor isn't enough, and you say you're always safe, that you don't do . . . what Mark did."

Her disapproval came through; she couldn't hide it. She honestly didn't understand the attraction of such a private matter like sex happening in a park or a public restroom. When Fenton didn't respond, she added, "Or were you not telling me the truth?"

Pain clouded Fenton's face. She knew he thought of her not just as a friend, but as a big sister figure. In light moments, he called her "Sissy" as a joke.

"I don't lie to you," he said slowly. "I may have . . . forgotten an incident with Mark. One time when I wasn't quite as safe. Mark may have written about it. In a diary the police have."

Gen's spine straightened. "Tell me this wasn't on campus."

His eyes welled up and spilled over, a stream of tears that distorted his face. In her experience, men didn't cry. Fenton had wept in front of her once before, several years back when his grandfather died, but that had been much more restrained and polite, a few drops he could wipe away with his pocket hanky. Then, she had patted his back in comfort. Now, she restrained the urge to smack him, keeping her hands securely on her glass and saying nothing.

A few minutes ticked by rhythmically. When Fenton's crying subsided, she asked, "What happens next?"

He blew his nose, and the trumpeting echoed off the walls. "I should look for a lawyer. Lord, I can't believe I just said that. You know anyone besides Darrell?"

"Just Frank Johnson at the NAACP." Negro lawyers didn't defend white men in their part of the country—or likely anywhere. "I could ask him about white lawyers."

She thought for a few more moments, then continued, "How about men you know in Richmond? Could you ask around?"

Fenton scowled. "I need to keep my distance from those fellas," he said. "They're not going to want to see me anyway. Some of them have wives and families."

They faced each other in silence as the second hand of the clock ticked and ticked. The weight of her uselessness sat heavily on Gen's chest. "I've been no help," she said finally.

"You let me come over. You gave me meatloaf and bourbon. You are the best friend I have."

Guilt filled her to bursting. She was a terrible friend, judgmental and unkind.

"Do you want to stay over?" she offered, and he jumped at the chance. He had slept over before, when their evenings went late or he'd drunk too much. He claimed the sofa bed in her office was comfy, and in fact he was the only one who had ever used it.

Gen had tested the sofa bed at the store, picturing her parents visiting, maybe during the fall when the trees produced a breathtaking canopy of colors in the surrounding mountains. But she never invited them and they never broached the topic—a sort of mutual agreement of silence.

The next morning, Gen heard Fenton padding around in the kitchen. Her nightstand clock read only 6:20. Soon the aroma of coffee hit her nostrils, and she threw on her bathrobe.

Fenton was already fully dressed, his shirt even more wrinkled, as if he'd slept in it. "I'll be out of your hair in a jiff. Don't want to get you in trouble with the nosy neighbors."

At the front door, Gen donned a big-sister face, concerned but smiling, to buck him up. "I'll be thinking of you today. Let me know what happens?"

His old Dodge didn't start right away; the cold engine took several tries to turn over. She hoped Mrs. Carr wasn't up, that the racket didn't attract her attention.

Chapter Eight

Fenton

Fenton had never been to the provost's office. Light spilled through the arched windows and landed on the two secretaries positioned like sentries at either side of the doors to his private sanctum. The older of the two barely acknowledged his presence, while Kathy Yost, the younger one and a former student he had mentored, smiled at him reassuringly. He took the seat Kathy suggested, one of several matching chairs with red and gold patterned cushions, even on the arms, like something out of a formal dining room.

A few minutes past the appointment time, Provost Ramsey flung open his double doors and waved Fenton inside.

"How is it we've never met?" Ramsey asked after they shook hands. He smoothed his silver hair, which, despite his age, was still thick and lustrous. Fenton felt the thinning of his own in that one gesture.

"We did meet once," Fenton said. "At your welcome reception. But you met so many people."

"Of course." Ramsey smiled, displaying a set of perfect white teeth. His appearance and comportment suggested an upper-class pedigree. Fenton pictured him hailing from a grand house shadowed by an allée of live oaks.

Fenton settled into his chair, a manly leather that sighed under him.

"An issue has come up, Mr. Page. It is *Mr.* Page and not Dr. Page, correct?"

The provost somehow intuited that Fenton was self-conscious about his lack of a doctorate. But he'd been hired for his position based on his hands-on theater experience, not because of an advanced degree. Fenton opened his mouth to point that out, then shut it quickly.

The provost consulted notes on a legal pad. "I've had a call from Provost Loomis over at our brother school. A pesky situation that I hope you can shed some light on. It appears some parents have complained about the play we're putting on with Davis and Lee this fall." His eyes narrowed. "*Charley's Aunt* by . . . Brendan Thomas?"

Fenton cleared his throat, which was scratchy as sandpaper. "Brandon Thomas. Yes, he wrote about a d-dozen plays, but *Charley's Aunt* was his hit."

Ramsey nodded with a tight smile. "The assistant provost looked it up in the library. A comedy, I take it."

"A very broad one. More of a farce. All good fun and mistaken identity-type humor, the kind of things the Victorians lapped up. I take it you didn't see the movie? My students didn't either."

Ramsey frowned. "Mrs. Ramsey likes farces, but when it comes to comedy, I'm more of a Shakespeare man."

The provost steepled his hands over the legal pad. "From what the assistant provost could find out about it, it's an odd little thing, what with a lot of cross-dressing and innuendo and all."

Fenton cast his eyes down and examined his palms, which glistened with sweat. He rubbed them quickly against his trouser legs. *Shakespeare used cross-dressing and innuendo,* he thought but couldn't say.

"It seems you've had some other curious choices in your time with us. Lillian Hellman. Oscar Wilde even. Thomas appears to be a contemporary of Wilde's. You like the Victorians, I take it."

"We've done a number of classics, but students prefer more

63

recent works," Fenton hurried to point out. "Next semester is *Our Town*."

"Good family fare. Always a solid choice," Ramsey said, rubbing his chin.

The silence that followed was achingly long.

"Given the atmosphere these days," Ramsey went on, "all the talk about morals and lewdness, and then the situation with Mr. Patton, it doesn't look good for us to do this particular play. I'm afraid Provost Loomis and I agree that it's best to cancel *Charley's Aunt*."

"But we're up in two weeks," Fenton blurted out. "Most of the students are off-book."

He flashed to all the rehearsals, the hours spent blocking the pratfalls. Andrew and Margaret were particularly strong in their roles, as was the girl playing Donna Lucia. How would he ever break the news to them? In his mind, he heard a chorus of groans.

"It would be cruel to shut it down," he said finally.

Ramsey's lips twitched. "And yet that's what you're going to do."

Fenton noted the emphasis on *you're*. Someone as high up the chain as the provost only meted out instructions. He wouldn't do anything as distasteful as informing students about an unpopular decision.

Fenton rose from his chair, but Ramsey wasn't finished. "Tell me something. No one advises you on your choice of plays, is that correct?"

The question shouldn't have startled him, but it did. "There's no theater faculty except for me. That's common at small schools."

"Yes, well, from now on, I'd like to get more people involved," Ramsey said. "Dean Rolfe for one, and someone from Davis and Lee since we do joint productions. You can run your ideas by them."

"Does Dean Rolfe *know* theater?" Fenton instantly regretted the question, which burst out as arrogant and then couldn't be stuffed back into his thoughts.

"I'm sure he'll welcome the chance to get to know it better," Ramsey said, dismissing him.

The dean's involvement in play selection was an insult to his professionalism, a punishment for sure. But wonder of wonders, the provost had never mentioned the police. Fenton found himself flashing a smile at Kathy on his way out.

Before the students arrived for rehearsal, Fenton got down on his hands and knees and peeled the spike tape off the stage, since there would be no scenery or props to place. Normally, the stage manager and crew would remove these markers at the end of the run, but Fenton found the ripping action cathartic.

"Hey, Mr. Page!"

Per usual, Margaret was early. He had never divulged that Susanna Carr didn't want to stage-manage with her. To spare her feelings, he had claimed it was his decision to stick with the first girl who accepted the job.

Throughout the rehearsals Margaret was a brick, laughing at his jokes, playing her role as he directed, perfecting her British accent. She occasionally annoyed him, too, the way she got, as Gen had put it, "underfoot," like a puppy.

Now Margaret stood on the stage looking down at his hunched back. "Everything okay?"

He pried up the last line of tape with a satisfying rip and stood up. "I'm just generally in the dumps today, Margaret. Rough week."

She fished in the pocket of her windbreaker and produced a pristine roll of butter rum Life Savers. Over the weeks of rehearsal, they'd discovered a mutual love for the flavor.

"Here, keep the roll. I have a spare."

Fenton wadded the tape into a neat ball and accepted the candy with a smile. "You're a peach."

Margaret regarded him like a jigsaw puzzle with pieces missing. "Which scenes are we going over today, Mr. Page? Act Three is pretty loosey-goosey, if you ask me."

"We aren't rehearsing today." He held up the ball of tape for her inspection. "I picked off all the spike tape. Took no time at all and made only this ball. Half a semester's work down the drain. We've been shuttered, Margaret, as they say on the Great White Way."

Fenton lobbed the ball of tape past her toward a trash can, and Margaret watched it sail by and miss.

"I don't get it."

"Happens all the time," he said, although he couldn't think of a single instance in his career when it had. "Things aren't going as planned and the producers—" He made a slitting motion across his throat.

"But we all thought we were doing well," Margaret protested. "You *told* us we were good, just the other day. We've got Act One down, you said."

"My dear, I never flatter actors," he said. "The minute you do, they start dropping lines and missing cues. I *believe* I said I was pleased you wouldn't embarrass me opening night."

"But now you're saying it's over? There's no opening night? My family already bought tickets!"

The dejection on her face tugged at him, and it was time to stop joking. "There will be refunds. This is no reflection on you or any members of the cast, Margaret. When the others arrive, I'll explain. This decision came from high up the ladder."

As Fenton related Ramsey's decision, the students' disappointment unfolded, from shouts to tears. He kept a special eye on Andrew, whose chin drooped toward his chest. Fenton had already suspected that Andrew's parents led the charge to quash the production, and the boy's apparent shame seemed to confirm his hunch.

"I know this isn't what we wanted to happen," Fenton said, "but y'all will be top of my list for tryouts for *Our Town* in January. I do hope you'll give that a whirl. It's already approved by the provost, so that one will fly."

Susanna performed her final stage-manager duties, staying to help him shelve props that wouldn't be used until whenever the next Victorian-era play went up. "Want me to turn on the ghost light?" she asked as she threw on her cardigan to leave.

"No, I'll do it. You go."

He hauled the light from the wings, a tarnished brass floor lamp minus its shade, and plugged it in. No one had died in the Baines college theater that he knew of, so there were no ghosts waiting to perform when the house went dark. Still, the tug of history compelled Fenton to leave a single light glowing on stage each evening.

"Good night," he said to no one in particular.

On his walk home, Fenton tapped his inner pocket for the roll of Life Savers from Margaret and dropped several rings onto his tongue.

He knew he was odd to chew them, but they tasted better that way, like the topping of a butterscotch sundae. With the candy crunching in his mouth and the fall leaves crackling under his feet, Fenton slipped momentarily out of his troubles. He was not in jail, and he still had a job. His good fortune had held for another week. He was about to pop several more Life Savers when a bitter, metallic taste permeated his mouth.

In the morning, after a night of bourbon shots to quell the pain, he telephoned the dentist's office and coaxed the receptionist to wedge him into the afternoon schedule.

"I teach Dr. Sutter's daughter, Margaret," he said. "She's one of my favorite students."

In the waiting room, anxiously anticipating the novocaine that would wipe out his pain, Fenton sighed at the dearth of reading material, back issues of *Field & Stream* and *Time*.

He chose the news magazine, thumbing ahead to the theater pages to read about Broadway plays, all of which he'd seen the previous summer. Skimming backward, his eye caught a headline in the medicine section: "The Strange World: A Psychoanalyst Interviews Thousands of Homosexuals."

He glanced around the waiting room. Two people had entered after him, a grandfatherly man who appeared to be dozing off in his seat, and Kathy Yost, the provost's secretary. She caught his

eye and smiled, and Fenton nodded back. He shoved the magazine closer to his face, as if she could pierce the periodical cover
with her x-ray vision and read the shocking headline.

Dr. Edmund Bergler, a psychoanalyst, had published a book
about his years-long study of sexual deviance in men, with the
astonishing title of *1,000 Homosexuals*. He theorized that homosexuality stemmed not from desire for deviant sex but for self-
punishment. One of his patients labeled homosexuality "misery
concentrated" and "guilt heightened." Some men, Bergler reported,
had hundreds of sexual contacts, with few lasting more than a
couple of weeks and the shortest only five minutes. "The homosexual unwittingly yearns for exposure," Bergler told the reporter.
"He's drawn to the allure of danger." Risky behaviors, like quick
sex in public places, were common.

Fenton's eyes rested on the word *danger*. His thoughts roamed
to an encounter back in the summer. A friend in New York had
invited him to the beach at Cherry Grove, introducing him to a
thickly wooded area where men congregated for sex. Fenton had
ventured into the copse and within moments had found a willing
partner. The incident between them lasted five, maybe six, minutes
while sounds of other men's pleasure drifted around them. He saw
his partner's face only briefly, and they had exchanged smiles but
not names.

Since Mark's arrest, Fenton hadn't frequented any of his usual
haunts in Richmond. His contacts who knew him as "Fred"
might have thought he died. In a way, a piece of him had.

Fenton continued to scan the article, which described a patient
called "Mr. X," a married man whose wife had found his not-so-
hidden cache of pornographic photos of men. Eager both to save
his marriage and to avoid imprisonment, the man sought out Dr.
Bergler, who had cured him in eight months of psychiatric treatment. All that had been required, the doctor claimed, was "the
will to change."

Could it really be such a simple formula? The children's librarian hadn't worked out for him, although she had the amazing

ability to hold her bourbon like a man. He had loved her repartee, her endless collection of amusing, off-color stories. But after two months of keeping company, she had tired of chaste dates and expected more. The night they planned for him to sleep over, he begged off over the phone, feigning an ulcer flareup. Although he said they'd reschedule, he never called her again.

The following week, he had returned to Richmond and his favorite bar. He'd met a lovely man whose left ring finger had a lighter band of skin where his wedding ring would normally be.

"If a man wants to persist in self-punishment, homosexuality is certainly the most efficient means to that unhappy end," Dr. Bergler said at the end of the article.

When Fenton lowered the magazine from his face, he saw that Kathy was staring at him. "They called your name, Mr. Page," she said.

He flashed a grin. "Must be my subconscious warning me, 'Don't go in there!'"

"You looked so engrossed. Must be some article."

Fenton tucked the magazine under a tattered issue of *Field & Stream.* "I was reading about the spring season on Broadway," he said, standing and buttoning his jacket. "Only it's an old magazine, so I'd already seen everything."

"You're so cosmopolitan!"

Kathy was in her early twenties, a perky brunette who had graduated from Baines a few years back. After a production of *The Little Foxes*, she'd confided to Fenton that her dream was to live in New York. He wrote an effusive letter of recommendation for her to the American Academy of Dramatic Arts, but she decided to finish her education at Baines and, worse, to snap up a secretarial job after graduation.

Her choice of "cosmopolitan" played directly into his vanity, and Fenton gave her a low dramatic bow. "You are too kind," he said. "And you really should call me Fenton."

Kathy colored an attractive peachy-pink and wished him luck with the dentist.

That night, Fenton called directory assistance in Manhattan for Edmund Bergler's address and number. He got all the way to the closing of his letter to the doctor before he balled it up and threw it in the trash. He'd be thirty-five on his next birthday, technically middle-aged, and it would take a miracle to change now.

Later, though, he lay awake thinking about the dark jail cell reeking of bleach that Mark had described in vivid detail. Fenton switched on the lamp, retrieved the sheet from the trash basket, and tried again.

Chapter Nine

Margaret

The Baines campus sprawled across hundreds of acres. From the quad of antebellum buildings at Baines's heart, the campus fanned out in a leisurely way, to the gym, student union, and library, crisp new structures erected when Margaret was a toddler. Beyond those buildings lay a manicured lawn for impromptu games and sunning when the temperatures rose. Farther out still sat the stables where students boarded their horses, surrounded by winding trails.

Margaret didn't own a horse, which was one of many reasons she didn't fit in at Baines. Neither did her roommate, Polly, a biology major with a keen sense of humor. But Polly did own a bike, a Schwinn Varsity she'd inherited from her older brother, which she sometimes let Margaret take for a spin.

The bike offered Margaret freedom, even though straddling the bar took some getting used to. Margaret told Polly she took it to town on errands, but she actually rode it on the horse trails. Bikes and walkers weren't forbidden on the trails, merely frowned on by the equestrians who considered them their private domain. Margaret purposely went at odd hours when she rarely spotted any living creature but a bunny or doe. Nowhere else outside of Westminster Presbyterian could she find such a serene place to think.

And her sophomore year at Baines required a lot of time to think about what she was doing wrong and why she didn't fit in. Margaret's efforts to make friends hadn't panned out. Except for Polly and another girl who joined them for meals in the dining hall, Margaret stayed pretty much to herself. The history honors society—a small group that her favorite professor, Dr. Rider, presided over—was dominated by a few snobby girls, and Margaret rarely spoke. Who even knew why Lee-Anne Blakeney was majoring in history and not something genteel like music or art.

Then she'd lucked into the school play. How excited Margaret had been to get a speaking role, even though the boy's part was hard to explain to her parents. They seemed relieved by the play's cancellation. "Maybe it's for the best, Margie," her mother had said. The one positive thing to emerge from all the time spent in rehearsals was her kinship with Mr. Page. Without the play, Margaret would have to manufacture reasons to visit him at the theater. She already planned to try out for the spring show.

The morning after Mr. Page broke the news, Margaret borrowed Polly's bike. She wanted to ride and ride and ride. The trail she chose was dry and smooth from a dearth of rain and amazingly clear of the usual horse shit; a stable hand must have come through to shovel it away. Margaret pedaled faster and faster, strands of hair blowing across her face. She even laughed aloud a few times because no one was around to gossip that she was odd or "funny," the word some girls muttered about her. Margaret shook her head to dispel the image of Lee-Anne Blakeney, who riled and fascinated her at the same time.

As Margaret rounded a bend leading back toward the main campus, a rhythmic clip-clop of hooves reached her ears. She slowed and coasted toward the edge of the trail to get out of the way of whatever massive animal was heading toward her.

The sound of trotting came louder and faster, more like a gallop. Margaret applied her brakes too quickly, swearing as the Schwinn tipped over. She tried to hop off before the bike careened into an embankment, but her foot caught on the center bar of the boy's bike, and she landed in the leaves with the bike half on top of her. She managed to pull herself out from under it, but placing weight on her right leg brought a mewl of pain.

The clip-clops halted. "You hurt?"

When she looked up, Lee-Anne was appraising her from a majestic roan. She was outfitted for her morning ride in a hip-length tweed jacket, black velvet cap with a strap secured under her chin, and knee-high boots.

The sight of someone as perfect as Lee-Anne made Margaret's insides shrivel. Lee-Anne often giggled with Susanna while staring directly at Margaret. Maybe Lee-Anne sensed her crush or found her ridiculous for some other reason. Even Polly had witnessed Lee-Anne's tittering in the dining hall and said, "What's with her?"

Margaret brushed fragments of leaves off her jeans. She always wore clamdiggers for her rides, even when it was chilly, and the flesh on the bare spot above her ankle was scratched and torn. "I'm fine," she replied. "Just getting used to the brakes."

"You're bleeding."

"It's nothing, really."

"I could ride back and get help."

Lee-Anne Blakeney offering to help *her*? When this was the longest exchange they'd ever had? Margaret worried it was a trick, that she'd accept and then wait and wait for help that never arrived.

"I'm *fine*, I said."

"Well, a girl's bike would be better." Lee-Anne laid a slight emphasis on the word *girl's*.

"You're right about that. Thanks, Lee-Anne."

Lee-Anne continued to assess her from on high, her face lit by a pool of morning light. "Is Dr. Rider your adviser?" she asked out of the blue.

Margaret hesitated before answering. Was this another trick? "Yeah. Why?"

73

Lee-Anne shrugged. "I was thinking of switching, that's all."

The statement made no sense to Margaret. Late in freshman year, Lee-Anne had boasted of snagging Dr. Thoms as her adviser, when he accepted only one sophomore.

"But I probably won't," Lee-Anne added. "Why are you looking at me like that?"

Margaret raised her hand to shield her eyes. "Must be the sun."

Lee-Anne's gaze turned away from Margaret and down the path. "You know, these trails aren't really for bikes." She clicked her tongue, either at her horse or at Margaret, and cantered off.

Despite the tumble, Polly's bike wasn't hurt, not the slightest dent or scrape. Margaret walked it back to her dorm one step at a time. The throb in her leg slowly dulled, and by the time she reached her dorm she wasn't hobbling. Her ego was more bruised than anything. Lee-Anne would likely spread the story about "funny" Margaret who couldn't manage to navigate a three-speed bike.

Chapter Ten

Gen

The whine from the phone cut through Gen's concentration. The latest copy of the *Mississippi Valley Historical Review* rested open in her lap as she devoured an article written by her grad school mentor, Muriel Whitbread. Female historians so rarely saw their names on anything but book reviews.

The intrusion persisted. No one she knew phoned her late at night, and as she glanced toward the gossip bench near the kitchen, her thoughts jumped to the hang-ups that had become more frequent. As a rule, those calls interrupted her at supper, but maybe her harasser had missed their own schedule. She found that if she waited it out, the anonymous caller gave up at about five rings.

Her phone continued to squeal, though, prompting Gen to abandon her comfy spot on the sofa. What if it was Fenton's plea from jail to bring his bail check?

On the seventh ring, Gen took a deep breath and picked up the receiver, steeling herself for the outcome. The voice on the other end was so unexpected, it made the room too bright, the overhead light blinding her.

"I was just going to hang up. I was beginning to think you were out on the town."

Gen held herself back from falling into the light repartee of their past, when she might have quipped: "In Springboro? There's barely a town to go out *on.*" Instead, she said, "What do you want, Carolyn?"

"I guess I deserved that." Gen heard the scrape of a match, the quiet inhale of a cigarette from Carolyn's end. She waited, letting Carolyn exhale, conscious of making whatever it was she wanted to ask for harder.

"It's that time of year, is all," Carolyn said.

Gen lowered herself onto the bench cushion, her wobbly legs welcoming the support.

"You know—the Southern," Carolyn continued. "You going?"

She and Carolyn hadn't missed a Southern Historical Association convention since they met at the conference in Columbia. Every November it was their special time together, as cherished as a wedding anniversary. This year, Gen had almost decided she couldn't face it alone, but she'd sent in her registration and reserved a hotel room in Atlanta just the same. It hadn't occurred to her until now that Carolyn might go, too.

"Yeah," she replied. "You?"

"Too far." The answer filled Gen with relief.

A pause followed, with nothing but the sound of Carolyn's smoking. "Is that it?" Gen asked finally.

"Please don't get off yet," Carolyn said. "I didn't call to talk about the Southern."

While she waited, Gen had wrapped the phone cord so tightly around her fingers it made indentations.

"Gennie, could I see you over the Thanksgiving break? Unless you're going home, of course."

Carolyn's affectionate nickname for her made her throat dry. Gen badly wanted a sip of water, but the sink was too far from the bench. Her voice came out raspy and weak. "*See* me?"

"Maybe I could drive down."

"Why would you do that?"

"We—I ended it badly," Carolyn said after a long exhale.

Gen imagined her stubbing the cigarette into the ceramic ash-tray she'd found in the curio store in Springboro—a scantily clad woman lounging poolside, probably from the 1930s. Fenton agreed to make the purchase to spare Gen the embarrassment, and she'd presented it to Carolyn for her thirty-eighth birthday.

"I've regretted it every day," Carolyn continued.

"The badly part or the ending it part?"

"All of it."

Gen stood up, ready to bring the conversation to a close. She could almost taste the burn of the Campari she'd need to calm down. An emergency call from Fenton would have almost been easier to handle. At least she would have known what to do.

"I can't talk about this tonight," she said.

"Hell, any time would be fine with me. I'm grateful you didn't hang up or curse me out."

"When did I ever curse you out?"

Carolyn sighed. "Not once, Gennie."

"You don't get to call me that anymore. I have to go."

"When can we talk again?"

Gen ran a hand through her hair. Should she end it now or end it later? Or should she not end it at all?

"This weekend," she said after a long pause, and then laid out her stipulations before dropping the receiver into its cradle.

Gen poured Campari and soda water over ice and sank back down onto the gossip bench. The bitter scent hit her nostrils as she lifted the glass. On the message pad she kept there, she scratched out a list of questions with a hand that quivered at first, then became surer as the spicy liqueur did its work:

Why now?

How long would the visit be?

Where would C stay?

Does this mean sex?

Why would I do this?

Ripping off that sheet, Gen started a second list—why she should never let the visit happen.

I'm still not over it.

I'm still hurt.

I don't trust C.

I can't draw attention to my private life.

And then she penned a third list, noting why she should agree to the visit, despite all the minuses.

We had 6 years together.

I still think about C.

I'm lonely, damn it.

After underscoring the last line twice, she freshened her drink and brought it to bed.

Gen carried the anticipation of Carolyn's next call with her from class to class, to meetings with students, to the grocery store, to the bank, to coffee with Ruby, and back home. She found herself savoring its arrival like a tart from the Barrington Tea Shoppe— one not to be shared, not even with Fenton. He was so distracted these days anyway, his worries tumbling out of him whenever they spoke, that he might trivialize her news.

Just the thought of talking to Carolyn again made Gen's skin warm and tingly, her toes curl in her pumps. All because the very evening Carolyn had called, the evening Gen had compiled her pros and cons lists, she had decided she would take Carolyn back in a heartbeat.

She didn't want to be so easy or predictable. She should make Carolyn work to get her back. But when it came right down to it, Gen had to force herself not to pick up the receiver herself and call earlier than their scheduled appointment.

On Saturday she dusted the gossip bench, straightened the message pad and pen. She changed her clothes twice, even though Carolyn couldn't see what she was wearing through the long-distance line.

The phone rang twenty minutes early—not like Carolyn, who was more often late. When she heard Juliet's clear voice on the other end, Gen's disappointment pinched like a tight belt.

"I wonder if you have any time this weekend to meet for coffee or a drink?" Juliet asked after some small talk. "This damn tenure packet has me wanting to slit my throat."

Gen smiled, the memory of being overwhelmed by her own application fresh in her mind. Still, the clock read six minutes to two, and she needed to keep the line open.

"Can I call you back later? I'm expecting another call."

"Oh, sure. And if this weekend's bad for you, it can wait."

Guilty at her own abruptness, Gen tacked on a lie that slipped out as easily as if it were true. "My sister's calling soon. About our father's health." Her sister *had* written to Gen with a brief mention that their father was retiring, and he *had* suffered a heart attack a few years back; but there'd been no mention of his health in the letter.

"How horrible! Well, I won't keep you another minute. I'll be wishing the best for your family."

Gen got a tumbler of water and repositioned herself at the bench, crossing and uncrossing her legs, trying to find a posture that was natural. The action made her feel ridiculous. All the evenings and weekends she and Carolyn had talked when they were a couple, Gen had never considered how she sat. They spoke so often and so long that a few times Gen had to pay her phone bill in installments.

At two, the phone didn't ring, and it didn't ring at 2:10 or 2:15. Gen got up and walked the perimeter of the kitchen once, then a few more times to steady and calm herself. She checked the wall calendar where she'd printed "CAROLYN 2 PM" in Saturday's block. Had she said two-thirty or three, but written two by mistake?

At 2:17, she wondered if Carolyn had gotten stuck on another call, the way she almost had with Juliet.

At 2:19, she considered that her clock might be running fast.

At 2:22, she downed her water in a long gulp.

At 2:25, she walked to the front door, thinking about throwing on her coat and leaving. If she did ever call, Carolyn would hear the phone ring and ring. At 2:29 Gen decided taking the phone off the hook was better because Carolyn would get a busy signal that said *I'm far too busy to talk to you.*

But she hesitated, and the wall clock read 2:31 when the phone finally rang. Gen let it squawk several times.

"Oh, thank God I haven't missed you," Carolyn said. "I am so, so sorry, Gen. I ran out to get cigarettes but there was an accident in town and all this traffic, and I just got back."

She held her thought: *You needed cigarettes more than you needed to keep an appointment?* "It's fine. I didn't notice."

"Phew! I had an image of you fuming over there."

"I was writing and lost track of time." She lowered herself onto the bench. "So."

"So. Here we are."

The *pro* and *con* sheets lay in a neat pile on the bench. Gen lifted the top sheet, the one that ended with *I'm lonely, damn it* and spotted *I don't trust C* on the list underneath it.

"Have you given any thought to what I asked? About coming to see you?"

Gen pushed the lists away, embarrassed how often and how much she'd considered Carolyn's request.

"I have."

"And?"

"And I'm not clear about why you want to. All of a sudden."

Carolyn lit a match. "I understand," she said. "I was a beast, springing the information on you the way I did. You deserved better."

"A better breakup?" Gen laughed at the audacity.

"Better treatment."

"I deserved someone who wasn't going to leave me."

"Things weren't perfect between us—"

"We had our difficulties, I know, but my parents did, too, when I was young, and my father didn't just up and move to another state." She didn't know she still felt these things, or more accurately, that she intended to say them. She had thought this call would go down smooth, like a fine brandy—a heartfelt apology, then a warm reconciliation. She didn't know, either, that the

80

analogy to her parents, a couple together since the nineteen-teens, would glide out so easily.

"What do your parents have to do with us?"

"I thought we were in it for the long haul. Like them."

"But they're married—"

"It doesn't matter." Her throat scratched, but she went on. "*You* had someone else."

Carolyn took in a deep, audible breath. "I don't know how you know, but I won't lie to you. There *was* someone. It was brief and unfortunate. I actually knew her before you and I met. She always dazzled me, and it just sort of happened. It was a huge mistake. One I'll regret for a very long time."

And there it was—the infidelity Gen had wondered about. She had hoped she was wrong, that Carolyn would hasten to deny it.

"Patricia Ormond." Gen didn't mean to speak the name out loud, but it escaped on its own. The year before, when she arrived at Carolyn's for Thanksgiving break, an unfamiliar Chevy with Maryland plates had occupied the carport. When Carolyn helped Gen carry in her weekend case, she had whispered in a rush, "Don't be mad, but my friend Pat from grad school came to town unexpectedly with her fiancé. She doesn't know about us."

That stung like a slap. "We've never had to hide *here*," Gen pointed out.

Carolyn colored and added mischievously, "We'll still have plenty of time together, late at night." Despite Gen's annoyance and disappointment, they had an enjoyable holiday with Patricia and her fiancé. Gen thought she remembered his name as Ken or Kirk, something crisp and monosyllabic. She hadn't given Patricia another thought until Carolyn announced the move to Towson.

Now, Carolyn's "I'm sorry" confirmed Gen's suspicion.

"So, what? She ended it, and now you're alone again and you want to come back?" Gen couldn't keep the bitter edge out of her tone. "And then when you're dazzled by someone else, you'll do it all again."

81

"I understand that you can't trust me right now," Carolyn said in a measured voice. "I get it. But we had almost six years together in which I was completely faithful. I swear it, Gen. I had lots of opportunities in Richmond, women I met when you weren't in town, but I never, ever did anything about them. I didn't want to! I don't know what happened with Patty—with *her*. It was like being caught in a riptide."

An image flashed into Gen's mind of Carolyn bobbing in a swirling current of water off Rehoboth Beach.

"And I want you to know that she didn't end it. *I* did."

"Did she lose her dazzle?"

"I'm sorry I used that word," Carolyn said. "I think the whole thing was more about me, anyway. That probably sounds ridiculous." She struck a second match, then a third and fourth in quick succession. Gen pictured the matches going out one by one as Carolyn struggled to steady her hand.

"It's too hard to explain on the phone," Carolyn said, defeat heavy in her voice. "There are things—I thought if I could see you, maybe that would help, but I've made such a mess of everything, I understand if you don't want to."

Gen smoothed her lists, which she had folded and refolded into squares without even realizing what she'd done. She'd been so sure she would take Carolyn back, but now her resolve wavered.

"There's too much going on right now," she said. "I'll make a decision after the Southern."

Chapter Eleven

Gen

The NAACP meeting took place in the assembly hall of Grace AME Church. The modest red-brick building hovered at the edge of a clump of businesses and shotgun houses in the Negro neighborhood of Slocum Point. Some white folks called it Colored Town. The church's elderly pastor no longer served as the chapter president, but he still volunteered his space, a long, skinny room that had assumed a shabby air since Gen was last there six years back. The walls wore a thin film of gray dust, and some of the venetian blinds were missing slats. But as Gen waited in a long entry line with mostly Negroes and a handful of white people, she noted the cracked linoleum floor that sparkled as if someone had scrubbed it to a high gloss that very day.

With pen poised to check off the attendees, Mae Johnson, the chapter secretary, greeted Gen warmly. "You'll have to remind me of your name," she added. Mae's tightly waved hair was the same hairstyle Gen remembered, but the strands of white were new.

"I'm probably not on there. I've been remiss with my dues." She reached into her wallet for a dollar bill, which she handed to Mae.

"It's two dollars now," Mae said.

Gen muttered an apology. She had stopped paying her dues

while she was working on tenure, when Virginia ordered the NAACP to file its membership lists with the state—a technique used by Southern states to intimidate the organization and its members. Gen drew out another dollar and apologized again for not keeping up.

When she heard Gen's name, Mae's face tensed, assuming an *I remember you* look, and the air between them cooled. Two years back, as part of a wave of integration efforts, the NAACP chapter had backed an effort by Mae's daughter, a straight-A student, to gain admission to Baines, the closest four-year college. When Frank Johnson, Mae's husband and the chapter president, wrote to Gen to ask for an *amicus* letter on his daughter's behalf, Gen had disposed of his note without replying. Her action had shamed her and nagged at her conscience, but she had not wanted to risk an association with a legal case like theirs in the middle of her push for tenure. To Mae and Frank, though, her silence surely looked like garden-variety bigotry.

The Johnson girl lost her case when the college administration successfully argued that her enrollment would require a rewriting of the school charter, which stated that Baines was founded for Christian white women.

Now, Gen was desperate to ease the tension. "Mrs. Johnson, I never got to tell you how sorry I was about the outcome for your daughter at Baines. She was more than qualified."

Mae nodded stiffly.

"I hope she landed somewhere she can use her talents."

Mae took in a stoic breath. "Bennett's a good school, but she's all the way off in Greensboro. I don't see her but a few times a semester."

"Let's hope Baines will be more forward-thinking someday."

"Someday won't be time enough for *my* girls." Mae glanced past Gen to the next woman in line.

Guilt rushed through her, and Gen fished in her purse for an extra three dollars—what would normally pay for a week's gas. Mae took the bills without looking at her and stuffed them into the metal cash box with a respectful "much obliged."

After the uncomfortable moment with Mae, Gen felt too embarrassed to speak to Frank Johnson directly, but she caught his eye and smiled. A compact, light-skinned man, Frank, like his wife, looked older and more drawn with the passage of time. Gen didn't remember him wearing wire-framed glasses, which gave him a scholarly air. She and Frank had enjoyed several lively conversations about integration in the past, and just before she stopped attending meetings, they'd graduated to a first-name basis. This evening, he nodded at her in courteous recognition but then turned his back and continued talking to the group of men that circled him.

The lengthy agenda included everything from updates about school integration efforts to routine reports from the Church Work Committee and the Women's Committee, which reminded Gen of a history department meeting. When Frank opened the floor to new business, a young man at the other side of the hall spoke up, and the meeting heated up.

"Mr. Johnson, no disrespect, but the sit-in at Darnell's lunch counter me and Theo proposed didn't make the agenda. You told us last time it would."

Frank pressed his lips together. "We can talk about it now if you want, Marcus, Theo."

The pastor cut in before the young men could respond. "No need for that, Frank. I can tell you right now that a sit-in is not a strategy this board wants to pursue."

"Why's that, Reverend?"

"We can't invite violence against our members," the pastor continued. "We can't support our folks going to jail. You see what just happened to Dr. King."

"We're not talking violence. But sometimes you got to take risks to get results. Dr. King knows it. Y'all know it."

"You might not be talking violence, but you could get your head bashed in just the same."

Marcus shook his head, and a hush descended over the room. After a pause, Frank interrupted the silence. "Marcus, we appreciate you and your desire to shake things up. We wish change

85

would come more quickly, too. On the matter of the lunch counters, however, the strategy that the national association advocates seems like the safest strategy."

The younger people in the hall groaned audibly.

"Now just wait, y'all. Boycotts have been successful. We've passed out fliers in the neighborhood asking folks to boycott Darnell's and Woolworth's and volunteer to picket if they can."

"Yeah, my mama got hers," Marcus said. "But seriously, Mr. Johnson? You talk a good game about change, but how you gonna get change if you don't demand it?"

"Not with all deliberate speed, that's for sure," the young man next to him quipped. Gen recognized the phrase immediately as the Supreme Court's vague directive when the *Brown* decision ordered the states to integrate their schools.

"Change ain't coming to us on a silver platter," Marcus continued. "And you wonder why young folks like us are heading over to SNCC."

With that, Marcus said something to the other young men, and they rose and left *en masse*. The chapter had not experienced rifts in strategy when Gen attended meetings before. There had been peaceful agreement on all the major issues. She wondered if the younger members like Marcus were students or recent graduates from the Negro school, Lincoln Junior College. The Student Nonviolent Coordinating Committee, founded the previous spring, advocated lunch counter sit-ins and other direct actions.

A wave of grumbling traveled up and down the rows of chairs. Frank maintained order with a gavel. "Don't you mind those young folks, Mr. Johnson," a woman called out. "Some young folks be the death of us all. You just keep doing what you're doing."

"Mrs. Combs, those young men are our future. There's room for everyone in the movement."

The name Combs sounded familiar to Gen. She thought that had been the name of the man caught with Mark Patton.

The final bit of business was the presidential election.

"I've asked some of our white members to act as escorts if they can. They did a wonderful job in the first weeks of school, transporting our children safely, and they have contributed mightily to helping register folks to vote." Frank gestured to several white men sitting at the side of the hall.

"There's a clear choice this year, and Negroes can make a difference. I know many of you listened in to the presidential debates and heard Senator Kennedy speak about Negro rights. His meeting with Dr. King last summer surely influenced his thinking."

"But where was he when they arrested Dr. King? Why'd it take him so long to say anything?"

Heads bobbed. News of Martin Luther King Jr.'s arrest at an Atlanta department store sit-in hadn't surfaced in the Springboro paper, but Gen had read the story in *The New York Times* at the college library. Kennedy had remained mum about the arrest for a week.

"I'm not going to second-guess the candidate so close to the election," Frank said. "The fact is, the senator has finally called Mrs. King to offer his help, and that's good enough for me."

After Frank gaveled the meeting closed, Gen mustered the courage to speak to him. She had several items on her personal agenda. When she offered her hand shyly, Frank paused before shaking it.

"Dr. Rider," he said, the use of her title a wall between them.

"I'm sorry I haven't been around, Mr. Johnson. Work . . . interfered."

Frank was too much of a professional to point out how she'd fallen short. "I'm thankful you're back."

"I have a few questions for you," she ventured. "The first one's for a friend."

Frank leaned an ear toward her, but his eyes skimmed the room.

"He's in need of a civil rights attorney, a white attorney, and I wondered if you might suggest someone. The only lawyer I know besides yourself is retired and, besides, he specialized in taxes."

"What's your friend's trouble?" Frank asked.

Gen hesitated for a moment and lowered her voice. "It's . . . he wasn't part of it, but he may get caught up with the men arrested on Labor Day."

Frank's face clouded. "I see. Mrs. Combs's boy is in the same trouble. I can give you a name, but he's not in town. Tell your friend to call my office tomorrow and talk to my wife."

He started to move away, but she touched his sleeve lightly.

"One more thing and then I'll let you go. I wonder if you might spare some time soon for an interview. I'm undertaking some new research on the founding of the NAACP, particularly on Miss Mary White Ovington, and I'd love to talk to you."

Frank's eyes flashed with what Gen assumed was surprise, and she wondered if he didn't recognize Ovington's name.

"She was the first secretary—"

"You don't have to school me in my own history," Frank snapped, and Gen shrank back from the rebuke. His lips formed a tight line.

"Of course not," she said.

"Anyway," he continued, in a slightly less harsh tone, "I wouldn't have much to offer. I never met Miss Ovington. You'll want the folks in Washington."

"Yes, I just—sorry." There was no easy way out of the hole she'd dug for herself.

"Excuse me now." Frank brushed past her. "Lamont, can I get a word with you?"

Her cheeks burned with shame, and only the crisp night air cooled her face. When Gen crossed the street to her car, she noticed a couple of white men lurking in the darkened doorway of the barber shop. One was whistling what sounded like "Tallahassee Lassie," a catchy song Gen knew because Carolyn owned the 45.

"What's a nice lady doing at a nigger meeting?" the other man asked her as she fumbled in her bag for her keys. He looked familiar. His hand gripped something long.

She almost snapped, "None of your business" out of instinct but remained quiet as her hand located the key ring.

"Seems like a lady should know better." A baseball bat emerged at his side.

Gen laced her keys between her fingers like Carolyn had taught her. Carolyn had lived in a seamy neighborhood in graduate school, which put her on alert for trouble. "You can poke somebody's eyes out with keys," she had said, matter-of-fact.

"Ah, let her go." The man who had been whistling pointed his chin toward the church. Over her shoulder, Gen followed his line of sight to a group of people exiting the church hall, including Frank and Mae Johnson.

She scrambled into her car and clicked down the lock button. The key turned in the ignition, and Gen sat revving the engine while her mind darted. With little time to ponder her options, she leaned heavily on her horn, letting it scream into the night.

The horn blast did the trick, shifting Frank and Mae's attention away from their companions and toward the imminent danger across the street. Within seconds, Frank had hurried the group back into the building.

The white man with the bat spat out something she couldn't hear through the closed window, and then he swung at her passenger-side door. Gen pressed her foot heavily to the pedal, but the car wasn't fast enough to miss the crunch of contact.

On Halloween, the campus rippled with exuberance. From her office window, Gen watched students crossing the quad in cowgirl holsters and hats, ghost sheets with eyes cut out, nurses' uniforms, and ballerina tutus. She hoped the Aunt Jemima in blackface wasn't one of her own students.

A girl walking with Margaret Sutter wore a lab coat smeared with gory daubs of red paint. Margaret's costume gave Gen pause: she was outfitted as a Girl Scout, complete with a beret and sash. Discomfited at the memory of the cookies someone had left for her, Gen lowered her window shade and turned her attention back to the open newspaper on her desk.

The morning edition of the *Gazette* spotlighted Mark Patton's purported "ring of perversion" as the lead story. Mark and James Combs now faced sodomy charges. The article mentioned other parties who might face indictment, which made Gen's foot tap double-time. She tossed the newspaper into her trash can and left for class.

The night before, she had stuffed a slightly bent cardboard mask with gold streamers and black feathers into her briefcase— a leftover from a gay costume party in Richmond she had attended the year before. Now Gen slipped the elastic band over her hair just before entering her classroom. Her students broke into a round of appreciative applause.

"Love the feathers!"

"So cute!"

"You look like Marie Antoinette!"

"Let's hope I keep my head." Within seconds, she yanked the mask off in such haste that the band snapped. "I usually bring cookies to class for Halloween, but I forgot to order them at the bakery. I'll get some for next time."

The chatter of her students subsided as she wrote the words *PLESSY V. FERGUSON 1896* on the blackboard in all caps and underlined them.

"Today we're looking at a landmark Supreme Court case from the last century," she said. "This is the case that was overturned in 1954 by *Brown v. Board of Education*."

Pens scratched across notebooks.

"This case had its start down in Louisiana, where the state passed the Separate Car Act in 1890. Who can tell me what that law said?"

The girls flipped open textbooks and kept their heads down. No one would catch her eye. Below the name of the case, Gen wrote *SEPARATE CAR ACT* and underscored it as well.

"Okay, here's a refresher. The Separate Car Act said that there must be separate railway cars for whites and Negros. And what happened as a result?" Only the rustle of pages and one sharp cough met her ears. "All right, then, what was the Committee of Citizens and what role did it play in this case? For those of you studying French, it was called the *Comité des Citoyens*." The words came out slowly and uncomfortably. She'd asked Juliet for the correct pronunciation.

In the silence that continued, Gen's frustration mounted into annoyance. She placed her chalk in the tray and brushed white dust from her hands. "Girls, I'm getting the distinct feeling you're unprepared."

One student's hand inched up.

"Go on, Lois."

"It's just . . . well, it's Halloween, professor, and everyone's having fun. Are you really going to make us talk about old *Plessy*?" Titters from the other students brought a smile to the girl's lips.

Gen crossed her arms. "I'm truly sorry to inconvenience you by expecting you to learn something in my classroom. And I'm also sorry you have such low regard for . . . old *Plessy*, did you say?"

"I didn't mean it nasty like that."

Gen nodded, trying not to lose her temper. "All right, Lois, why don't you tell us what you remember about Mr. Homer Plessy?"

The student fumbled with her notebook. "He was a colored fella—no, wait, a mulatto—who demanded to ride in the white car of a train. And they wouldn't let him because of the law." She seemed confident of her assessment of the case at first, then added quickly, "I think."

"You *think*? And is that what the rest of you took away from the reading, too—that some Negro had the audacity to want to ride in the white car?"

A few heads bobbed, but most eyes fell back to their text-books. More pages riffled.

"How many of you did the reading?"

A handful of students volunteered that they had.

"But most of you spent time putting together costumes for today, quite elaborate ones in some cases, and didn't bother to read the assigned pages? And for those of you who did, your understanding of Mr. Plessy's case is so rudimentary that you've reduced him to an uppity mulatto who didn't know his place?"

Gen turned to the blackboard and struck out *SEPARATE CAR ACT* with the eraser, rubbing ferociously at the ghost streaks left behind until they were gone. She wasn't sure what angered her until her mind flashed to the faces of the white men lying in wait for the NAACP members just days before.

"I honestly can't believe you, girls," she said, turning to them again. "Can you even imagine the courage it took for Mr. Plessy to take a seat in a whites-only car?" Spittle gathered at the corners of her mouth, and she wiped at it with her index finger. "This is 1960, not 1860. Negroes still face horrible discrimination and unspeakable violence. If you are the future, you make me despair for this country!"

She'd taken students to task before but never in such a belittling tone, and their faces registered their shock. Gen glared at them for a long moment, then said, "Read your text. I need to get something from my office," and exited the classroom.

She hadn't left anything behind, she just needed to rest her weight against her desk and take in some deep breaths. Her rebuke of the students was rash. They were little more than children, clinging to old beliefs learned from their parents. She would calm herself, apologize, and start class afresh with a patient smile. Her class notes always outlined alternate plans for when students were less than prepared.

The breaths soothed her, and in a few minutes Gen opened her eyes. She heard shuffling in the hallway and through her open door saw Lee-Anne Blakeney scurrying from Henry Thoms's office. The girl wore a flouncy, sleeveless white gown suitable for a debutante ball, with a rhinestone tiara topping her blond ringlets. Gen might have ignored her, but Lee-Anne had nearly tripped into the hallway in her haste, and her chest heaved with exertion. She wore one silver high heel, but the other was gripped in her hand.

"Everything all right, Lee-Anne?" Gen called from the doorway.

"Oh, yes, ma'am, just late for class."

Lee-Anne balanced on one foot while hiking up the right side of her skirt. Gen's eyes traveled to her exposed calf as the girl stuffed her bare foot into the spare shoe.

"I hope Cinderella doesn't have far to go," Gen remarked as Lee-Anne flinched in pain.

The girl smiled sheepishly. "They're my mom's and I wear a half-size larger."

Henry Thoms emerged from his office and stopped in his tracks, his mouth clenched like he'd bitten into a lemon. He nodded in Gen's direction, locked the door behind him, and retreated down the hall. Lee-Anne took off in the opposite direction.

Back in the classroom, the girls were suspended in silence as if they had been playing Simon Says and had frozen in place for ten minutes.

"I apologize," Gen said. "Snapping my mask like that must have put me out of sorts. Let's return to *Plessy*, shall we?"

Geoffrey Huston, an avuncular Brit who had served as history chairman for a dozen years, scheduled a department meeting the last Monday of each month. The distance between meetings suited Gen. The only woman in the history faculty, she didn't merit a spot in the men's club. Most of her department colleagues, although jovial enough, treated her like a kid sister who invaded their treehouse. Huston was the exception. In intermittent spurts of collegiality, he invited her to his office for a chat and a cup of tea. He expressed genuine interest in Gen's research into the NAACP's history.

Professors and instructors trickled into the department's conference room, occupying the same seats around the long oak table every time—creatures of habit, just like their students. With six full-timers, the department was larger than most at Baines.

"Didn't we just have a meeting? I could have sworn I saw all y'all not a month ago." Roscoe Babcock plunked his briefcase down next to Gen's. He made the same crack every month, and by now the faculty barely acknowledged it.

Henry Thoms was noticeably missing when Huston entered

at the appointed meeting time. "Anyone seen Henry?" the chairman asked. When silence followed, he pressed, "Roscoe?"

Roscoe dismissed the question with another quip. "Am I my brother's keeper?"

Huston huffed, glancing up at the wall clock, then launched the meeting without the senior-most professor.

The mimeographed agenda carried the same items every month with only slight variations. Gen often wished she could read surreptitiously, but Huston expected full attention from everyone.

Neither of Gen's committees was very active in the fall semester. The college-wide Admissions Committee and the history department's Academic Awards Committee picked up speed in the spring, so when her turn to report arrived, she passed her time to Roscoe. Along with several other important positions like Tenure and Privilege, Roscoe served on the executive committee of the Faculty Senate and required more than his allotted time for substantive comments interspersed with the occasional lighthearted remark.

In the middle of Roscoe's report, Thoms ambled in, apologizing for his tardiness. "Couldn't be helped," he muttered.

"I'm happy you could join us, Henry," Huston said, his tone dry and clipped. Gen had observed growing friction between the two men, but there was no one in the department she felt comfortable enough to ask about it.

When prompted for his report, Thoms rearranged his papers with exaggerated importance. He chaired the department's powerful hiring committee, which was accepting applications for the position vacated by a professor who had retired.

"Many fine Renaissance men to consider," Thoms said. "Damned hard to narrow it to ten. Oh, pardon my French, Virginia."

Gen didn't react. She knew there were likely Renaissance women who had applied but who didn't make Thoms's cut. He preferred giggly girls to serious women scholars. When Gen gained seniority in the department, she planned to put herself forward as possible chairwoman. If Huston still headed the department, he might be fed up enough with Thoms's reign to let her run.

Huston's updates closed out the meeting, as routine as usual. But then he surprised them with a piece of unsettling new business.

"Congressman Duke will be visiting campus tomorrow afternoon." Huston puffed out his fleshy cheeks. "A last-minute campaign swing, I imagine. The mayor will host him. He'll be talking to the administration, but he's asked to meet with faculty at four o'clock."

Huston twisted his pen in his hands. "Attendance isn't mandatory, just suggested. If you don't have time to spare, I understand, but it would be good if at least one of us was there to report back. I'd go myself, but office hours and all." A flimsy excuse, easily circumvented.

"What's on the agenda, Geoff?" Thoms said.

Huston cleared his throat. "The dean says the congressman shares the mayor's concern about deviancy. He wants to talk about it as a problem on campuses and lay out some sort of program to put an end to it."

Gen's heart thumped, matching the rhythm of her foot under the table. A legislative committee in Florida was ferreting out homosexuals among faculty, staff, and students in that state. A friend of Fenton's from his acting days had been interrogated by officials at the University of Florida but kept his job when he suddenly obtained a girlfriend.

"Put an end? As in take out a hit on someone?" Roscoe harrumphed. "Those fools in Washington have nothing better to do than trump up problems and meddle where they don't belong!"

"Yes, it seems like a load of codswallop to me," Huston said. "But I was asked to inform you about the visit. There may be further instructions coming down from the dean or the provost after this, and we don't want to be caught off guard if that happens."

"I don't see why *this* department needs to get involved," Thoms added. "Nothing but family men and our own lady professor here. Let the other departments police their culprits and weed them out. It's no secret who's who."

"What does that mean, Henry?" Gen's mouth tightened around her words.

Thoms lifted his shoulders and made a little *pfft* sound.

"I take it you won't be going then, Henry," Huston said.

Thoms leaned forward as if ready to change his mind and volunteer, so Gen jumped in. "I'd be happy to go, Geoffrey," she said. "I'll take notes after and share them with y'all."

Chapter Twelve

Fenton

Dean Rolfe scheduled the faculty meeting with the congressman for the largest space on campus—the theater. When Fenton entered from his office under the stage, the house lights were up and the auditorium was half full, with professors and instructors scattered through the rows. Heads swiveled his way as he hastened up the side aisle and plopped into an end seat behind a row of female faculty that included Gen and Ruby. The bulwark of women soothed him.

"Fancy meeting you here," he whispered into the space between Gen and Ruby.

"Best to hear firsthand what the congressman has up his sleeve," Gen said.

"My thoughts exactly."

Dean Rolfe introduced the mayor, dapper and polished as always. If Fenton ever encountered him at a bar in Richmond, he wouldn't be shocked. The mayor liked to gush about his lovely wife, the childhood sweetheart who grew up down the block from him in Springboro. *The lady doth protest too much*, was Fenton's thinking.

According to coverage in the *Springboro Gazette*, the incumbent was engaged in a close mayoral race against the former county prosecutor. Both men had put forward anti-vice platforms, with the prosecutor arguing that his experience better positioned him to tackle the town's recent problems. Fenton had listened to the challenger on the radio and found his tough-guy stance both convincing and terrifying. Coupled with the current police chief, a prosecutor-turned-mayor boded ill.

The mayor spoke briefly, reminding the audience about his determination to smoke out deviants but careful not to veer off into a full-blown campaign speech. He then introduced the eleven-term congressman, who also faced unexpected competition at the ballot box. In polls, he led his younger opponent by just two points, with a four-point margin of error.

Duke, whose white eyebrows met at the bridge of his nose, commanded the space with his baritone. "My office is working closely with your mayor and other local officials," he announced. "Today, we launch a daring pilot program called 'Know Your Neighbor.'"

That explained the baskets of paper a crew of young men proceeded to carry through the auditorium. Fenton took a sheet from the top and passed the basket down his row like a church collection.

"Just invested in a brand-new xerography machine for the office, so we decided to put it to good use," Duke said with pride.

"Our tax dollars at work," Fenton heard Ruby quip to Gen.

The sheet featured a drawing of a serious-looking man with a telephone receiver pressed to his ear. Below the picture a description set in large type couched the Know Your Neighbor initiative as a sort of block watch. Reading between the lines suggested something more nefarious—an effort to encourage citizens and coworkers to spy on each other and report potential "moral turpitude" to the police.

"So how does this work in Springboro and specifically for y'all at Baines College? I'll tell you. No one knows each other better than colleagues, right? Why, I could tell you what my aide ordered for lunch. You had the chicken salad on a bun, am I right, Dan?"

A young man whose slender frame was swimming in a cheap gray suit halted in the aisle and saluted his boss on stage.

"See there? It looked mighty good, too, I should add."

The joke brought snickers from the mayor and dean but no one else.

"We're hoping to make everyone just a little bit more aware of what's going on around us. If something smells fishy and you bring it to the attention of the authorities, then that takes away its power to stink up your fine school and the whole dang town, for that matter." The congressman winked toward someone in a front row.

When Duke ended his remarks, a handful of faculty members raised their hands, including Ruby, but the dean popped out of his seat and explained that Congressman Duke didn't have time to entertain questions. "You can address your questions to my office," Rolfe said.

Before being whisked offstage, Duke said, "I apologize for having to run, but my campaign staff has me booked solid, most likely through the Second Coming."

The tepid applause that followed reminded Fenton of an off-Broadway show he'd seen that bombed.

"Well, wasn't that informative," Ruby said when the faculty rose to exit. "I wanted to ask Mr. Duke if all this nonsense was just a hissy fit because he didn't get to chair the House Un-American Activities Committee."

"You wouldn't have!" Fenton said.

"Someone should. He seems to have made a quick U-turn from hunting down Reds to sniffing out—" She glanced at the flier, "—moral turpitude. Good Lord."

Ruby ripped her flier into perfect fourths and tossed the pieces into a trash bin at the back of the theater. With her secure position at the college, a respected husband, and three married sons, she could afford to be cavalier about the menace of Know Your Neighbor. For Fenton, the danger burned in his gut like wildfire.

Gen folded her own flier neatly and slid it into her purse. Fenton caught her eye and mouthed *talk later* before returning to his office.

Fenton reread the letter from Dr. Bergler as the minutes ticked away on the clock in the waiting room. The good doctor had responded with admirable speed, referring him to a colleague in Richmond named Dr. Thorne. Bergler claimed Dr. Thorne had enjoyed "great success" with cases such as Fenton's. "Even at your advanced age." The words pricked at Fenton's pride. He was mature, certainly, but thirty-four hardly qualified as "advanced."

His hand trembled as he returned the letter to his satchel. The gay grapevine teemed with horror stories of forced hospitalizations, lobotomies, and chemical castration. Dr. Bergler's response, however, had assured Fenton his treatment was merely a talking cure undertaken several times a week. It sounded harmless enough, and Fenton certainly had no trouble talking about himself. Given the new level of anxiety Congressman Duke had introduced with his "Sell Out Your Neighbor" initiative, as Gen called it, he hoped the doctor might offer strategies for avoiding suspicion.

When the door to the inner office finally opened, Dr. Thorne's easy smile greeted him, radiating benevolence.

"Mr. Patterson? Please come in." As with Bergler, Fenton had used the pseudonym Frederick Patterson, even though he trusted their sessions would be confidential. He was less sure if a doctor's records could be impounded if he was ever arrested.

Dr. Thorne motioned Fenton to a scratchy-looking gray couch and settled into the fashionable Eames chair opposite him. The psychiatrist said nothing at first but continued smiling while Fenton's eyes took in the diplomas and Rothko-like paintings on the walls, the Kleenex box on the coffee table, the thick medical tomes on the bookshelf. Fenton swiped his damp palms together and tried to get comfortable, but the couch's stiff cushion reminded him of a mattress in a cheap motel.

"Let's start with why you're here, Mr. Patterson."

The intimate history he'd shared in his letter to Dr. Bergler gushed out of him, but he added depth and perspective, including his police interrogation and Duke's campus visit. He drew the Know Your Neighbor flier from his pocket and handed it to Dr. Thorne, who jotted notes into a leather-bound book.

"Is your stomach upset, Mr. Patterson?" Fenton glanced down; he hadn't noticed that his hand had traveled to his gut, which churned like a cement mixer.

"I had a bleeding ulcer a few years ago. It might be back."

"An ulcer."

Dr. Thorne closed his notebook but kept a finger between the pages to mark his place. Fenton assumed he would now offer advice, something for the fifteen dollars he was paying him, but all he seemed to want to do was repeat what Fenton said and state the obvious.

"So, then," Fenton said, "I've laid out the sordid details of what's happening. I'm wondering what you'd suggest for someone in my pr-predicament."

"You see your life as sordid."

"Most everyone around me thinks it is," Fenton snapped.

"What about you?"

The question made Fenton's eyes well up unexpectedly. "Sometimes," he admitted.

"You've come to the edge of a cliff," the doctor said.

The statement made the tears spill out. He grabbed a handful of tissues and dabbed at his wet cheeks.

Dr. Thorne made another notation in his book. "Mr. Patterson, homosexuality is indeed the quickest means to an unhappy end. If you decide to work with me, our goal would be to stop you from taking further steps toward your own oblivion."

The words *end* and *oblivion* jumped out at him. Fenton knew men who'd been beaten to within an inch of their lives for just looking like fairies, but so far he'd been spared. His father took a strap to him when he was young, but didn't all fathers? And suicide hadn't crossed his mind since his early teen years.

"Happily, I sense something positive in you. You desperately want to find a way out of all the degradation, filth, and debauchery."

The trio of condemnations landed like a pile of manure.

"You may have noticed we are just blocks from an area frequented by homosexuals."

Fenton nodded haltingly, afraid to admit he knew the exact location of every bar and cruising place in Richmond.

"The choice was intentional. I've helped many men like yourself, but only those who commit to hard work. If you undertake this therapy, it will require the utmost fortitude. You may be tempted to leave here and go for a drink or find someone in an alley. However, to be cured, you will have to refrain from all homosexual encounters for as long as you are in treatment."

Fenton balled the tissues in his hand into a tight wad.

"There will be no physical contact with men. No drinks in bars, no public toilet encounters, no kissing or hand-holding, no penetration, fellatio, mutual masturbation, massages, or stroking."

A nervous laugh escaped him. "You've thought of everything."

"This isn't a joke, Mr. Patterson. Needless to say, self-pleasuring is also off limits. No magazines or movies that might trigger unnatural passions. No thoughts about men you've been with or desired."

"Doctor, I don't see how I can possibly stop my thoughts."

"There is a proven scientific method for that. I use a small machine similar to a lie detector."

Fenton's throat constricted. "How much p-pain is involved?"

"Oh, none at all. It simply trains the mind. I've had wonderful results. Why, recently, a man about your age married a lovely young woman and impregnated her on their honeymoon!" The doctor smiled almost proudly, as if he had supervised their intercourse.

"Children— I don't—"

"You needn't worry about passing your tendencies along to your offspring. Homosexuality isn't genetic. It results from absent fathers and mothers who wean their sons prematurely."

"B-but my father wasn't absent," Fenton protested in a weak voice. If anything, his father had been omnipresent, a force to reckon with. Although dead twelve years, his cruelty lived on in Fenton's memories.

"Perhaps not physically, but if we dig deep enough, we'll see he withheld from you emotionally."

He had no rejoinder for that or the doctor's assertion about breastfeeding, and he would die of embarrassment asking his seventy-year-old mother when she weaned him.

"My recommendation would be three sessions," the doctor said.

"That's all?"

"A week."

Fenton swallowed hard. "For how long?"

"At least a year, possibly more."

Fenton reached toward the wallet in his breast pocket. "I don't see how I could manage the fees and the gas. It's a long drive from Springboro."

The doctor shrugged and stood up, signaling the session's end. "You have a choice to make. The wrong choice could have dire consequences."

Dr. Thorne moved to his desk and quickly and efficiently wrote out a receipt. Fenton handed him three crisp fives, which the doctor tucked into a drawer.

"What do you say, Mr. Patterson? Would you like to mull it over and let me know?"

Chapter Thirteen

Ruby

Except for the female faculty gatherings, Ruby and Darrell rarely entertained. For election night, Darrell talked her into inviting folks to watch the Huntley-Brinkley coverage. It made sense to host, he said; they had the biggest house and the biggest television. Mostly, she thought he wanted to show off the TV, a new purchase.

"Zenith Space Command 400," Darrell told guests who asked about the model. "The sound is incredible. Double speakers." Until Darrell retired, neither of them had considered it important enough to own a TV, but now her husband treated the Zenith like their most prized possession.

For the election night party, they moved their kitchen and dining chairs into the family room to supplement the sofa and lounger. Ruby unfolded metal snack trays and scattered them around the room to discourage wet rings on her cherry tables. They stocked the bar and laid out an array of snacks—popcorn, potato chips, pretzel sticks, onion dip, and a chocolate sheet cake with buttercream frosting from the bakery that read: "And the winner is . . ." in swirls of red, white, and blue.

Darrell had suggested two competing cakes, one for his man, Nixon, and one for hers, but Ruby vetoed the idea. She and

Darrell had had minor dustups during the debates, and Ruby didn't want to foment discord among her guests. Aside from Gen, she didn't know how any of her friends and colleagues voted and didn't plan to ask.

Guests began trickling in around seven, with Gen leading the pack. Juliet May followed soon after. Juliet had not been on Ruby's original guest list. She was still annoyed about the young woman's refusal to heed her advice, but Gen said they were becoming good friends, so Juliet made the final cut.

"What happened to your car door, Gen?" Juliet asked, catching Ruby's attention. "Looks like Willie Mays took a swat at it."

"Nothing that exciting," Gen said with a nervous laugh. "Just my bad driving."

"I've driven with you. You're an excellent driver," Ruby objected.

Gen shrugged. "Distracted lately."

Slowly, seats filled and all the available floor space was taken, too. Everyone—even the younger folks—chuckled at Chet Huntley's opening remark: "I hereby speak for all those Americans who have adjusted to the immutable fact that, come what may tonight, we shall be older than the president of the United States."

"Well, this old fossil couldn't be more pleased," Ruby said. "Here's to a new generation taking charge." The guests raised their glasses in the first toast of the evening.

Returns took their sweet time rolling in. Guests snacked and talked over NBC's long-winded and prideful explanation of its RCA 501 computer. Reports from the two campaign headquarters landed with a thud, too.

"Now that's a scintillating detail," Darrell said as the reporter covering Nixon told of the candidate's solo drive that afternoon into Mexico.

"Yes, but don't you want to know what he was picking up in Tijuana?" Juliet asked with a crafty grin.

Around eight o'clock, the real excitement came not from the TV screen but from the late arrival of another guest, whom Darrell led into the family room.

"Who won?" Fenton asked, hoisting a bottle of Cold Duck.

A young woman entered a few steps behind Fenton, over-dressed in a black cocktail dress and nubby wool bolero jacket. Ruby's thoughts raced, trying to place her. Did she work on campus, or was she a student? She looked young enough to be.

Then Fenton introduced her around as his "friend," Kathy. Ruby remembered her finally as a former student, a fairly recent Baines graduate—at least ten years Fenton's junior, she reckoned.

As they refreshed their drinks in the dining room, Darrell whispered to Ruby and Gen, "I always thought Fenton was, you know—" He let his wrist hang limp, and Ruby smacked his hand down.

"Behave," she said. "People . . . change."

Gen mumbled, "Not unless they have to."

Darrell shrugged and retreated back to the family room, while Ruby and Gen lingered at the bar as if hunting for more ingredients for their cocktails.

"Is this Kathy thing . . . new?" Ruby asked. It seemed like a legitimate question to ask Fenton's best friend.

"Let's say it's new to me," Gen said, her forehead creased with worry.

Ruby surveyed Gen's face. It had never occurred to her that Gen could harbor any deeper feelings than friendship for Fenton. But he *was* an attractive, single man—an oddity in Springboro.

"Sorry," Ruby muttered, to say something. It came out hollow, like perfunctory condolences to a widow she barely knew.

Gen turned a puzzled look to her. "Oh, Lord!" she said. "It isn't *that*. It's just, he never said a word, and I'm in shock."

Fenton appeared beside them and picked up two cocktail glasses from the selection Ruby had set out.

"Because your man won Connecticut?" he quipped.

Gen's attention remained fixed on the bar. Ruby sipped her whiskey and soda, her eyes flitting between the two. She wasn't sure if she should provide a buffer for a possible argument. When Gen continued to hang back, Ruby decided to leave with a breezy, "See you back at the tally board!"

As she withdrew, she heard Gen's low, baffled voice: "What are you *doing*?" Fenton's response was too muted to make out.

The party dragged on into the late hours. The NBC computer divined the winners of various states—Huntley and Brinkley called them "projections." With the nail-biter returns, Ruby and Darrell ran low on drinks and snacks. Even the cake had only one ragged corner left, and Ruby wished she'd taken Darrell's advice to buy two.

At eleven-thirty, the computer was predicting a slim Kennedy win, but the news anchors warned that final results would likely not come in until the following day. A groan rose from the guests, most of whom made excuses and took their leave.

"School night," Juliet said. Gen left soon after, blowing kisses to Ruby and Darrell but merely waving to Fenton. What had passed between them after Ruby left the bar?

After midnight, the only guests left were Fenton and Kathy. Fenton looked settled in, but Kathy stifled yawns behind her hand. Darrell disappeared from the room for longer than it took to visit the bathroom, and after a while, Ruby heard sounds of water running in the kitchen sink.

"I suppose we should be getting along, too," Kathy said—one of the few comments she had made all evening. She had a low, breathy voice that surprised Ruby. "Could I help you clean up?"

"Oh, no, we're fine, dear."

Still, Fenton appeared hesitant to leave the sofa. To urge the two of them on, Ruby asked, "Would you like the last slice of cake to take with you?"

Kathy rose from her seat, her hand skimming the narrow waistline of her skirt. "I couldn't possibly, Dr. Woods, but thank you. And thanks for including me. I'm so honored. You know, I was too shy to tell you, but your nineteenth-century American lit class was one of my very favorites."

"Thank you, Kathy," Ruby said. She might have added, *Call me Ruby,* but stopped short of doing so.

Darrell was dipping glasses in a soapy dishpan when Ruby came into the kitchen.

"Thanks for starting," she said. "I can't believe how late it is."

"Damn, I thought they'd never leave!"

"Fenton acted like he wanted to spend the night." Ruby put on an apron with a nervous laugh. "He reminded me of Pete on his first date. Remember how scared he was?"

"Yeah, he could barely get it out when he asked me if he should kiss the girl at the door. I don't remember her name, do you?"

Ruby shook her head slowly, but her thoughts lingered on Fenton, not her youngest son.

Chapter Fourteen

Gen

Gen hadn't been to Atlanta since her senior year in high school, but the city carried a distant bad memory as the site of her first heartbreak.

That spring, she had set out on a bus from Charlotte to visit her best friend, Laurette Sparks, a freshman at Agnes Scott College. They'd been planning the rendezvous since Christmas. Laurette's roommate would be out of town visiting family, and they could finally share a bed without fear of anyone's mother popping in. Gen had already been accepted at Agnes Scott for the fall, so the weekend held the promise of what the next three years with Laurette would be.

When she arrived at the dorm, Laurette hugged her coolly, as if they were just friends and nothing more. She pointed Gen toward her roommate's bed. After a day of polite distancing that stung, Gen pressed for an explanation, and Laurette admitted she'd fallen in love with a girl in her composition class. "You'll meet someone, too," Laurette had assured her. "College is different." Gen returned to Charlotte early, switched her admission to Queens College, and never saw Laurette again.

This trip didn't require her to go anywhere near Agnes Scott. For the long weekend of the Southern Historical Association conference, Gen would be ensconced at the Biltmore Hotel, whose porticoed entrance presided over West Peachtree Street like a dowager. Gen had never checked into a hotel alone. With all the male historians swarming the gilt lobby and no Carolyn as a buffer, she wondered if she should have chosen a guest house instead, as she had for that first conference in Columbia. Something about collecting her own room key, though, filled her with an electric charge of both excitement and terror.

The man behind her in the hotel registration line looked familiar. She recalled sitting next to him at a panel the previous year, exchanging thoughts about one of the papers.

"David, isn't it? Good to see you again." He smiled with a confused expression that said he was trying hard to place her without the aid of a name tag. "Gen Rider, Baines College?" she added.

"Yes, of course. Is that devil Henry Thoms here, too?"

The man glanced past her expectantly, but Gen explained that her colleague couldn't make it. Thoms had stopped attending the Southern, complaining that the conference had become too political. The gathering in Memphis a few years back had featured both a fiery pro-integration speech by novelist William Faulkner and a mixed-race banquet that shocked and alienated segregationists like Thoms.

The awkward exchange was an ill-omened start. The speakers and sessions should thrill her, but the idea of enduring the weekend on her own was daunting. She would force herself to socialize.

Gen followed the bellhop onto the elevator and to her seventh-floor room, where she changed clothes and pored over the conference program. She ran her finger down the pages, locating a reception hosted by two women whose husbands were on the local planning committee. It rankled Gen that the female historians were sent off to a genteel tea with faculty wives in the solarium of someone's house while at the same time the men engaged in meatier discussions in the hotel's banquet hall. But, of course, she would attend the tea; all the female association members would be there, and none would dare venture into the men's space.

110

Gen continued searching the program for names she recognized until she saw that Muriel Whitbread was moderating a panel the next day. Muriel didn't attend every year, and her presence in the program sent a wave of relief through Gen. A pioneer of Southern social history, Muriel had served as Gen's dissertation adviser at Ohio State. More than that, she had championed Gen's early career, helping her secure the position at Baines and later advocating for the publication of Gen's first book review in the *Mississippi Valley Historical Review*. Whenever Gen and Muriel met up at the Southern, Carolyn joked that she felt superfluous: "Y'all are like a mutual admiration society."

At the women's tea, Gen spotted Muriel's distinctive froth of white hair. At just five feet tall, Muriel was dwarfed by a ring of faculty wives transfixed by her words. Although it was bad manners to butt in, Gen did so anyway, softly touching the sleeve of Muriel's serge suit jacket. As she did, she caught the tail end of the conversation, a swapping of tips about travel to Miami Beach.

"I will have to look up that hotel when we go in January," the woman next to Muriel said. "We are always desperate for a charming place to stay."

"It will suit you, I'm sure," Muriel said.

Gen left her hand on Muriel's sleeve until the older woman acknowledged its pressure and her face lit. She pecked Gen on the cheek, careful not to tip her teacup, and introduced her to the circle of women as "my dear friend and colleague, Dr. Rider." When the talk shifted to research and teaching, the faculty wives wandered off to other conversations, leaving Gen and Muriel on their own.

Muriel stunned Gen with the news that the spring semester would be her last at Ohio State. She wanted to travel more while she still could, she explained, visit far-flung friends and family, do research in New York City. Although Gen had known the professor for almost twenty years, her private life remained a mystery. Muriel didn't have a husband or an apparent "friend." Instead, she'd owned a series of cocker spaniels, often two or more at a time, whom she referred to as her babies. Still, the

111

older woman never showed surprise that Gen and Carolyn were annual conference companions, that they always shared a room and negotiated the sessions like a matching set.

It seemed odd, then, when Muriel didn't inquire about Carolyn during their lengthy conversation. The three of them had enjoyed dinner or drinks at several conferences.

Muriel asked if Gen was staying at the hotel, and that was how Carolyn's absence—almost as palpable to Gen as Muriel's presence—edged its way into the conversation. "Sadly, I'm by myself this year. Carolyn took a new job in Maryland. Goucher College."

Muriel nodded. "Yes, I know."

Gen made a concerted effort to remain unfazed by this news and act as if Carolyn confiding her move to Muriel was business as usual. Even though her heart had picked up a beat, she managed to say, "I didn't know you and Carolyn were in touch."

Muriel took a delicate sip from her tea. "We talked about jobs here last year. She said her department had gotten uncomfortable, and she probably wouldn't get tenure. She needed a letter of recommendation. You were off at a panel, and she suggested we have a drink." She leaned in and whispered conspiratorially, "And you know I much prefer a martini to tea any day!"

Gen remembered the occasion because it had struck her as odd. A panel on the Jacksonian era should have drawn them both, but Carolyn had begged off, saying she had conference fatigue and urging Gen to go anyway. What she had actually done was to seek out a separate *tête-à-tête* with Gen's former mentor.

"She wrote over the summer to tell me she'd landed on her feet," Muriel continued. Her eyes took on a look of concern. "My dear, did I say something wrong? You just lost all your lovely color."

Gen struggled to regain her composure and concoct a story at the same time. She didn't have a teacup to occupy her hands so she squeezed them together behind her back. "Oh, it's childish. I just remembered how jealous I was that Carolyn got so much more of your time last year. And I hadn't seen you since Memphis."

112

"You and I must have dinner to make up for it. Unless your dance card is already full."

Gen forced a smile. "I'll ring you in your room to set a time. But if you'll excuse me now, I do have to be somewhere else."

After her series of lies, Gen dashed out. She knew Muriel would soon be surrounded by admirers and then swept away to other events.

Back at the hotel, Gen intended to go straight to her room and put a washcloth on her now-throbbing head. Instead, she took a detour past the closed doors of the men's gathering, where she listened to the dull hum from inside the hall. A distinguished older man emerged as she was standing there.

"I wouldn't go in there if I were you," he said with fatherly concern. "Unless you fancy a lot of smoke and noise."

Gen smiled tightly. She could just see past the man into the ballroom as he held the door for her. Under the glistening chandeliers, a sea of gray and brown suits filled the space between the columns; voices rose in a chorus of baritones and basses. The sound made her lightheaded, and she thanked the man but hurried toward the elevator.

In her room, she decided to skip the evening's keynote address and order room service, although it was an extravagance Baines wouldn't reimburse. She was disappointed with herself and suspected Muriel would be, too. Where was the Gen Rider who had learned to navigate academia in a men's field, who had persisted until her department granted her a permanent spot?

Under her embarrassment ran a current of renewed anger at Carolyn—for leaving her, yes, but more for mapping it all out and telling Muriel, and probably others, about the plan. And if Carolyn had fears of not getting tenure, why hadn't she bothered to tell her lover?

She could scan the conference program again for familiar names, attend panels of interest and introduce herself to scholars whose work she admired. She could seek out Muriel and pursue the dinner invitation. Anyone could force herself to make it through three days of an uncomfortable conference.

113

The other option was to leave—the way she'd done all those years earlier when Laurette's news toppled her confidence. Although she hated her cowardice, the very idea of escaping comforted Gen and lulled her to sleep. The next morning, she left a note for Muriel at the front desk, claiming a sudden cold, and slipped back to Springboro.

On the long bus ride home, Gen made up her mind. A Thanksgiving meeting with Carolyn was off the table. Gen would drop her a note and let her know her final decision.

Gen imagined that the anonymous gifts she received at the beginning of the semester had ended with *Girls' Dormitory*. But soon after her return from Atlanta, she found a greeting card in her home mailbox without a return address or stamp. The card's cover featured a picture of two cuddly kittens in a basket festooned with ribbons and forget-me-nots. The verse inside read, "Thinking of You—Three little words/Mean so much/When sent to keep/Good friends in touch." Printed at the bottom was "xo—M," and taped to the blank side of the card was a "gold" ring set with cracked green glass, possibly an old Cracker Jack charm.

She traced the ring with her finger and contemplated the initial. Several of her students had first names beginning with *M*—Martha, Melanie, Millie, Monica, and others. Of these girls, only Margaret Sutter displayed a special fondness for her. Fenton said the girl had developed an attachment to him, too. "She's a needy thing," he had said, "but aren't we all?"

The ring and the "xo" didn't jibe with the Margaret Gen knew, who mostly sought her out for advice about the Civil War class or her major. Maybe someone was playing a trick on both of them. Gen couldn't decide whether to ignore it or dig deeper.

She'd spoken once to Fenton since they exchanged terse words about his choice of date for Ruby and Darrell's. He called when she was back from Atlanta, inviting her for coffee or a drink. "I miss you," he said, though it had been little more than a week. She asked for a rain check. She couldn't avoid him or his side of the story forever, and the situation with Margaret offered an opportunity to clear the air and make peace. The truth was, she missed him, too.

Fenton gushed when he heard from her and extended an invitation for breakfast in his rooms. When she arrived, the smell of fresh paint hit her nostrils before the aroma of coffee. In the corner she noticed a closed gallon of paint with a brush set across the lid.

"Sorry, I thought the stink would be gone by the time you got here. I cracked a window so we don't pass out from the fumes."

"It's so . . . white," she remarked. One of his walls, which had once been a bold magenta, was now devoid of color.

"Things were too pink," he said quickly.

Fenton's double hot plate and pint-sized refrigerator didn't permit much cooking, so the meal consisted of orange juice, coffee, toast, and plain crullers from the bakery. "Trying to keep my weight down," he explained as to why he hadn't selected his preferred breakfast of jelly donuts.

Gen almost said, "For Kathy?" but kept the thought to herself.

Fenton set his tiny bistro table with a lace-edged tablecloth and a vase of fall-colored blooms. "I hate carnations and mums, but they're all you can get," he explained.

When they were settled with their food, Gen showed him the card and ring. She'd left the charm taped to the card, fearful that removing it would acknowledge it.

"It doesn't seem like Margaret," Fenton said, rereading the card. "Well, maybe the kittens. I could see her giving you candy. She always brings me Life Savers. But the ring confounds me. I can't imagine her being so forward. I think she'd die of embarrassment before actually signing this."

Gen's thoughts skittered back to the candy kisses and Girl Scout cookies, which she had never mentioned to Fenton. She told him now about the three gifts, including the copy of *Girls' Dormitory*, and how at Halloween, Margaret's Girl Scout uniform had unsettled her.

Fenton returned the card to its envelope. "These girls . . .

They're all bursting hormones, aren't they? If it worries you, I'd talk to her."

"That will be an unpleasant conversation," she said. His cavalier tone bothered her, for reasons she couldn't put a finger on. "Have you noticed her being teased by other students?"

"There was some snickering about her getting a male role in *Charley's Aunt*, but that's not unusual." He paused, digging further back in his memory files. "One student told me she didn't want to co-stage manage with her. I figured they were feuding over some boy."

"Which student was that?"

"Your neighbors' girl, Susanna Carr."

"Ah."

Gen wasn't sure why she said "ah" as if everything had fallen into place. The gifts still puzzled her, and the idea of another student setting Margaret up over a boy stretched believability. Besides, Susanna didn't strike Gen as a vindictive prankster. Gen had whittled away at the girl's bigoted beliefs as the semester progressed, and Susanna had chosen to write her term paper on Andrew Johnson's failures as president.

"I suppose there's no way around talking to Margaret."

Fenton refreshed their coffee cups. "Well, I myself prefer to dodge anything like that," he said.

They shifted to small talk. Gen itched to ask him about Kathy, but every time she hinted at personal topics like Ruby's party or what was going on with Mark's case, Fenton veered away and peppered her with questions about something else, like her trip to Atlanta. After an hour, she'd done most of the talking, laying out how she'd learned from Muriel about Carolyn's duplicity.

"At least it's over and done with," he said. "Nothing muddying the waters now."

"I mailed a letter to her this morning, telling her not to come."

"Brava! A courageous move." He placed a hand over his heart. "'I never yet was valiant.'"

Gen stared at him, unfamiliar with the quote. "King Lear," he explained.

"Well, *I'm* hardly valiant."

"It's brave to take some sort measure of control when things are spinning," he said. By the way his head drooped toward the table, she thought he had shifted gears to his own spinning life.

"I've been worried about you, Fen," she said after a pause. His head bobbed back up. "I'm sorry I lashed out at you at Ruby's. It wasn't compassionate. I don't know what you're going through right now."

"Neither do I." He frowned. "I'm seeing a shrink in Richmond. Three times a week."

Her mouth fell open. "Wow."

"Wow indeed."

"How's it going?" The question burst out as simplistic and uncaring, but Gen had never known anyone who had visited a psychiatrist except an aunt by marriage whom her mother pronounced "loony."

"It's mostly talking," Fenton said. "But sometimes he attaches this machine to my wrist and leg. He shows me slides."

"A *machine?*"

"Oh, just a little one." He spread his hands shoulder-width to approximate the size.

"And what are the slides of?"

"Naked men and women. If I . . . if I get aroused by the men, I feel this shock."

She watched his throat constrict, as if it were hard to swallow. "Fenton, that's terrible. That's cruel."

"Oh, there haven't been that many jolts. It's hard to get aroused when everything's so clinical. I'm not making progress, so the doctor wants to send me home with the machine."

"Fenton—" She reached over and clapped his hand, which was cold. "Did he suggest dating Kathy?"

"No, no, he'd say I'm not ready. I thought if I had a lady friend, the police might leave me alone." His eyes watered. "And Kathy likes me for some reason. She wants to spend time with me. I'm cosmopolitan, she says."

Gen withdrew her hand from his. "You shouldn't lead her on, Fen."

"Oh, you think less of me now, don't you? I hear it in your voice. I can't b-bear it." Tears coursed down Fenton's cheeks and dripped off his chin.

He wasn't wrong. Gen had always thought of them as being on equal footing, having to negotiate their secret lives as best they could, sharing their struggles. "We're members of the same church," was Fenton's euphemism for gay people.

Now, pity for him welled inside her. She struggled to clear her emotions from her face.

"That is just like you to be so dramatic." She fished a clean hanky from her purse and handed it to him, then fetched the box of crullers. "Better not to wallow."

She hadn't answered the question, and she knew he'd recognize the dodge. Still, after a few more sniffles, he blew his nose like an obedient boy and helped himself to another cruller.

Chapter Fifteen

Gen

"Margaret, got a minute?" Gen asked after class. The girl's face lit like she'd been hand-delivered an A-plus.

Gen closed her office door behind them with a quiet click—something she rarely did because she didn't want to alarm students by having them think they were in trouble.

And like clockwork, Margaret asked, "Did I do something wrong, Dr. Rider? I still have your book—I just keep forgetting to bring it to class." She bit a thumbnail, and Gen noticed for the first time how raw the tips of her fingers were.

"No, it isn't that, Margaret. Your paper on Brady's legacy was outstanding. Bring the book back any time you can."

Gen sat down at her desk and withdrew the kitten card from her top drawer. "This was in my mailbox at home, and I wondered if you knew anything about it."

Margaret opened the card, her lips parting as she read the verse and inscription. She glanced at the Cracker Jack ring next, then back at the verse.

Gen was no detective, but the girl's confused expression suggested she'd never seen the card before. Margaret closed it quickly, like it might explode, and handed it back to Gen. "I— sorry, no, I don't. Sorry."

Gen slid it back into the drawer. "Is there anything going on that's troubling you, Margaret?"

The girl's eyes widened. "Dr. Rider, I swear I never saw that before. And there are lots of girls with *M* names!"

"Oh, I believe you." Gen reached over and patted her shoulder. "I just meant, is there any reason someone might be playing a trick on you? With a card like this."

Margaret shook her head.

"I ask, because I've gotten some other anonymous presents recently. Candy and a box of Girl Scout cookies. Then a book." She held back the title, afraid of frightening Margaret more. "And I do remember you dressed like a Girl Scout for Halloween."

"It isn't me!" Margaret's breaths became shorter, heavier.

"Please, Margaret, try to calm down. You're not in trouble. I'm beginning to think we may have a prankster, and I wanted to see if you had any idea who it might be."

Margaret's head wagged *No* more slowly.

"No one's causing you any trouble?"

A third shake of the head. Margaret's hands curled into her sides. "Can I go now? I have another class."

Gen knew that was a lie because Margaret so often came to see her at this very hour. But there was no point in torturing the girl further. Margaret's discomfort was clear. She was holding something back but wasn't going to divulge it to Gen.

"Sure. Sorry to keep you."

Margaret fled from the office, letting the door flap open roughly.

On the path to the college library, Gen jerked her head at a sudden squeak of bike tires. A beaming Juliet rolled up next to her.

"Didn't mean to scare you," she said. "I just couldn't wait to tell you I submitted my tenure portfolio."

"Today?"

"Ten minutes ago. You're the first person I've told." Juliet was wearing her hair down, held back by a tortoise-shell headband, and it fanned attractively over her shoulders.

"Congratulations!" Gen said. "I have a good feeling about it."

"I don't want to jinx it, but I do, too. Ruby probably won't." Juliet gripped her bike handles. "I kept the spring end date for my housemother stint. I can't tell you how many times I retyped that page, taking it out and putting it back in. But no matter what they decide, I'm a free woman come May. I can always go back to high school teaching."

Gen wondered what it would be like not to feel so invested in her career. In the final countdown to her own tenure decision, she had slept fitfully, when she slept at all. Many nights, she read into the morning hours and rose before dawn, padding around in a haze of worry and calling Carolyn way too early. She wasn't sure which she'd feared more: the loss of income and security or the humiliation associated with being denied the promotion. Like gossip, shame traveled quickly on a small campus.

"We'll have to celebrate," Gen said to Juliet.

She meant they should acknowledge the milestone of submitting the application, but it sounded like a premature victory celebration instead. Juliet shook her head.

"I don't feel *that* good," she said. "But hey, why don't you— Oh, never mind. I know you like to clear out for Thanksgiving." Her foot met the bike pedal again, as if ready to head out.

"I'll be in town this year," Gen said.

She had always reserved the holiday weekend for Carolyn but told most people that she went home to Charlotte. This year she had nothing written in her calendar, and the disagreeable choice between *actually* spending four days with her parents and being alone loomed large. Fenton was heading to family in Valdosta. Ruby had offered Gen a warm invitation, which she hadn't yet accepted, as any holiday at Ruby's meant a house full of sons, daughters-in-law, and grandchildren.

"You planning something?" she asked Juliet hopefully.

Juliet smirked like a mischievous kid. "I'm hosting a Misfits Thanksgiving. The house empties out on Wednesday, so the plan is a potluck supper for anybody with no place to go . . . or no place they *want* to go. Probably a small group. It would be so much more fun if you could come."

Gen snapped up the invitation, offering to bring a pie from the bakery and a bottle of cream sherry that was calling for someone to drink it.

Chapter Sixteen

Lee-Anne

Lee-Anne's hand hesitated before knocking on the office door that read "Professor H. Thoms III." The rhythmic click of typewriter keys floated through the open transom. Other male professors had their wives or secretaries type their articles, but Dr. Thoms liked to pound away at his Underwood himself.

"My wife may object, but I will be buried with this beauty," he said with pride. Lee-Anne couldn't understand the attachment to a noisy piece of machinery so old her grandfather might have owned it. Her own typewriter was a sleek Olympia portable her parents had bought for her freshman year.

She rapped twice on the door, then listened, but the typewriter clattered on. Relief rushed through her, and instead of knocking again more loudly, she turned to leave. Lee-Anne was halfway down the hallway, almost to the rear door of Waylon and escape, when Dr. Thoms's voice called out, "Lee-Anne! Where are you going?"

Lee-Anne pivoted, offering him a sheepish smile. "I didn't want to bother you. Sounds like you're hard at work on something important."

"Just a book review. Nothing that can't wait. Come on back now."

The professor flapped his hand at her until she moseyed to his office. His space was enviably roomy, the equivalent of three professors' offices put together, with a round conference table and a comfy sofa.

Her mother said she was lucky Dr. Thoms took an interest in her studies. He hailed from one of western Virginia's most distinguished families, and the Civil War statue of Big Beau in the town park commemorated his ancestor.

"Such a handsome man, too," her mother added, explaining he'd been a heartthrob when she was in college. Now Dr. Thoms had salt-and-pepper hair and a close-cropped beard that accented his profile. But it was his honeyed voice that appealed to Lee-Anne more than his looks.

The door behind them closed. All the girls knew about Dr. Thoms. He'd divorced his first wife to marry one of his students, but his eye continued to rove.

It had landed on Lee-Anne last spring, when she enrolled in his American history survey. Late in the semester, he suggested she major in history because of an innate talent at not only absorbing information but synthesizing it. He offered to be her adviser. Until that moment, she had planned on music as her major—she'd studied piano since she was six—but the interest he showed in her flattered her.

This fall, they began meeting once a week. When she asked around, no other girls met with their advisers in private so often—maybe once or twice a semester.

They'd begin at his desk, talking about her studies, but the conversation would coast into other topics. Dr. Thoms showed an inordinate amount of interest in Dr. Rider. He was either disgusted by her or in love with her; Lee-Anne couldn't tell which. He was especially intrigued by Dr. Rider's "History of the South" course, but Lee-Anne only had secondhand knowledge of that. She did, however, share her syllabus from the Civil War class.

"Good girl," he said approvingly when he perused it.

During those initial fifteen or twenty minutes, Dr. Thoms scratched out notes while they talked. Lee-Anne focused her attention on a handsome photo on his desk of him, his wife, and their two young sons in a casual pose on their front porch, happy grins lighting their faces. With the younger boy perched on his knee gripping a floppy stuffed rabbit, Dr. Thoms resembled any affectionate father. He once commented with amusement that the little boy "will not let go of that thing, not even to let his mama wash it."

Eventually, their meetings would shift. Her professor pushed back from his desk and said, "Let's move our *tête-à-tête* to the sofa, shall we?"

The first time he used the phrase, Lee-Anne asked him for the definition. "It sounds French," she said.

He smiled in a leisurely way and said it meant a private conversation for two. Later, she looked it up in the library dictionary, scanning the page hurriedly for more explanation but finding nothing about the way his hand had traveled up her thigh.

Now, his question always made something lock up inside her.

Chapter Seventeen

Gen

When Ruby pressured her about Thanksgiving, Gen found herself juggling two invitations.

She stopped first at the Woods's house, where Ruby had taken over the cooking responsibilities from her husband and cordoned herself in the kitchen with her daughters-in-law. The young women shooed Gen into the family room, where Darrell and his sons watched football.

"My money's on the Lions," Darrell Jr., who liked to be called Dave, said. "How about you, Professor?"

Ruby's oldest son handed her a whiskey sour. She had known Dave and his brothers since before any of them could drive, and it felt odd to be drinking socially with them now.

"Dave, it's really okay to call me Gen."

He looked embarrassed, as if she'd asked him to call her *darling*.

Between polite exchanges of adult conversation with Gen— "What're you teaching this semester, Professor?"—father and sons shouted at the players on the TV screen like they were in the room. Ruby's middle son paced the floor anxiously, carrying his infant girl like a football. Dave's boisterous boys darted in and out of the room and ignored their father's weak entreaties to "stop that running, y'all. I'm not going to say it again."

To make matters worse, Gen didn't understand the game and didn't care to. She'd learned the basics from long-ago Thanksgivings with her father and brother-in-law, but aside from touchdowns and field goals, she wasn't sure why the men were screaming so much. She drank her cocktail in silence, the screen a blur in front of her. By the end of the game's first quarter, she had slipped away into the kitchen.

"Is it absolutely dreadful?" Ruby asked. "I can hear the shouting even with the door closed." She smiled at Gen as she inserted a meat thermometer into a plump, golden turkey.

"I don't appreciate football, I guess," Gen said.

"Isn't it just the dumbest game?" one of the daughters-in-law said. "And it makes Peter so anxious. I bet he's out there wearing a hole in the rug right now."

Gen offered to do something, anything, but Ruby assured her they had the menu under control. She stood out of the way and watched the preparations, the proverbial third wheel. In all her dinners at Ruby's, time had never ticked by so awkwardly. She would have to make her exit to Juliet's before she got trapped.

"I think I'll just slip out now," she said to Ruby after the women had wrestled the bird from the oven onto a serving plate. Gen placed her empty drink glass in the sink like a final notice.

Ruby wiped her hands on her apron. "You don't mean you're leaving?"

"I have a second dinner I have to get to."

The confusion and hurt on Ruby's face stung. "But you haven't eaten *here!*" she protested. "I'm sorry the bird took its sweet time. We'll eat in just a shake. Why don't you call the men to the table?"

From the hallway, Gen phoned Juliet to let her know about the delay. The silence from the other end of the line was hard to read. Gen didn't know Juliet well enough to gauge if it was distraction, disappointment, or displeasure.

"We'll try to save some booze for you," Juliet said in a clipped tone that made it clear.

When Ruby's meal was finally served, the family ate in a

whirlwind without much conversation except for passing dishes. Gen was grateful for the rush in which Ruby's sons and husband raced to return to their TV viewing stations with plates of chocolate chess pie and Reddi-wip.

"I really have to go," Gen said.

"Take a piece of pie to go," Ruby urged, but Gen waved it off. A whole sweet potato pie sat on the back seat of her car, waiting to go to Juliet's.

At the front door, Ruby helped her into her coat. "You're being mighty mysterious," she said.

"I don't mean to be." Without explaining, she pecked Ruby on the cheek and made her escape.

The first-floor lights of Cavendish House were blazing when she arrived on the front porch. In all her years at the college, she had never been inside the stately antebellum residence, which had once been the home of a Baines family member.

Juliet answered the doorbell after a long minute. "Oh, Gen," she said with feigned nonchalance. "I thought you ditched us."

"I'm sorry. I had a hard time getting away from Ruby's." In the grand foyer, graced with a chandelier and winding staircase, Juliet took the sherry and pie as Gen shed her coat.

A middle-aged woman was sitting alone in the parlor off the foyer, which smelled of fresh-brewed coffee and pumpkin pie spices. Juliet introduced the other guest as Fay Purdy, who ran the children's room at the town library.

"We've met, I think," Gen said but immediately realized they hadn't. She'd heard her name somewhere. "On second thought, I'm not sure."

"Happens to me all the time," Fay said. "I have not-met so many folks!"

Fay was about Gen's age, with lines around her mouth and curvy hips that strained at her nubby wool sheath. A dimpled grin gave her a youthful air.

"Sorry we're such a small crew," Juliet said. "Clay, a French instructor from D and L, was here earlier, and Rhonda from the Baines library, but they both had another engagement."

"Probably with each other," Fay added with a wink in Gen's direction.

Juliet blushed. "I don't think so, Fay."

They sipped their Harvey's Bristol Cream, which they agreed was a bit too sweet but gave them a nice buzz anyway. Fay was a talker with a laugh that came in gusts. She regaled them with anecdotes about townspeople "who shall remain nameless." She seemed to know everyone, having lived in Springboro all her life. Her marriage to her high school sweetheart had ended tragically when he was killed on Iwo Jima, and she hadn't found another love.

"What about you, Gen? You a widow, too? Or are you married to your career?"

Heat flooded Gen's face as she cast a *save me* look at Juliet. She hadn't trotted out her deceased fiancé in a while, and the mixture of drinks in her bloodstream made her fuzzy-headed.

Juliet rushed in to fill the awkward pause. "Gen lost her fiancé in the war, too."

"I don't like to talk about it," Gen rushed to add, so Fay wouldn't press her for details she could no longer remember manufacturing.

Fay reached over and patted Gen's hand. "I know how it is, dear," she said. "I've never had a greater love than my Johnny."

Carolyn glided uninvited into Gen's thoughts, and her eyes misted over. Fay offered to bring her water, but it came out with an unladylike burp that shattered the somber moment and made them all laugh.

The topic of men returned later, after a break in which they refilled their drinks and helped themselves to dessert. Fay said, out of the blue, "You know, I had a fella a few years ago who taught here at Baines. We were an item for just a slip of time. I often wonder how he's doing. I don't suppose either of you know him. Fenton Page? The theater director?"

That was why Fay's name seemed familiar; Fenton must have mentioned her at some point. Gen avoided looking up from her slice of pumpkin pie. "He's a friend of mine," she replied.

129

Fay eyed her curiously. "Well, if you see him, would you give him my best? Tell him Fay says, 'Don't be strange!' He'll get the joke." Her tone was wistful, and Gen felt a pang of sadness for her.

After Fay left, Gen lingered behind, nursing her sherry. Juliet's voice fell to a hush, even though they were alone in the house. "Do you think Fay really doesn't know about Fenton being—you know, gay?"

The conversation had careened into private territory. In public, Gen was accustomed to addressing Fenton's sexuality in coded terms, avoiding the actual words that described him. He was a confirmed bachelor, just as she was a career woman. She proceeded cautiously, surveying Juliet's face for subtle signs of disapproval or distaste that didn't appear.

"Maybe she likes him too much to care," Gen offered.

"Like that young secretary . . . I forget her name. The one he brought to election night. I found it so odd, didn't you? Like he was trying to prove he's *not* family." Juliet fixed her eyes on her plate and proceeded to finish her slice of pie in rapid bites.

Gen started at *family*, such a clear signal for gay people. She and Fenton used both that word and *church* when they referred to people like themselves. Carolyn preferred to say "she bats for our team" because she enjoyed softball.

Juliet had dropped a broad hint when she admitted wearing an engagement ring to "keep the men at bay." Although Gen had responded with her own fake fiancé, they hadn't proceeded any further. In the past, Fenton had kidded Gen about being slow to pounce on obvious clues.

"You got your head in those history books when it could be somewhere else," he teased—a dirty joke she dismissed because she was exclusively Carolyn's at the time and not in the market to date.

Now Gen felt foolish drawing too much attention to Juliet's revelation—as if she hadn't known all along! She picked at the Fenton thread instead. "He told me he's trying to change himself," she said.

Juliet looked up from her plate, now dotted with flakes of crust. "Oh, that's terrible."

"I said the same thing. He's actually going to a psychiatrist to train himself to prefer women."

"What a waste of time and money," Juliet said. "Why is he doing that to himself? He's a grown man. He knows it's impossible."

"I think he's banking on other folks not knowing that. He's been afraid of losing his job. Or worse, going to jail."

Juliet slapped down her plate. "If I were ever in a spot like that, I'd just—"

Gen swallowed hard, half-expecting the solution "kill myself." But after a dramatic pause, Juliet continued, "—I'd pick up and move somewhere else. A big city that's not under the microscope. *This* town—"

Juliet didn't need to finish her thought for Gen to understand. "Is there any more sherry?" Gen asked.

Juliet hopped out of her seat with a smirk. "There is. But what say we switch to something stronger?"

Gen stayed at Cavendish House into the wee hours, reveling in an open chat with "family." Over shots of Jim Beam, she and Juliet discussed everything from when they first recognized their attraction to women, to women on campus they suspected were gay ("Frances Palmer, for sure!"), to the ghosts of lovers past. Although she was Gen's junior, Juliet's list of exes was longer.

"What can I say? I had a wicked youth," Juliet said.

Although she matched Gen in belts of bourbon, Juliet never got drunk. "Hollow leg," she explained, "inherited from my daddy." For Gen, after a certain number of shots, the parlor of Cavendish House started to spin, and she feared driving home.

Juliet suggested she stay the night, and Gen agreed although she wasn't sure what Juliet had in mind. When Juliet said she'd sleep on the sofa in her first-floor suite, unexpected disappointment flashed in Gen.

"*I'll* take the sofa," she insisted, embarrassed that she had mistaken Juliet's invitation for interest.

"I can't let you. It's not that comfortable."

"Well, why don't we share the bed?" Gen suggested.

"As long as you don't mind. I don't think I snore."

Gen watched Juliet fumble through her dresser drawers for an extra nightgown.

"Here, wear this, it's my nicest one." The flannel cascaded over her ankles, which made them giggle like girls at a slumber party. "You are just too short, Dr. Rider."

Lying within inches of each other in bed, they talked more and kept collapsing into uncontrollable laughter when they attempted to be quiet and sleep. After they caught their breath, Juliet reached out for Gen's hand, squeezed it, and let it rest there. Gen lifted Juliet's hand to her lips and gave it a butterfly peck.

They rolled toward each other. Juliet's hand brushed Gen's cheek, cupped her neck. When their lips met, the kiss started soft before catching fire, like they'd become characters in a movie— as if anyone made movies about women doing things like that.

Their gowns caught on their chins and heads as they hurried to shed them, which made them giggle all over again. When Juliet's fingers found their way inside her, the only sounds in the room were Gen's moans and Juliet's reassuring whispers.

A different noise, a whining ring, cut through their private moment. Gen hoped it was some distant phone they could ignore, but Juliet bolted upright.

Gen recognized it, too, then. Cavendish boasted a brass doorbell, the old-fashioned kind you twisted. She had admired it when she came to the door that evening.

Their breaths came in anxious puffs. They waited for it to stop, but someone kept turning the bell, over and over, demanding Juliet answer the door.

Juliet threw on her nightgown and robe. When Gen offered to come with her, she waved her off.

"Probably just campus security," she said. "They look out for us on holidays especially."

132

Gen flicked on the table lamp and strained to listen. Juliet greeted someone by name, but then she couldn't make out their low voices. Within minutes, Juliet returned to the bedroom with a look that Gen couldn't read.

"What?"

"Campus guard, like I thought. He saw the parlor lights on at four in the morning and got curious. And then he spotted a car in the driveway, and he thought I was being raped or something." Juliet sat heavily on Gen's edge of the bed. "Damn. I should have asked you to pull it around the back."

"I'll leave." Gen hung her legs out of the covers, then crossed her arms over her bare breasts.

"No need, I got rid of him. Told him I had *family* staying over. Not even a lie." Her tone was light, but Juliet's hands on the quilt balled into fists. "This is why I couldn't listen to Ruby and Frances about living here. Jesus, May can't come soon enough!"

"Juliet, I'm going to go," Gen insisted. She found her wool dress where she'd left it, folded across a flowered armchair.

In the bathroom, Gen splashed water on her face and stared at her disheveled reflection, her face devoid of makeup, her hair sticking out in odd peaks. Thirty minutes earlier she'd felt alive, vibrant, desired. Now she looked like the middle-aged woman she was quickly becoming. She combed her fingers through her hair, but the attempted grooming didn't help.

Dawn light peeped through the leaded glass in the Cavendish House front door as Juliet helped Gen into her coat.

"I've dreamt about being with you," Juliet whispered as they hugged. "I want to try again."

Gen slid out of the embrace first, replying that they would see each other soon. On the short drive home, Juliet's romantic words, so full of longing and hope, echoed in her thoughts.

Chapter Eighteen

Gen

A hangover pulsed behind Gen's eyes. She forced her lids to open and tried to read the time. Ten-something, it looked like. She squinted at the alarm clock until she made out the second hand pointing to the space between five and six. In the medicine cabinet, she located the Bayer aspirin and downed three.

Somehow the milk had gone sour, and black coffee was her only choice. She drank the bitter brew down anyway, standing at the kitchen table in her bathrobe. If she didn't wake herself up, she might be tempted to crawl back into bed until Saturday.

The ring of the phone jolted her, and she wondered if it was Juliet. The night before had been exhilarating, sexy, but in the brassy morning light Gen worried about becoming involved with someone right in town, on campus. Someone who said she'd been dreaming about her, but whom she hadn't dreamt about in return.

"Did I wake you?"

Gen sank onto the telephone bench at Carolyn's voice.

"I've never known you to sleep past seven, not even on vacation."

"Late night," Gen replied, fussing with a pulled thread on her terry robe.

"I hope it was fun," Carolyn said, fishing for information Gen wasn't going to give her.

She waited.

"I got your letter, obviously," Carolyn said, "or I'd be on my way right now."

Gen waited again.

"I thought I'd check and make sure you hadn't changed your mind. I could hop in the car and be there right after lunch."

Gen had located Towson on a road map and knew it was twice the distance from Springboro as Richmond. Carolyn couldn't be calling from home.

"Where are you?"

"Peggy and Lorna's. We had a gay old dinner last night with some of the girls."

Peggy was one of Carolyn's exes from years back, a high school gym teacher with an infectious laugh. Lorna, her partner, worked at the state archives and shared a lot of interests with Gen. In the months since the breakup, Gen hadn't realized she missed the couple and the many "gay old dinners" they'd hosted, but Carolyn's casual mention of them broke the wound open.

Gen stifled a yawn. She'd had only a few hours of sleep, her head continued to throb, and the game Carolyn was playing exhausted her.

"So if you'd like to reconsider," Carolyn continued, "I might come tomorrow. For the day."

Gen rested her chin in her hand. "Why in the world do you think I'd reconsider?" she demanded. "My letter was very clear. I'm done, Carolyn. There's nothing to say."

Carolyn sniffed on the other end of the line. "The girls took a vote last night. They said I should try anyway, that maybe you'd had second thoughts. And I'm so close . . ."

Gen shivered. The group had discussed her private letter, in which she had poured out her fury at discovering Carolyn's lies. Worse, they seemed to have passed it around to weigh if Gen's words sounded serious and final. She imagined one of them dismissing it with, "Ah, we all fly off the handle sometimes," and another woman calling for a vote. *All in favor, say* aye.

"It's too late, Carolyn," Gen said. She wanted to cut her as deep as she'd been wounded. "Tell your friends I've found someone else, and this was a waste of your dime."

She clicked the receiver into place without saying good-bye. Putting Carolyn in her place did not feel as good as she'd hoped. It both satisfied her and brought stinging tears. Gen plodded back to the bedroom and tucked herself under the covers.

Gen woke again when the sun was just beginning its slow crawl toward nighttime. Her head was less fuzzy and pounding than it had been in the morning, but now her stomach grumbled its complaint. She'd stayed in bed all day without anything more than a cup of black coffee.

She had left both of her Thanksgiving dinners without taking any leftovers, and her refrigerator was almost bare. At the back of one shelf, she found a new container of port wine cheese spread that Fenton had given her on one of his visits. An untouched sleeve of Ritz Crackers sat in the cupboard. She ripped it open and mounded cheese onto a cracker and, while she was still chewing, prepared two more just like it. She preferred her cheese and port separate, but at that moment nothing had ever tasted so good. She considered eating the whole tub, possibly with a spoon.

The doorbell buzz interrupted her snack. She didn't think it could possibly be Carolyn, not after she'd told her to stay away. Through the window panel in the door, she spotted Juliet, and her heart picked up a beat. With cracker crumbs on her bathrobe, sour breath, and matted hair, Gen didn't cut an attractive figure. She held a hand over her mouth self-consciously as she waved Juliet in.

"I haven't showered or even brushed my teeth," she said. "My breath smells like port wine cheese. Give me fifteen minutes to be a real person again."

Juliet smiled broadly and gave up her coat. "I think I can spare the time."

"Make yourself at home," Gen called out. She didn't want Juliet to see her stuffing her coat into the chaotic hall closet, where purses were poised to tumble off the top shelf, while an assortment of shoes, slippers, and galoshes littered the closet floor, along with loose garments that had slipped from hangers.

But Juliet spotted the closet anyway. She clucked her tongue as Gen gave the door an extra push to close it. "Gen Rider! I never knew."

"It's my darkest secret." Gen motioned to the liquor cabinet. "But my alcohol is in perfect form."

"You have your priorities straight."

The hot water soothed her, but Gen didn't dawdle in the shower. Her mind weighed the options of what to say to Juliet. *Do you think it's wise for either of us to date someone in town?* was the most direct and accurate, but there was also the cowardly, *It's too soon after Carolyn,* which would shut the topic down more quickly. Juliet could offer a competing opinion about dating in Springboro, but how could she dismiss Gen's feelings for an ex?

With hair combed but still wet and no time for makeup or lipstick, Gen opened the bedroom door expecting to see Juliet on the sofa, reading or thumbing through a journal.

Instead, Juliet had made her way to the kitchen table, where she helped herself to the cheese and crackers still lying out. She wore her hair braided again, and it hung neatly between her shoulder blades. The sight of it charmed Gen and sent a ripple through her core, a sharp memory of the things they'd done the night before.

"Looks like you didn't eat much today either," Gen said, standing beside her at the table.

Juliet stuffed the rest of the Ritz into her mouth sheepishly. "I actually ate like a pig today," she said after swallowing. "Turkey, pie, you name it. I eat when I'm nervous, and I can't think of anything else to do." Her scowl was teasing and not genuine. "And

137

you only have history journals lying around. Not a single *Life* or *National Geographic* in the house!"

Gen's cheeks warmed. Copies of the *Mississippi Valley Historical Review* hardly invited casual reading. "You caught me being vain," she said. "I had a book review published in the fall issue."

"Well, then I'll have to read it." Juliet smeared another cracker with cheese and piloted it toward Gen's mouth. Gen's lips parted to take a bite, and Juliet promptly polished off the other half. They chewed slowly and in silence, watching the shadows outside the window dim as dusk set. Across the backyard, the overhead light in the Carrs' kitchen, which faced her own, flickered on.

"Juliet—" Gen said finally, but then she wasn't sure where to go from there.

Juliet brushed her hands together, dusting off the crumbs. "Well, that doesn't sound good," she said, a tremor in her voice.

Gen cast a sideways glance at Juliet. Her profile was lovelier than Gen had noticed before, with high cheekbones and delicate ears that her braided hairstyle complemented. Subtle lines accented the corners of her blue eyes, which Gen had made brim with tears by just saying her name. She took Juliet's hand and started to speak, but Juliet raised their joined hands to cover her lips.

"I know what you're going to say." A little choking sound escaped her throat. "You're going to say you're still in love with Carolyn. Or if not that, you're going to say you aren't attracted to me. I'm not sure which is worse."

Gen lowered their hands, and her own eyes filled. The emotions welling up confounded her. She could so easily dissect and interpret documents, craft a convincing historical argument, but she was sinking through the sludge of her feelings.

"Neither of those. It's—I'm scared to be with someone right here, in town."

Gen meant because of the risk of exposure, but Juliet pegged the excuse as something completely different. She dropped Gen's hand.

"You're scared of someone getting too close."

Gen shook her head but stopped short of objecting. On spring break the semester of their breakup, Carolyn had accused her of that very thing. Gen had laughed it away as preposterous, given they'd been a couple for six years. But Carolyn objected to playing house on weekends and vacations. She wanted a real relationship, like Peggy and Lorna's.

"There's nothing for me in your neck of the woods, but you could easily get a job here," Carolyn had suggested. "This crazy Confederate town could use a historian like you."

Lorna had told them about an archivist job. And although Gen reluctantly applied for the position, when they called for an interview, she declined—something she didn't admit to Carolyn.

"Guess my resume wasn't good enough," was what she said.

"*Good* enough? How could that be? Gen Rider is so good she's *too* good." When Gen took offense, Carolyn said she was joking, but her words rang with bitterness, not amusement.

Now Gen's tears fell harder and faster, until Juliet took pity on her and drew her into an embrace. She wept freely into Juliet's shoulder. But when her tears beaded up on the angora sweater, soft as a baby's blanket, she knew she had to stop. It was too embarrassing, crying in her kitchen like a little girl, and she didn't want Juliet to mistake it for something it wasn't—desire for Carolyn.

Gen made a move to disengage from Juliet's arms, muttering, "I'm all right now." Her eyes were still wet, though, and Juliet continued to clasp her tight, whispering something soothing into her ear that Gen couldn't make out. Pressed against her, Gen caught the clean, familiar scent of Juliet's shampoo—Halo, like her own.

And when their lips met, it was as dizzying as Gen remembered from the night before. The kitchen spun like a classroom globe. Gen leaned further and further into the kiss, wanting more of something but unsure what.

Then a light flashed behind her lids, making her eyes pop open, and she lurched away from Juliet.

Her kitchen shade was still raised, and the Carrs' kitchen had gone dark. Gen dove for the cord and lowered the shade clumsily, unevenly, her hands tensed.

"What's wrong?" Juliet said, out of breath from the kiss.

Carolyn had occasionally chided her for being over-vigilant when it came to shades and curtains. "Not everyone wants to watch you, Gen," she said, only half teasing.

Gen thought of that now as she replied, "It's nothing" and drew Juliet from the kitchen to the bedroom, where the curtains were securely closed.

Chapter Nineteen

Fenton

The story occupied no more than five inches at the bottom corner of the *Gazette*'s front page. Fenton read it twice as he sipped his coffee in the theater the Monday morning after Thanksgiving.

Having pled guilty, Mark had received a year's probation, and the three other white men arrested on Labor Day also received mild sentences. The judge leveled a stiffer punishment of two years in prison on James Combs, Mark's Negro companion. The investigation that had pursued leads for weeks had so far yielded no other arrests, the paper reported.

The mayor, who had won reelection handily over his opponent, told the *Gazette* he was satisfied that justice had been served. "The Know Your Neighbor program has yielded a few names," he said, "but nothing of great concern. Our citizens can feel safe in Springboro. We'll be closing the investigation down." He didn't need to mention that Congressman Duke had lost his bid for a twelfth term to a young man who had no interest in weeding out vice in a sleepy town at the corner of his district.

The news took a big bite out of Fenton's worries, and he felt like celebrating. He reached for the phone to call Gen, but his superstitious bent told him not to jinx anything.

Later that day, he heard from Mark, who was rooming in the

Slocum Point Motor Court on the edge of town near the Negro neighborhood. At night, its attached diner served as an unofficial pickup place for gay men, which Fenton knew about even though he had only ventured there once. It was too close, too dangerous, too seedy. When Mark asked to meet him there, Fenton countered by suggesting the bar in the lobby of the Hotel Jeff Davis in nearby Leesville, which had no associations with anything gay and was a safe three miles away.

Fenton dressed for the elegant bar in a suit and tie and arrived ten minutes early to take a table in a far corner, away from prying eyes and ears. While he waited for Mark, he ordered bourbon, neat. Time ticked by, and before long he ordered a second.

Mark arrived a half-hour late, wearing a garish plaid tie that he was still adjusting under his shirt collar. He wasn't wearing a jacket under his navy peacoat.

"They wouldn't let me in without a tie," he complained. "To a bar! The coat check girl took pity on me and gave me this hideous loaner."

"I would have warned you, but I thought you knew."

The waitress set down Fenton's drink and took Mark's order, side-eying him. With hair so long it curled over his collar, Mark looked more bedraggled than the day he and Fenton had met in the town library—no longer the natty art historian who prided himself on his grooming.

"Silly me, I guess I forgot," Mark said. "I've had other things on my mind."

His biting tone stung. Mark looked away from Fenton and helped himself to a handful of peanuts.

Fenton waited for Mark's scotch to arrive before he spoke again. "I was happy to read about your sentencing," he said.

Mark snorted. "If anyone can be happy about sentencing."

Everything was coming out wrong. "I don't know what to say to you," Fenton admitted.

Mark turned a fierce glare toward him. "How about a simple thanks?" he said. "My lawyer wanted me to give people up, but I thought that was despicable."

142

Fenton swigged his bourbon. "I didn't know."

"You could have guessed when you were still walking around without any charges against you."

Mark gave the peanut bowl a shove, but his voice remained low and modulated.

"It was tempting, Fen. They would have expunged my record after three months. They would have gone lighter on Jimmy." The tender nickname leapt out. "But who turns on other guys like that? I couldn't do it. Now I've got this permanent stain on my record, and I probably won't see Jimmy again. I can't even move away from this fucking town and start fresh."

Fenton was aware of the waitress hovering nearby, attuned to the shrinking levels in their glasses, and he waved her off.

"I do thank you, Mark," he said. "I don't know if I'd have been that noble in your shoes."

"I wasn't looking for praise, Fen. Maybe I was stupid and I'll regret missing the chance to throw you all under the bus." Mark sniffed and finished his drink. "I asked you here because I need a job. I'm a little desperate. You know anybody hiring convicted sex offenders?"

Fenton couldn't laugh at the sad joke. He pulled out his wallet and thumbed through his slim stash of bills. "Would twenty help at all? I'm kind of short right now. I've had to pay—" He stopped, not wanting to burden Mark with his therapy story, or to hear his disapproval.

Mark tilted his head curiously, as if he expected Fenton to finish his sentence with "for sex."

"Not that," Fenton said with a frown. "Consider this a gift from a friend."

Mark glanced around before pocketing the tens that Fenton slid across the table. "I appreciate it. This will keep me at the Slocum another week." With a nervous laugh, he added, "I've actually considered committing myself to Western State so I'd have someplace to live."

Fenton shivered at the mention of the asylum in Staunton. Horrible things happened there, everyone knew: lobotomies, straitjackets, shock treatment—the real kind, not the mild jolts Fenton got in therapy.

"Please tell me you won't do that," he said. "We'll figure something out. I'll give you more on payday. We'll stay in touch."

They finished their drinks in silence, and Fenton emptied the remaining singles from his wallet to pay the tab.

With the threat of arrest lifted, Fenton decided to break up with both Dr. Thorne and Kathy.

He reasoned he could call the psychiatrist's office and leave a message with the receptionist, a sweet-tempered lady who reminded him of one of his aunts. Because he had never agreed to the doctor's plan of taking an electrode machine home, there was no reason to see Dr. Thorne in person ever again. What joy! Fenton could avoid the doctor's "Do you think this is a wise idea, Mr. Patterson?" which bounded into his head.

"I guess you'd like to reschedule," the receptionist continued.

Fenton hadn't anticipated having to lie. "No, not r-right now," he said.

The receptionist paused. "Would you like the doctor to call you back?"

"I— Well—" He couldn't finish the thought, so he slipped the phone softly back into the cradle without replying.

But what to do about Kathy?

Fenton had played her beau on less than a handful of dates, if he included Ruby's election night party. On the most recent one, just before the holiday, he had worked up the courage to coax his tongue into her mouth. Her cheeks were amazingly soft against his. He wanted to ask about her moisturizer, but then her hand slid to his crotch and he surprised himself by hardening.

In bed, Kathy's naughty suggestion that he take her from behind worked well for him, especially when she agreed to switch off the lamp. After the sex, he wondered if Dr. Thorne was mistaken and the right woman could guide him toward a semblance

144

of heterosexuality. But when Kathy mounted him, cajoling him for a second go-round, he went soft.

"We shouldn't stress an old man's ticker," he said, feigning exhaustion.

Unlike the men he'd been with—even months-long relationships, like Mark—Kathy turned possessive after one roll in the hay.

"I don't see why you can't come home with me for Thanksgiving," she had said. "I want to show you off to my parents!"

"Don't pout."

"I'm not pouting."

"I'm looking right at you and believe me, you're pouting. And it's not pretty." When her bottom lip quivered, he regretted the insult and took her hand lightly in his. "Look, hon, I planned this trip back home long before we started going out. I don't get back there much, and my mother's expecting me. I can't back out now."

Once he'd called Dr. Thorne, Fenton decided to try the breakup-by-phone technique with Kathy. She didn't cooperate.

"You don't see us having a *future* together?" she repeated. "Tell me you didn't just say that. God, Fenton, I let you *fuck* me on our second real date! I slept over at your apartment. I've never done that with a guy."

"Now, hon, I know for a fact I wasn't your first—"

"I didn't mean I was a *virgin*." She spat out the word. "I mean I always held out longer, and I've always insisted the guy stay at *my* place."

The distinction was lost on him, but there was so much he didn't understand about women from his own lack of experience. There had only been one girl before Kathy, and they'd slept together as freshmen in college, almost twenty years earlier. He and Fay Purdy had never gotten past second base.

"You introduced me to your landlady, for God's sake," Kathy went on.

He had, but only because they'd run into her on the front porch and it had seemed the polite thing to do. That, and she might provide cover if he ever needed someone to testify that he wasn't queer. He couldn't admit either of those things to Kathy, though.

"I told my parents and my friends about you! Do you want me to look like a fool? You want everyone saying even old Fenton Page doesn't want me?"

Fenton bristled at the implication of her last question. Even with the age gap, he knew Kathy found him attractive. On one of their dates, she had asked playfully, "Why haven't you been snapped up yet? You're such a catch." He had shrugged off the question with a bashful smile.

In his mind, he had hoped this breakup would proceed smoothly. Maybe she'd sniffle, ask to see him one last time, and he'd relent to coffee or a drink. He owed her something. He hadn't anticipated a verbal lashing.

"I'm sorry," he offered, but she had already hung up.

Part II

Winter 1960–1961

Chapter Twenty

Gen

Although her schedule was full to bursting in the days before finals, Gen labored to shift her thoughts away from the weekend with Juliet and toward pressing academic tasks. At unwanted moments, while she prepared her final lectures, collected term papers, and created exams so they could be mimeographed, the first blush of a new love affair filtered back into her consciousness in delicious Technicolor.

Once, a moment with Juliet flashed to mind during a meeting with a student. Gen didn't hear half of what the girl said and, in too short a tone, asked her to repeat it—twice. The student looked crestfallen, and Gen had to apologize, blaming the end of the semester for her frayed attention span.

And then Huston requested a meeting, to discuss what, she wasn't sure. "This and that," the chairman said vaguely, making her wonder if a student had taken complaints about her teaching to a higher authority. "As soon as you can," he added, and the stipulation made her palms sweat. She wished she knew how to prepare.

The department secretary, Linda Sue, popped out of her seat when Gen arrived for the meeting and asked if she could get her anything. "Anything at all?" Then she quickly tailored it to

"Coffee, Dr. Rider? I just made a fresh pot." Linda Sue had never offered Gen coffee. In fact, she had never paid much attention to Gen at all, although she did her mimeographing with a smile and greeted her pleasantly when she picked up her mail. Gen never solicited anything more from her—unlike Henry Thoms, who had a habit of perching at the edge of Linda Sue's desk while he regaled her with humorous stories about his sons.

Gen glanced toward Huston's door, which was open a crack. She wanted to be on the other side of whatever unpleasantness was in store.

"I think I'll just go in, if he's ready for me."

"Let me check," Linda Sue said—something else she never did. The young woman scurried to Huston's office and poked her head in. "Dr. Rider's here," Gen heard her say before she motioned her in. Linda Sue clicked the door closed behind her.

Huston was already on his feet behind his desk, his fingers tented on the blotter as if the furniture were holding him erect. His eyes blinked rapidly before falling to the chair across from him. "Gen, please sit."

He continued to stand for a long moment after she took her chair. Finally, he crossed in front of his desk and settled himself in the leather armchair beside her. He'd done this before when he'd invited her to tea, and Gen felt her body loosen.

"I don't really know how to begin," he said.

A knot tugged at her belly. She sat up straighter and took several measured breaths.

"I had a visit from the mother of one of your students. Mrs. Blakeney. You know her?"

"Lee-Anne's mother? No, we've never met."

Huston cherry-picked his words. "She was . . . upset. Distraught, you might say. Linda Sue had to help calm her down. I haven't had such a visit from a parent before. It was . . . unnerving."

Gen coughed once to clear away her mounting anxiety and take charge of the meeting. "If this is about my Civil War class, Geoffrey . . . well, Lee-Anne has made it abundantly clear all semester that she doesn't understand why we talk so much about

150

Negroes. I'm fully aware of her discomfort. But what could she possibly want this late in the semester? Special dispensation from the final? She had a B-plus on the midterm, which I consider respectable, but she wasn't happy. Or is she just raising a fuss to try to get me to change the syllabus going forward? You can't expect me to do that." She cut off her rambling and paused for his reply.

The lines in Huston's forehead creased. "Of course not. I wouldn't call you in here for *that*."

A slight taste of bile rose in her mouth. Something worse than *that* had brought her to this moment.

Huston's words and sentences scrambled in her ears: "...kitchen window ... the shade ... her friend, Mrs. Carr ... with a female ... compelled to report ..."

Gen's neck and face burned. The kiss, which had thrilled her, now flooded her with shame.

"... never encountered anything like this ..."

Gen wanted to be anywhere else, with Huston's damning words out of her ears. She grabbed the arms of the chair but found herself rooted in place.

Since her hiring at Baines, Gen had known that the college could snatch away her career at any moment, that she had to conduct herself in a way that didn't apply to other faculty. People like her and Fenton had to take special precautions. They weren't allowed mistakes. The unspoken code of conduct demanded vigilance and sacrifice.

But then, one lapse in judgment, one passing failure to be on guard had brought her to this sickening moment. Gen Rider had been caught being human—not on campus or with a student, but with a willing adult in her own kitchen.

"... appointment with Provost Ramsey ..." she heard Huston continue. And then the first complete sentence since he'd begun speaking: "I wanted to tell you first."

All those years of diligent hiding churned in her, and a bitter resentment she didn't know she was capable of bubbled up. Her hands curled into fists on their own accord. *I was in my own home,* she could have sworn she said, but nothing came out. She tried again, a tremor in her voice, a shaking at the back of her throat.

"I was in my own home, Geoffrey. In my *kitchen.* I shouldn't have to account for what I do or don't do there on my own time." The room seemed important to stress; nothing too untoward ever happened in a kitchen.

Huston's head bobbed in agreement, but his next words didn't match the action. "It's a serious charge. I must say, I'm deeply disappointed."

The chairman leaned forward, his elbows on his knees, his full cheeks drained of their ruddy color. He didn't specify that he was disappointed in *her,* but he didn't need to. "Your research draws enough attention," he said, "and now this."

"I was in my own home," she repeated, reasoning that he didn't understand. But her assertion came out soft and weak—the "female" voice she hated and encouraged her students to rid themselves of.

"Mrs. Blakeney said if I didn't speak to the provost, she would. That it was her duty."

Gen's thoughts tumbled over each other.

"It's better coming from me than from a hysterical mother," he continued. "I thought maybe you could explain to me what happened and I could frame it more delicately. I'm not asking for an explanation now. Tell me tomorrow. Maybe it was an accident, or maybe the female was a relative you were hugging. It was Thanksgiving weekend, after all. I'm willing to accept that it was purely innocent and Mrs. Carr made a mistake in what she saw."

Her neck was on fire now, and she tugged at the collar of her blouse. "I was in my own home. With whom or doing what is no one's business. That's all I have to say."

Huston punctuated his response with a sigh—the impatience of a parent whose child refuses direction. "You'll have to say something besides that. Mrs. Carr is likely just following the

Know Your Neighbor guidance. And after what happened with the Patton fellow . . . well, the provost won't let this matter drop."

Gen ran her damp palms over her skirt and stood. "You haven't given me enough time."

"It's what we have," Huston said.

As the light drained from the day, Gen pulled up to the curb in front of her bungalow but remained in the driver's seat, hands fastened on the steering wheel. Beside her on the passenger's side was a stack of papers she'd grabbed from her desk before racing from her office to the safety of her car. She wasn't even sure what was in the messy pile, some of which had pitched forward onto the floorboard when she jammed on her brakes at a stop sign. She decided to abandon it all and get inside the house as quickly as she could.

Gen glanced at the liquor cabinet but bypassed it. She had too much to do, too much to think about, too many people to call to allow herself the luxury of getting drunk. Instead, she forced herself to enter the kitchen and down two glasses of water from the tap in rapid succession. Her throat scratched like sandpaper. She let her eyes wander across the yard, where the light was on in the Carrs' kitchen. At almost dinner time, Mrs. Carr was sure to be home.

Gen continued to watch out the window, her heart tapping out a frenzied beat. After some time passed—five minutes? ten?—she spotted what she'd been waiting for: Irene Carr's outline in her own window. Gen straightened her spine and willed Mrs. Carr to look back at her. As if she could sense Gen's stare, Mrs. Carr's eyes remained cast down, fixed on something in front of her, likely in the kitchen sink.

"Yes, wash those hands," Gen muttered. "Get them nice and clean."

And then Mrs. Carr glanced up—so fleetingly, Gen wondered if she imagined it. Within seconds, her neighbor had closed her flouncy cafe curtains.

Gen's legs turned to rubber. If she called Ruby, if she related the situation to Darrell, he would likely tell her not to engage her neighbor in any way. Her better judgment agreed with his imagined advice, but her heart also weighed in. Without donning her coat again, Gen left her house through the kitchen door, crossed her backyard, and found herself standing on the Carrs' porch.

She jabbed the doorbell once, twice. She crossed her arms to keep herself from shivering in the evening air, then punched the bell again. The fixture wasn't broken—she could hear the melodic chime from where she stood—but no one came to answer it. Mr. Carr's Lincoln wasn't in the driveway, so his wife must be alone. The woman had bemoaned to Gen, more than once, her empty nest since Susanna had enrolled in Baines.

"I know you're in there," Gen said loudly, not caring who else heard. She switched to the door knocker, a polished brass lion's head, and rapped it in a forceful rat-a-tat-tat.

Still, nothing. Gen trudged down the walkway and back to her house, letting the door slam behind her. Inside, she rested her forehead against its heavy wood.

She needed to warn Juliet and Fenton, but the pain of having to tell her gay friends that she'd let them down was intolerable. Gen sank onto the phone bench and dialed another familiar number.

Not long after the call, Ruby stood in Gen's foyer bearing a fragrant roasted chicken Darrell must have cooked for dinner. She hadn't stopped to cover the bird with tinfoil, and it listed precariously to one side of the serving platter. The sight of her distinguished friend, hair in disarray, coat sliding off her shoulders, holding a chicken, made Gen half-laugh, half-cry.

Chapter Twenty-One

Gen

Frank Johnson had only a few hours before his bus left for Washington, Mae explained. "No appointments today at all, Dr. Rider."

Gen understood how rude it was to show up at the law firm first thing in the morning, without an appointment, expecting a busy attorney to carve out a slot for her in his schedule. Still, out of desperation, she had risked the discourtesy and detoured to Johnson & Waldron on her way to campus.

"I won't take but five minutes of his time, Mrs. Johnson, I swear."

"He said not to disturb him for anything," Mae replied. "Big meeting to get ready for."

"Please." It sounded like begging, even in Gen's own ears. "I wouldn't ask if it wasn't urgent."

Mae's face softened, and her hand inched toward the intercom button of the phone on her desk. She didn't have to make the choice, though, because Frank emerged from behind his closed door.

"It's okay," he said. "Just this one interruption. Dr. Rider, good to see you again."

He extended a welcoming hand that Gen shook gratefully. Since the fool she'd made of herself with Frank in October, she had been to a second NAACP meeting and even volunteered for the women's committee, all without asking for anything in return. Now Frank's warmth suggested they might soon return to a first-name basis.

"I won't take but a minute," she assured him as he motioned toward a seat across from his desk.

He shot her a polite smile. "What can I possibly do for you?" His slight emphasis on *possibly* wasn't lost on Gen.

"I'm in a bind. At the college. I need an attorney's advice—" Frank's eyebrows lifted, and Gen stumbled to explain. "I was hoping just—I hoped maybe you could refer me to a lawyer for my particular case."

He pushed his glasses up his nose. "What is this bind you're in?"

Gen bit her upper lip before continuing. As she related the conversation with Huston, she watched the lawyer's face closely but didn't notice a change, not even a flinch. At the end of her story, Frank steepled his hands in front of his mouth but didn't speak.

"I have to talk to the chairman this morning, and I wrote this statement that I would like a lawyer to look at in case it's a mistake to put it in writing. I can't afford to make things worse for myself."

Frank held out his hand for the sheet she'd withdrawn from her purse.

Dear Dr. Huston:

Per your request, I am furnishing a response to an allegation put forth against me by Mrs. Blakeney, which I believe is an invasion of my privacy. At the time Mrs. Blakeney alleges the incident took place, it was a Sunday evening and I was in my own home.

156

Also, as you yourself noted, Mrs. Blakeney made this scurrilous charge based solely on hearsay and second-hand information.

Thank you in advance for drawing this matter quickly to a conclusion.

Sincerely,

Virginia Rider, Ph.D.
Associate Professor of History

He scrutinized the short statement, appearing to read it twice, then passed it back to her.

"Legally, I don't see any problem with it," Frank announced. "I might have left off *scurrilous.*"

Gen sensed a "but" somewhere in his statement. "Is there some other problem, aside from legal?"

Frank rubbed his mouth and took his time answering. "I find it unlikely to satisfy anyone in a position of authority. You said you were asked for an explanation that the chairman could take to the provost. You haven't given one."

"My explanation is that it's none of that woman's business to spread rumors about me because of something she thinks happened in my home. I don't care what cockamamie idea she got from the Know Your Neighbor campaign."

The attorney drew in a long, patient breath. "Privacy is a tricky defense, Gen. The Constitution doesn't outright guarantee it. There's some judicial precedent, but if someone accuses you of committing a crime in your home—"

"Kissing someone is a crime?" She laughed, but Frank's face remained impassive.

"It's not sodomy, but there *are* laws against homosexual fondling and lewdness."

"In private?"

"In public."

"Which this isn't a case of."

Frank glanced toward his desk clock, an ornate brass piece that resembled a ship's gauge. He clearly hadn't anticipated a circuitous discussion when he agreed to speak to her for five minutes.

"What would you do, Frank?"

He held her eyes but paused for a long moment. "I'd go with your first instinct. I'd hire an attorney." He picked up a pen and scratched onto a legal pad. "Let me give you some names."

After Gen delivered her statement to the department secretary, Huston did something he had not done in all the years she'd taught at Baines: He came to her office. Not bothering with a hello, he blurted out, "I was hoping you'd give me something more substantial."

"And I was hoping to put the matter to rest," she replied, as evenly as she could. She motioned him to her visitor's chair, but he remained just inside the door, his face as pale as the letter flapping in his hand.

"It isn't a question of me. You have an impeccable record as a teacher, and far be it from me to pry into your life at home. But this complaint has come from a *parent*, a prominent alumna and donor who's capable of making a fuss out of nothing at all, and if I don't address it with the provost, Mrs. Blakeney will. I'm afraid that could go very badly for you."

"Just so you know, Geoffrey, I spoke to an attorney this morning."

That brought a hint of color back to Huston's cheeks. "Oh, very good. Excellent move." His firm agreement buoyed her. "And what did he think?"

"We didn't get that far. We'll talk again soon," she lied. Huston nodded as if satisfied that she'd taken action. She didn't mention that she would need to work her way through the short list of white attorneys Frank had created off the top of his head, people he'd collaborated with on NAACP business.

Before noon, when she knew Huston's meeting with the provost was scheduled to begin, Gen drove herself to the Barrington tea shop. Juliet was already waiting at a table facing the picture window. It was the same table they'd chosen on their first rendezvous, but this time when Gen sat down she noticed it wobbled a little.

Her eyes misted over, and Juliet's face blurred. "I don't think I can—" Gen began.

But then she heard Juliet's calm, clear voice as the waitress placed a menu in front of each of them.

"Well, thank you. What looks good today?"

After the beverages and sweets Gen didn't have any taste for, they sat in Juliet's ancient Buick outside the tea shop. She rarely used the vehicle, preferring to go everywhere she could on two wheels.

"I'll come forward," Juliet said. "We'll say it was all innocent and that Mrs. Carr needs glasses."

Gen shook her head adamantly. "One of us in trouble is enough. Better me than you."

"But it might clear you!"

She almost laughed but stopped herself. "You spent the night," Gen pointed out. "That hardly seems innocent."

Juliet twisted the end of her braid. "They don't know that. Even if they did, they wouldn't know *where* I slept. You've said Fenton stays over on your sofa bed. A guy sleeping over looks worse than a woman."

Fenton had encouraged Gen to lie, too, and Huston in his way had hinted broadly at the possibility. But she'd been so outraged at the invasion of her private space that when pressed for an explanation, she could only tell the truth. She was in her own kitchen, and what happened there was no one's business.

"Here's the thing," she said to Juliet. "I was in my own home. I would have thought you of all people would get how important that is."

159

Juliet gripped the steering wheel. "You keep repeating that, and I do get it. But Gen, your job's at stake, your reputation. Why not deny the whole thing and throw the blame on Mrs. Carr? Then maybe you could continue on as always. *We* could continue on."

Gen rolled down her window a few inches for air. "It would be awkward to take back my statement now. The provost already has it. What do I do—say, whoops, I just remembered?"

Juliet sighed heavily and started the engine.

Chapter Twenty-Two

Gen

Gen waited for word from Huston or a command to appear in the provost's office, all while trying to focus on grading student papers. Everything proved a distraction, even going into the kitchen to prepare a quick meal. Each time she spotted the window, so innocently facing the Carrs' house, memories flooded back. That window mocked her even in her dreams, jolting her out of sleep. Soon, Gen stopped going into the kitchen at all, drinking water from the bathroom sink and forgoing most food except the dry Cheerios, crackers, and apples she could keep on her desk. If the kitchen had had a door, she would have closed it off from the rest of the house.

She steered clear of her office at school, too, only venturing there after dusk on Friday, when faculty and staff had departed and students huddled in their dorm rooms cramming for finals. The campus at those times offered delicious quiet, the silence broken only by the insistent "who cooks for you" cry of a barred owl.

There was no avoiding administering her final exams, though. On Monday morning, Gen dry heaved into her toilet bowl. She brushed her teeth vigorously and ran a comb through her hair, adding a spritz of Adorn to hold it in place. Foundation and powder under her eyes covered the smudges from lack of sleep.

She made it to her office without encountering a single faculty member. The janitor sweeping the hallway greeted her with "G'morning, Professor," as if it were any other day. For a few minutes at least, she almost believed it was. Behind her closed door, she composed herself, gathered blue books from a stash in a file drawer, and reviewed the sheet of essay questions Linda Sue had mimeographed for her.

At the door to her classroom, she froze. Through the door's window panel, she could see the rows of girls with their heads bent over their textbooks. The rumor might have already rolled across campus, and the students she was about to face might have heard the gossip about her. She dismissed the notion with a determined intake of breath. After all, there'd been no summons yet, and the allegation against her remained just that.

Gen twisted the knob. She suspected her smile might look fake, but it was the best she could muster, and besides, the girls would be so nervous about the exam they would likely not notice.

"Good morning, everyone," she said in what she hoped was a cheery tone. She focused her gaze on Margaret, who was the first to return the greeting. "Please put your textbooks and notes away now so we can get started. You're a bright group, and I don't think any of you will find this test too challenging."

With a quick scan of faces, she located Susanna and Lee-Anne at their usual side-by-side desks, looking relieved at Gen's statement. Perhaps Mrs. Carr and Mrs. Blakeney had been too embarrassed to tell their own daughters the gossip, or maybe they wanted them to finish the semester without distractions that could damage their GPAs.

The two girls were among the first to finish the exam. Neither appeared to have an inkling of what their mothers had set in motion.

"I think I'll pull better than a B-plus this time, Professor,"

Lee-Anne whispered with a self-satisfied smile. "I really studied."
Leaving behind her, Susanna offered a pleasant, "See you next year!"

Margaret was the last to turn in her exam. She also slid the borrowed photography book onto the desk with a soft thanks. "I don't suppose you ever found out who sent you those presents," she said, her eyes fastened on Gen's stack of blue books.

With all that had happened since Thanksgiving, the pranks had slipped Gen's mind.

"I haven't," Gen replied. "I'm not sure I ever will. Don't worry about it, Margaret."

The girl's face relaxed. "I probably won't see you again before January. Are you doing anything fun over the break?" It was an odd question from a student, as if Gen were a peer and not a teacher.

"Just resting, I hope."

"That's nice," Margaret said, but her tone was laced with such melancholy that Gen patted her back as they exited together.

"You have a merry Christmas, Margaret."

Gen withdrew to her office to gather what she needed for the second exam. As with the first, the test went without a hitch, the girls unaware of the drama unfolding in her own life. When she announced, "That's it, girls—time," she felt the weight lift off her as she realized she could retreat home.

She had to brave the department office one last time to collect her mail. Linda Sue said, "Good afternoon, Dr. Rider," in a voice louder than needed for such a small space. As if on cue, Huston emerged from his office.

"Gen, would you please—when you have a moment."

Gen gathered her mail, mainly notices of meetings and a reminder about committee appointments for the spring. Mixed in with the other papers was a vellum envelope from the Office of the Provost with, *Dr. Virginia Rider, History Department* typed neatly across the front.

She didn't need to open it; she could almost read the message through the thick, watermarked paper. She walked as steadily as she could into Huston's office and planted herself in front of his desk.

"There's no hearing?"

"You haven't read your letter." He glanced down at the stack of mail in her hands, and she shook her head.

"It's suspension, not dismissal, pending an investigation by the provost's office. Very contained. Mrs. Blakeney and Mrs. Carr won't go to the press or contact Congressman Duke. The provost doesn't want parents pulling students out and all that."

She nodded roughly as she let the idea of suspension sink in.

"I believe just the provost and Dean Rolfe's office will be involved. The Tenure and Privilege Committee will also review the situation and send Dr. Ramsey its recommendation. That's very good news, Gen, very good news."

Which part is the "very good news"? she wanted to ask, but found her voice wasn't available.

"You can have an attorney present, and you said you contacted one already. He can call character witnesses, people to provide testimony on your behalf. And you have a good friend on Tenure and Privilege. Ruby will be invaluable. She's greatly admired and has a lot of influence."

Huston's words scrambled out, like they were ready to run for cover. He reached into his pocket for a handkerchief and wiped his brow.

"Nothing will happen until January, possibly February. Unfortunately, you know I'm on sabbatical at Cambridge. Can't be changed at this late date."

She remembered what Huston's sabbatical meant—that the department's only other full professor, Henry Thoms, would step in as interim chairman.

"I'll write you a statement of support, Gen, a strong one, I promise. I'll get right to that as soon as I submit my grades. If there's an opportunity for me to give testimony before I leave for Cambridge, I'll do that, too."

Tears formed at the corners of her eyes, and she blinked them back, determined not to let Huston or anyone at Baines see her cry.

"What about my spring classes?" she managed to ask.

"I've canceled the seminar. Henry and I are in the process of interviewing a part-time instructor for the pre-Civil War class. There's one impressive young fellow who's finishing his dissertation on Manifest Destiny. Of course, he won't follow your syllabus, but at least the class will run."

Of course they'd hire a man. Henry Thoms wouldn't have it any other way. "You've thought of everything," she said, unable to curb her sarcasm.

"This is all most unfortunate, but it's going to be fine. You have an impeccable teaching record and solid scholarship. This will be over before you know it."

His face clouded as he cast his eyes toward the door. Gen turned and saw a campus security guard hovering in the frame, a slender young man whose name Gen didn't know.

"Give us a minute, would you?" Huston said to the guard. "Now, about your exams—"

Gen turned away and pushed past Linda Sue and the guard, even as Huston called after her. The young man followed her down the hallway to her office and waited at her door while she grabbed her coat and shoved the provost's letter into her briefcase. She left her blue books on her desk, assuming that was what Huston was going to instruct her to do. She couldn't imagine someone else grading them. What would Henry Thoms make of her questions about "the Lost Cause" and Jim Crow?

Across the hall, Lee-Anne was waiting outside Thoms's door for his office hours to begin, and she stared at Gen with wide eyes, her mouth a perfect O of shock. Gen relocked her office, then hissed at the guard under her breath, "Whatever you do, do not touch me."

"Yes, ma'am." The guard's voice trembled. Not much older than her students, he had likely never imagined this sort of task.

He walked a respectful distance behind her to the parking lot, where he halted and continued to stand watch even when she was in her car with the motor running.

She lingered before shifting the car into reverse, making the guard stamp his feet in the cold while she withdrew the provost's letter from her briefcase and ripped it open. The envelope flap sliced a cut in her thumb, just deep enough to leave a thin red line on the creamy vellum. Gen pressed down on the wound as she read the dreaded words: *without pay*.

Chapter Twenty-Three

Ruby

Ruby assembled an emergency meeting of the female faculty group, but only three women showed up. She tried not to attribute the sparse numbers to anything but the end-of-semester timing.

When the women arrived, Ruby's dining-room table stood bare, without a cookie or glass of water in sight. "I apologize for my lack of hospitality," she said. "I'm not in a hostessing mood."

"Ruby, dear, what's the matter?" Vanessa Westergren asked.

Ruby informed them about Gen's suspension. At the far end of the table, Frances Palmer blanched and ran a finger repeatedly over a grain of wood. Juliet May nodded as if familiar with Gen's story. Ruby remembered that she and Gen had become friends in the past few months.

Vanessa demanded specifics. Ruby realized Gen hadn't given her much.

"Mrs. Carr, her next-door neighbor, thought she saw Gen in an improper . . . embrace. Through the kitchen window."

Vanessa grimaced. "What do you mean by an improper embrace?"

"With another woman."

"Who?" Vanessa demanded.

Ruby huffed with impatience at her colleague from the Music Department. Vanessa sang soprano beautifully, but aside from that, Ruby had never taken to her. "That's irrelevant. I'm not even convinced it happened. Gen won't say anything too specific, and that's fine. Her privacy is what's at issue. Why, your privacy and mine are, too, for that matter. What we do in our homes is *our* business, not the college's."

"Precisely!" Juliet noted. "Ruby, shouldn't the Faculty Senate have a say? And what good is tenure if they can do this to someone?" The young professor gripped the edge of the table.

"Tenure and Privilege will take up the matter as an employment issue and make a recommendation to the Senate," Ruby replied. "The Senate will relate the decision to the provost. As members of the committee, you and I will have to stand strong for Gen, Frances."

Frances continued to stare at the table without speaking.

"Tenure doesn't protect anyone when it comes to . . . behavior," Vanessa added, in response to Juliet's other question. Her slight hesitation before *behavior*—as if she'd considered inserting a descriptor—made Ruby press her hands together in her lap.

"Gen Rider is one of our most respected professors," Juliet said.

"Of course, that goes without saying," Vanessa agreed. "Her behavior on campus has been nothing but exemplary in all the years I've known her. But what if off-campus, she's . . . done something immoral? What if this so-called embrace was something . . . seamy?"

Frances lifted her head, finding her voice at last. "First of all, who decides what's 'immoral'? And second, why don't you tell us how any off-campus behavior would affect Gen's teaching?"

Ruby had always liked her bite. Frances had fought her way through the Biology Department, the only woman in a male-dominated field, and wore as many battle scars as Ruby. She had still not attained the rank of full professor, after all her years of service and a strong research agenda.

Vanessa snapped back. "You needn't get so testy, Fran. I *like*

Gen. But you have to admit that if a faculty member is caught stealing or brawling in town or something like that, it would make you question how morally fit they are to guide students. It seems Gen's done something that got her neighbor so riled up she wanted the administration to know." Vanessa leaned back as if she'd finished her summation.

"The Know Your Neighbor nonsense is over," Frances pointed out. "Her neighbor shouldn't be spying on her."

Ruby had lost control of the meeting. She hadn't meant to let the discussion drift toward the legitimacy of the charge against Gen or, worse, her moral fitness. Why hadn't she limited the meeting to faculty she knew would be sympathetic? Before she could try to steer them to an action plan, however, Juliet chimed in.

"If Gen's done something immoral, then so have I."

All heads swiveled toward the young woman, whose high cheekbones bloomed with rosy splotches.

"Gen and I were kissing in her kitchen," Juliet said. "We forgot to put the shade down, and Mrs. Carr apparently saw us."

Something welled up in Ruby and escaped as a little gasp. She tried to cover it with a cough, but the sound drew Juliet's attention. The active *were kissing* jumped out—not a hug or an embrace or a peck on the cheek, but an adult kiss that continued for a while.

"I thought you knew and were being discreet," Juliet said to Ruby. "I thought *embrace* was your euphemism."

Ruby shook her head. "Gen didn't give specifics, and I didn't ask."

"Well, it was completely consensual," Juliet continued. "I've wanted to speak up, tell the provost it was me, but Gen's worried that would make things worse. She thinks she can withstand this on her own just by claiming she was in her own house."

A long silence followed Juliet's admission. Vanessa twisted the wedding band and engagement ring on her finger, while Frances returned to staring at the table.

Over the years, Ruby had known plenty of female faculty who

set up house together—Frances, for one—but she always imagined the relationships as convenient, not sexual. On weekends, Gen drove all the way to Richmond to stay with a friend named Carolyn, and that behavior struck Ruby as odder. In public, Gen proffered the story that she'd lost her fiancé in the invasion of Normandy and then threw herself into work and friends. Ruby found it better not to think or ask about Gen's private story—or those of Fenton and colleagues like him.

Now, the charade had burst open. At least, in Ruby's dining room.

Ruby's voice wavered slightly when she finally spoke. "I doubt coming forward would clear Gen, and she wouldn't want you to risk everything so close to your tenure decision."

Juliet folded her arms firmly. "If faculty can be attacked like this, I don't want tenure."

Vanessa clucked her tongue but at what, Ruby didn't know. After another pause, the music professor rose and lifted her coat from the back of her chair.

"I'm sorry, I need to get moving," she said. "Can't leave Charles too long with the children. Let me know if there's something I can do."

At the door, Ruby took Vanessa's arm. "Everything we said today is confidential."

"I'm not someone's nosy neighbor, Ruby," Vanessa replied with a hint of distaste, but the assurance gave Ruby a modicum of comfort.

With Vanessa gone, Ruby brought an open bottle of red wine and glasses to the table. "I don't know about you, but I need a drink."

The three of them inched closer together and Ruby filled the glasses. Ruby resisted the urge to gulp hers.

"Does Gen have money to get by?" Frances asked after a sip.

The question chilled Ruby, who realized she hadn't bothered to ask Gen something so basic. The fact that Gen needed to support herself had gotten lost in a flurry of indignation. Suspension without pay was not only demeaning, but outright cruel.

"I would be willing to chip in each month to help her," Frances continued. "If more faculty got involved, I bet we could raise a decent kitty. No one has to know specifics." Frances fished in her pocketbook for her wallet and withdrew twenty dollars. "I'll start it off." She pushed several worn bills to the center of the table like she was anteing up in a poker game. Twenty dollars was a hardship for any female professor at Baines, but Ruby matched the amount and Juliet gave up the four dollars she had with her.

Juliet volunteered to approach other female faculty members about contributing and to take up the collection each month until Gen was reinstated. Frances shook her head firmly.

"Better not draw attention to yourself," she said. "Let me. No one looks too close at an old lady." Gratitude for Frances's commitment surged in Ruby.

After her colleagues left, Ruby thought about the rustic cabin in the West Virginia mountains that she and Darrell owned. They'd fallen in love with the area around Lewisburg on their honeymoon and had purchased the cabin with money Ruby's grandparents left her. Originally a family getaway, it now provided a summer retreat for Ruby's writing and Darrell's fishing. The rest of the year, the place sat empty.

Ruby dug out the cabin keys. It would be a good escape for Gen until the provost's hearing commenced.

Chapter Twenty-Four

Gen

Gen and Juliet hadn't seen each other since the suspension, but they talked on the phone most nights. Their exchange just before Gen left for Ruby's cabin didn't go well. Juliet voiced her unhappiness that all contact would end because the cabin didn't have a phone line.

"I could come with you," she suggested. "You can't have Christmas and New Year's by yourself in some godforsaken cabin."

"I don't mind." They still didn't know each other well. Holing up together in a remote cabin for weeks in the winter could feel claustrophobic, but she didn't say that.

"Well, *I* mind," Juliet said. "I don't like it."

Gen sighed. She found Juliet's needy side unattractive, like a student wheedling to get her grade changed. "You don't know who could be watching us."

Juliet snickered. "Sounds like we're starring in a spy movie."

"Look," Gen snapped, "someone was watching me and I didn't realize it and now I'm suspended. There's nothing funny about it."

The line went quiet and then Juliet said softly, "I'm sorry, Gen. I make stupid jokes when I'm on edge. Of course you're right."

She pictured Juliet's face, the way in a certain light her blond hair took on a reddish cast. "It's just three weeks, sweetie. I'll see you before you know it." The affectionate name slipped out without thinking. She'd never used it with anyone else.

The next morning, Gen took off early, gassing up at the Texaco on the edge of town. She expected the man usually on duty to try to make small talk with a regular, and her hands tightened on the wheel as she pulled up to the pump. When she didn't recognize the young man who bounced out of the station door, she loosened her grip and asked him not only to fill it up but also to check under the hood.

As she put more and more miles between her and Springboro, the roads narrowed until they became a series of complicated switchbacks in the West Virginia hills. A sign for "Folly Way" marked the spot where she turned left onto a gravel trail. The irony of the name made her smile for the first time in more than a week, but she quickly turned serious again when deep ruts in the road threatened to rip off the underbody of her car.

She negotiated her way inch by inch to the white wooden fence noted on Darrell's printed directions. Without a passenger, she had to jump out and prop open the barrier with a rock, pull in, and close it behind her again.

Transformed into a dirt path, the road snaked through a pasture to a woodsy area. With each tenth of a mile that clicked by on her odometer, Gen's courage foundered. The prospect of escaping had buoyed her, but now she wondered how difficult it would be to back out and head home.

At last, Ruby and Darrell's log cabin rose out of a majestic stand of red pines. "Rustic," her friend had described it. If it rained or snowed, Gen would be stuck for the duration. But she had nowhere to be, and at Ruby's suggestion she had piled the back seat with provisions. Her suitcases held three weeks' worth of clothes.

Remembering Mark Patton, she had also brought along the Belk's department store box in which she kept private souvenirs.

It had once held the silk blouse she'd splurged on for her inter-view at Baines. The blouse had long ago made its way to the Salvation Army with a frayed cuff and missing collar button. Now the tissue paper protected her mementos, the ones she didn't dare show anyone—photos, letters. Unlike her orderly files at school, kept with a historian's precision, the box resembled her hall closet, her keepsakes simply tossed inside.

If Gen's landlord got wind of the charge against her and changed the locks, nothing in her house would incriminate her. She slammed the car trunk over the box like the door of a safe.

Ruby had warned her about the temperamental front door key that had to be wiggled until it clicked into place. In the main room, lacy cobwebs and a pattern of mouse droppings across the kitchen counter attested to the fact her friends hadn't been in residence since August.

Gen unfolded Ruby's elaborate directions for opening the cabin. First on the agenda was to switch on the hot water heater and then crack open windows to dismiss the musty odor. The brisk outdoor air made the main room, a sort of kitchen and living room combined, even colder, so she considered making a fire. Through the window of the back door, Gen noted a stack of logs under a tarp.

She'd never constructed a fire on her own, but she had remem-bered to bring matches and newspaper with her. To guide her, she dredged up a visual memory of Carolyn sparking a fire on cool evenings at the beach cottage. Carolyn would have been amused at the pile of snapped matchsticks before the flames from the paper and kindling actually caught the logs. It was longer still until the air warmed so Gen could remove her wool coat. On a nail near the door, she found an apron that likely belonged to Darrell, given the chef's hat printed on the front. Without taking a break she scrubbed the counters so she could unpack her kitchen supplies.

Daylight was fading by the time she'd finished the main room, and Gen switched on all the lamps. With the crackle of the fire and the golden glow from the lamps, the place felt livable. "Cozy" was the other word Ruby had used. Standing at the kitchen counter, inspecting her work, she unwrapped cheese and crackers from her provisions and ate a few without tasting them. They brought up the sharp memory of Juliet in her kitchen, the kiss that had sparked desire and trouble at the same time; and loneliness surged in her. She shook it off and went to inspect the handsome record player, a Phillips portable in a vinyl case, which, unlike everything else in the cabin, looked brand-new.

Ruby and Darrell owned no peppy albums that she could dance away her sadness to—or if they did, they left them all in Springboro. Classical was the only choice. The Toscanini she chose faded into the background as she sat on the sofa with a glass of white wine and an article on the Freedmen's Bureau she hadn't found time to dig into. But she kept reading the same paragraph over and over.

The crunch of tires outside brought Gen out of her exhausted fog. Ruby and Darrell both pronounced the cabin completely safe, with no intrusions or disturbances in all the years they'd owned it. The nearest neighbor was at least a quarter-mile back, before she reached the wooden fence.

From the window, all she saw was the blinding flash of high beams. When the headlights dimmed, she recognized the black and white Bel Air and threw open the front door.

"What are you doing here?" she called out, expecting to see Ruby, but it was Fenton who emerged from the driver's side. They'd made plans for him to visit, but not till the following week.

"I'm early, I know. I couldn't call you. My car's sick, and the mechanic didn't think it could make the trip. Ruby let me borrow hers, but I had to come this week." He plunked down his suitcase on the stoop but held onto a grocery bag. "Oh, you thought I was Ruby! You're disappointed."

"Don't be ridiculous." In the moonlight, unidentified creatures navigated the spaces between the trees. "Get in here."

"I love it when you boss me around."

Inside, Fenton set the groceries on the kitchen counter and stripped off his coat. He scanned the rest of the room, rotating his glance from the fireplace to the sofa to the record player and back. "Aren't you the Girl Scout, making a fire. This place is something! Ruby said cottage, and I think I expected Fire Island, but in the mountains."

"I'm pretty sure she said cabin, which is different," Gen said, feeling defensive. "And it's a lot better now than when I first got here."

"I'm sure the mice think so, too."

The statement nicked her, even though the cabin wasn't her own. There wasn't a mouse dropping in sight after her diligent dusting and scrubbing, which left a crisp scent of pine behind. She had planned to tackle the two bedrooms the next day and suddenly worried about the dust bunnies that would come dancing out when it was time to turn in.

"I was just grateful to get away," was all she said. When Ruby had pressed the keys into her hand, Gen had teared up at the generosity. Ruby seemed to intuit that she needed to be somewhere where she wouldn't pass the college gate every day or run into Irene Carr on the street or at the grocery store.

"Oh, of course," Fenton said. "And you'll be happy to know I come armed with medicine. Gimlets!"

He withdrew bottles of vodka and lime juice from the grocery bag and set about finding glasses.

"I brought livelier records, too. I didn't trust their taste, and I was right. Go open up my suitcase. I adore Arturo, but I'm afraid this funeral dirge will have us slitting our wrists in no time."

Gen snapped open his mahogany-colored Samsonite and found a library of 45s in their sleeves—almost more records than clothes. She lifted the needle from the Toscanini and pressed a stack of singles onto the automatic turntable.

"Now that's more like it," Fenton said. "'Come on, baby, let's do the twist!'" He swiveled his hips while putting the finishing touches on their drinks. Gen joined in, gyrating to the music, laughing out loud, and not caring how awkward she looked.

After they'd twisted away some of their cares, Fenton turned down the music and they settled on the couch with their tart cocktails. Gen welcomed the way the gimlet stung her throat, almost as if it was burning away the bad things that had happened.

"Thank you, Fen. I didn't realize how much I needed this."

"Gimlets cure what ails you," he said, taking an appreciative sip.

She pressed her hand over his. "That's for sure. But what I really needed was to act silly."

He squeezed her hand in return. "And everybody knows Gen Rider is just *so good* at acting silly."

Gen let the sarcastic comment slide by without protest, knowing he'd meant it as a joke. She might be staid most of the time, but she had her share of silly moments. They'd danced the twist before, and her impersonation of Henry Thoms sounding like Foghorn Leghorn always sent Fenton into peals of laughter.

But when he used her full name and emphasized that she was *so good*, she'd heard Carolyn's voice instead. "Gen Rider is so good she's *too* good"—a remark that *was* meant as a barb and had cut Gen to the quick.

As the records dropped one by one onto the turntable, they ran out of lighthearted things to say and long silences ensued. The elephant in the room was her suspension, but she wanted to skirt around that. When the Everly Brothers started crooning, "Things have really changed since I kissed you, uh-huh. My life's not the same now that I kissed you, oh yeah," Fenton got up and switched it off.

"Sorry. Not sure how *that* one got into the pile."

"It's okay," she replied. "I'm not that fragile."

"You know, you never really told me what happened. Or who with." He took a long drag on his cigarette and eyed her through the smoke rings. "Do you want to?"

At his invitation, the story cascaded out of Gen—from Thanksgiving at Juliet's on through the next day and the lingering kiss in the window.

"Well, hon, I'm glad it was Juliet. You'd be cute together. And she's over twenty-one."

Gen started. "What does that mean?"

"Nothing." Fenton flapped a hand to sweep away the remark.

"Fenton. What have you heard?"

He shrugged, his feigned innocence making her body tense.

"Just something vague . . . about a b-bike at your house."

Gen took a long, even breath. "That was Juliet's."

Relief washed over his face. "Well, of course, it was! She looks just like one of the students riding it."

She pressed him further. "Has someone suggested I was inappropriate with a student?"

"No, oh no! I heard something about a bike, that's all, and I . . . I wondered." His eyes flicked to the record player, which had gone quiet. "Guess I should put on another stack. Want a refill while I'm up?"

She clapped a hand on his arm to stop him, and he recoiled. "Watch it, hon, that hurts. Let up with the witch's claw, okay?"

Gen released her grip. "I'm trying hard to understand you, Fen. You actually wondered if I was *preying* on a student?"

Fenton's laugh burst out fluttery and forced. "Preying? No, of course not! It's just . . . well, the male teachers suss out the willing ones. I always wonder about you gay girls. Aren't you even the teeniest bit tempted, ever?"

The toasty room, so cozy just moments before, now threatened to smother her. Gen rose from the couch, although she had nowhere to escape to in this small space except the bedroom. Retreating, slamming a door like she wanted to, might bring some relief, and she toyed with the idea.

"I thought you knew me better. You listened to me when I was worried about Margaret and that gushy kitten card. I've never once crossed a line with a girl!"

Fenton's eyes popped open wide. "Oh, hon, I'm sorry! This gimlet's gone right to my head. Please sit down. I've got an idea." He sprang to his suitcase. From a paper bag tucked under a change of clothes he withdrew a present in crisp green foil, elaborately tied with red ribbon. He waggled it in front of her. "Early Christmas? I know it looks like a book, but I promise it's not *Girls' Dormitory*."

Another joke. Gen recognized his style, the way he scrabbled to backtrack when he stepped on her feelings. And *her* style was to cave and let the careless comments slip by.

This time, though, his words had smarted like a precise paper cut she didn't notice until it hurt like hell. Gen's eyes traveled from the present in his hands to his hopeful face and back again.

She hesitated. She could give in and pretend he hadn't said the awkward thing about students. But worse than his actual suggestion was how it sent her thoughts tripping over themselves, made her second-guess herself. Could she *swear* she'd never crossed even the thinnest line with a girl—say, with a look or a touch?

"I think I'm exhausted," she said finally.

He lowered the package to his side. "I drove all this way and you're already calling it a night?"

Gen peeked at her wristwatch. "It's officially morning. You can stay up, but I've had it."

The wall clock read eight o'clock when Gen threw on her robe, inventoried the kitchen provisions she'd brought from home, and settled on scrambled eggs and toast for breakfast. Her stomach growled as she cracked eggs into a bowl, but she held off cooking them when she heard the sound of the shower.

Fenton wandered in dressed in a favorite maroon turtleneck and tweed jacket, like he was going on a date.

"You look handsome," she said.

He blushed a pink that complemented his clothing.

"Coffee?"

"Please." His joking mood from the previous night appeared to be packed away in his suitcase. At the table, he lit a Pall Mall, then nodded toward it. "You don't mind, do you, hon?"

She shook her head. He was indulging more than usual; he'd always been more of the type who stole an occasional smoke from his desk drawer.

They jockeyed for space for their plates, orange juice glasses, and mugs. "Sorry there's no bacon," she said, "but we can go to town and get some for tomorrow."

He left his plate untouched but took a long drink of black coffee. "Thanks, hon, but I have to take off again soon."

She put down her fork. "You said you were staying a few days."

"That was before. I can't keep Ruby's car long," he explained without looking at her.

"I'm sure Ruby won't begrudge us one more night."

"Well, the truth is I'm worried about what the Texaco guy will do to *my* car while I'm gone. I might come back to a whole new—what's it called?—transmission."

Gen balled up her paper napkin. The night before, she'd wanted to get away from him and his insinuation, but by the light of day she was glad for the comfort of another body in the cabin.

"You're mad at me," she said.

Fenton snorted. "Last night you were so mad at *me* you couldn't stand to be in the same room."

"I never said that."

"Actions speak louder, baby." He wiped his mouth even though he hadn't eaten a bite. "Look, Gen, we got off to a bad start. I wanted to help, not make it worse. Maybe I'm not the company you need."

She nodded. She didn't know what or who she needed, but Fenton didn't seem to be it.

"Let's exchange presents at least," she suggested.

Fenton had indeed bought her a book—a hard-cover copy of Kennedy's *Profiles in Courage*. She thanked him profusely, unable to admit she already owned the paperback.

"Mine's not so original." Gen watched him rip at the silver and blue-striped paper. She had slapped a premade foil bow on it because she could never tie them to her satisfaction.

He admired the skinny knit tie that matched the color of his turtleneck.

"Just what you need, right? Another tie."

"No, it's perfect. My favorite color."

The exchange passed for something like making up. When he drove off in the Bel Air, waving out the window, she already missed him.

Chapter Twenty-Five

From the file of Dr. Virginia Rider

Dr. Lowndes Ramsey
Provost, Baines College for Women
Old Main

Dear Dr. Ramsey:

I am writing this letter in support of Dr. Virginia Rider. I have known Dr. Rider since 1944, when she arrived at Baines as a candidate for an open position as instructor in American history. She was a doctoral candidate at Ohio State University, and I was a member of the search committee that brought the three strongest candidates to campus. Dr. Rider came with the highest praise from Dr. Muriel Whitbread of OSU, a distinguished scholar.

Dr. Rider stood out among the candidates for her dissertation on the writings of Albion W. Tourgée, a founder of Bennett College and lead counsel for the plaintiff in Plessy v. Ferguson. She has published several book reviews in refereed journals. In the time I have known her, Dr. Rider has also been a frequent attendee at the Southern Historical Association and presented two papers there. Her research interests never fail to elicit discussion of the highest intellectual order among the faculty.

In 1954, following consecutive contracts as an instructor, Dr. Rider applied for and was granted a tenure-track position in history. During her time as an assistant professor, Dr. Rider twice won the college-wide Lydia Baines Morrow Teaching Excellence Award, in 1956 and again in 1958. This, as you well know, is a highly competitive award that is difficult to achieve even once, let alone twice. I myself have observed Dr. Rider's teaching, and she demands academic rigor from her students while remaining kind and patient with them. In my informal meetings with Baines history majors, several have proclaimed Dr. Rider to be among their favorite professors.

In spring 1960, Dr. Rider was promoted to Associate Professor with glowing recommendations from faculty at institutions such as Ohio State University, the College of William and Mary, and Smith College. I understand she is now doing research that explores the life and writings of Miss Mary White Ovington, cofounder of the NAACP, and I fully anticipate that she will in due time be promoted to Full Professor.

I have nothing but respect for Dr. Rider. She is an asset to the department and the college, and I would miss her collegiality and intellectual passion should she leave Baines for any reason. I encourage you to reinstate her as soon as possible, so that her students and colleagues may once again benefit from her many gifts as a teacher and scholar.

Yours sincerely,

Geoffrey R. Huston, Ph.D.
Chairman and Professor, History

Testimony of Geoffrey R. Huston, Chairman,
History Department, Baines College for Women,
to the Provost's Committee on Values and Moral Standards

Interview conducted by Arthur Burnside, Esq.,
Chief Counsel, Baines College for Women

Arthur Burnside: And how do you know Mrs. Blakeney?
Geoffrey Huston: We attend the same church. We've been at some of the same social gatherings. That sort of thing. I have taught her daughters. Excellent students. Lee-Anne is a history major.

AB: And Mrs. Blakeney paid a visit to your office on November 30?

GH: It was just after Thanksgiving. I didn't write down the date.

AB: And could you tell us what Mrs. Blakeney was like?

GH: I'm not sure I understand.

AB: How was Mrs. Blakeney acting?

GH: If you mean what was her affect or how did she seem to me, I would say that she seemed agitated.

AB: What had happened to her to agitate her?

GH: Nothing had happened to her that I know of. A friend of

Mrs. Blakeney's, a woman who is a neighbor of one of our faculty members, thought she saw something disturbing and told Mrs. Blakeney about it.

AB: Go on.

GH: I don't feel comfortable going on, Dean. In all honesty, it was hearsay and gossip, like some women are wont to do. It came to me thirdhand.

AB: I understand. My wife herself is prone to gossip, but sometimes her gossip is remarkably accurate. So this hearsay. It was about Dr. Rider. [pause] Could you speak up?

GH: I didn't say anything because I didn't hear a question. But now that I'm speaking, I'd like the record to show that Dr. Rider received the Lydia Baines Morrow Teaching Excellence Award twice. I have observed her teaching myself and—

AB: Yes, that's all in your letter of support. But I'd like to get to the heart of this hearsay, as you call it. Now I know this is unpleasant, but we need to piece things together, and your testimony is vital. I greatly appreciate you agreeing to give it before you leave for your sabbatical. So let me rephrase that in case I have not been clear. What about Dr. Rider had so agitated Mrs. Blakeney? [pause] Dr. Huston?

GH: She heard that she had embraced another woman. Or someone who appeared to be a woman.

AB: Is that the word she used, embraced?

GH: With all due respect, you have a statement from Mrs. Blakeney and one from the neighbor, I've forgotten her name, which outlines what she thinks she saw. Why do you need me to restate everything?

AB: A fair question. The committee would like to establish if Mrs. Blakeney changed any of her story between the time she spoke to you and the time she submitted her statement. Maybe she embellished, added details she didn't tell you. You can understand how important that might be—to Dr. Rider, of course.

GH: All she told me was that Dr. Rider's neighbor thought she saw her and another woman [unintelligible].

AB: Could you speak up?

GH: Kiss, I said. Kiss. But I'd like to stress again that Mrs. Blakeney herself saw nothing.

AB: Yes, I understand. And what else?

GH: That was all she said. Oh, and that she would feel compelled to report it to the provost if I didn't. She said she approached me first because she felt comfortable with me, and the matter was so delicate.

AB: She said delicate?

GH: She may have. I didn't take notes.

CTR: So, am I to understand that Mrs. Blakeney didn't speak to you about other matters?

GH: As I said, that was all there was to it.

AB: And then what happened? The sequence of events.

GH: I asked Dr. Rider to my office, where I related the situation. I asked her to explain in advance of my meeting with the provost.

AB: And she refused.

GH: I gave her the day to consider it. The following morning, she said it was a matter of privacy, as it states in the letter she submitted.

AB: How did you understand her refusal?

GH: I wouldn't call it a refusal. And I don't see how my understanding of what she said is pertinent.

AB: Well, it's simply that you know Dr. Rider better than we do. Was she defiant, perhaps? Nervous? Did she not understand the gravity?

GH: As she says in the letter to the provost, she has a private life and what she does in it is no concern of mine or yours. Or her neighbor's, for that matter. That's how I understand it.

AB: Your letter in support of Dr. Rider is glowing. If you knew for certain that she had kissed another woman, or possibly even one of our students—

GH: I've heard no mention of that!

AB: Perhaps even had relations with her?

GH: I haven't heard that either. Really, this has gone too far.

AB: Just one more question, please. If you *did* hear mention of it, or if more evidence of moral turpitude presented itself, would you change your letter in any way?

GH: I cannot indulge in this, sir. If you have evidence like that, you'll have to present it, and only then would I consider your question.

From the file of Dr. Virginia Rider

Dr. Lowndes Ramsey
Provost, Baines College for Women
Old Main

Dear Provost Ramsey:

I was asked for a statement about the goings-on I witnessed on Friday, Nov. 25, from my kitchen window. I will try to be as detailed as possible.

What happened was Mr. Carr and I had my sister and her entire family, as well as our own, for Thanksgiving dinner, and I was quite worn out after. My husband had gone into the office to catch up, so I decided to pour an aperitif while I waited for him.

I was in the kitchen adding ice to my drink. My kitchen window faces the back of Miss Rider's house. I usually keep the curtains drawn after dark because you can see right in, but I forgot. Her shade wasn't down, so I couldn't help but see them in the window frame, standing close together. I'd seen Miss Rider with other women at her home before, and with Mr. Page from the theater. They've been seen out and about in town and at a barbecue in her backyard, and I thought little of it.

What was different this time was that Miss Rider and a woman were standing so close it felt strange to me. I could see they were talking. And that's when it happened. First they hugged, and then they kissed right on the mouth, not on the cheek like friends do. I dropped one of my mother's antique glasses and it broke into a million shards that took me forever to clean up. I was still finding them days later.

I was shocked and frankly disgusted. My husband and I have noticed a few times that Mr. Page has spent the night at Miss Rider's house, which is morally questionable in itself, but this crosses the line into perversion.

I closed the curtain right away. My husband came home, and we had dinner. I didn't tell him because I was afraid he'd call the police. It is my understanding that kind of thing is illegal everywhere in this country.

When I looked out the window before I went up to bed, there was a blue bicycle propped against a tree in the backyard, like something one of our students would ride, and that made me curious. I've never seen Miss Rider on a bicycle, so I don't think it was hers.

The bicycle was still there in the early morning, but soon I heard tires squeaking and saw a female speeding off from Miss Rider's. Whoever it was had spent the night. You can draw your own conclusions.

I asked my daughter, Susanna, if she knew anyone at school who rode a blue bicycle. She said no names came to mind but that she would ask her friends. The next day I continued to be so disturbed by the incident that I told my frequent bridge partner, Mrs. Amanda Blakeney, who then reported it to Dr. Huston.

Sincerely yours,

Irene (Mrs. Thomas) Carr
Baines College Class of 1936

Chapter Twenty-Six

Ruby

Ruby had served with the Faculty Committee on Tenure and Privilege for two and a half years, and her three-year stint would conclude at the end of the semester. She assumed that in a few years someone would nominate her again because of her status as the only female full professor on campus.

"We should just make it for life next time," Roscoe Babcock, the chairman, had teased when she embarked on this, her third term.

"You'll have to talk to my husband about that," she had joked in return. The jovial spirit of the committee, particularly in its latest configuration with Frances Palmer as a second female member, held a strong appeal for her.

Besides that, Ruby viewed the work as among the most significant she'd done at Baines. She appreciated the chance to advocate for young faculty members, especially women, and play her part in advancing their careers. This semester, she would advocate hard for Juliet May, who might face opposition due to stepping down as housemother.

The mood in the committee as the first semester of 1961 dawned was as dismal as the winter sky. Roscoe had convened an ad hoc session, with no tenure portfolios in sight. At Ruby's seat at the table, as at all the others, rested a manila folder reading *Dr. Virginia Rider* on the tab.

Roscoe called the meeting to order. He didn't usually bring a gavel, but today he withdrew a gold-accented wooden one from a green velvet-lined box and gave it a sharp rap to get their attention. No one made a quip, although at another time someone might have, even Roscoe himself.

Ruby cast her eyes around the table at the other committee members and tried to evaluate where they stood on Gen's suspension. She was grateful that Roscoe had supported Gen's tenure, even though he didn't approve of her research. She didn't think the distaste he felt about her research on activists like Albion Tourgée and the rights of Negroes would prevent him from seeing the injustice in her situation now.

Opposite Ruby sat Frances, who at the women's meeting had confirmed her support for Gen. Frances shot a weak smile at Ruby across the table, all the while turning a pen over and over in her broad hands.

The professors from Philosophy and Math always held their cards close to the vest, but they were decent men who looked like they were listening whenever Ruby spoke. Today, the Math professor didn't acknowledge Ruby when she walked in, a rarity on this congenial committee. His blank expression worried her as she caught the end of Roscoe's opening comments: "—this unusual and somewhat unsavory task. Shall we begin?"

Ruby watched the history department secretary jotting down every word Roscoe said, and she raised her hand.

"Roscoe, I'd like to ask that we retract the word *unsavory* from the record," she said, feeling all eyes fasten on her.

"And why is that, Ruby?"

"It could seem a bit prejudicial, don't you think? I mean, people at this table may still be forming their opinions on this matter." Frances dipped her head in agreement, and the Philosophy professor stroked his beard.

"Well, I've already gone and said it," Roscoe complained. "I wasn't trying to prejudice anyone."

Ruby hurried to backtrack. "Oh, of course not, Roscoe. I'm just asking to take it out of the record. It might look to the Faculty Senate like we'd already decided before we started discussing."

Roscoe muttered something under his breath and agreed to a quick voice vote. Four said "aye," but the Math professor abstained.

"Strike out the word *unsavory*, Linda Sue," Roscoe said to the secretary.

"We should probably also strike that we discussed it," Frances added, and Ruby smiled at her colleague's quick thinking.

The chairman sighed but took a second vote on striking the discussion.

Roscoe then moved on to the thin folders in front of them, leading them through the documents inside. On top was a letter from Geoffrey Huston, extolling Gen's teaching and service in effusive language, his sentiments weighing more than the sheer onionskin paper on which they were typed. Behind that was a transcript of Huston's testimony to the newly convened Committee on Values and Standards, in which he stood firm and didn't succumb to conjecture.

Next came a handwritten statement from Mrs. Irene Carr, who outlined in detail what she had seen—or thought she had seen—through her kitchen window. Mrs. Carr composed her account in a clenched script, each word jostling the others like passengers in a congested train. It filled three full sheets of heavy stationery engraved with *Mrs. Thomas L. Carr* in swirling gold letters at the top.

Several additional sheets offered tangible proof of Gen's exemplary record at Baines: letters in support of her tenure, her tenure letter from the president, and notices of her two teaching awards. Ruby had lobbied hard for those final pieces to make their way into the folder. Roscoe had at first deemed them unnecessary because, as he put it, "Good God, everyone knows Gen's about perfect."

Roscoe allotted fifteen minutes for them to read the documents to themselves before he called out for comments or questions. He stared down the table at each of them in turn.

"I think this is not even worth our time." Frances closed her folder with a slap. "What we have here is one dubious statement from a neighbor pitted against overwhelming evidence that Gen Rider, a tenured professor, has been nothing but a paragon at this institution for fifteen years."

"I agree wholeheartedly," Ruby said. "Plus, the woman admits she was drinking at the time!"

"Adding ice to a drink," Roscoe corrected. "It's not clear she drank any of it before she dropped it."

"You know, I did wonder if the neighbor had an axe to grind," the Philosophy professor chimed in.

Roscoe called on the Math professor, who flipped back through the documents, a stubby finger stopping on Mrs. Carr's letter. "Here's what concerns me," he said. "I'm willing to allow that maybe Mrs. Carr didn't see what she thought she saw. But then there's the bit about the bike. Whoever rode it spent the night. To me, that suggests a student."

Sweat trickled under Ruby's blouse collar. She had read Mrs. Carr's letter and silently cursed her for speculating on who owned the bike.

"It was Thanksgiving weekend," Ruby noted. "What student would be up at dawn the Friday after a holiday? I have three sons, and I can tell you for sure, not a single one!"

Roscoe chuckled. "I got to agree with you on that, Ruby."

"Plus," Frances added, "there's still the question on the table of whether Mrs. Carr had some other motive."

Roscoe leaned back in his chair and withdrew his pipe and tobacco from his jacket pocket. Ruby groaned audibly at the prospect of sitting through the rest of this meeting under a literal cloud of smoke, so he placed the paraphernalia on the table in front of him like a promised reward.

"You know," Roscoe said, "four or five years back I had a neighbor across the street, a renter, who liked to keep his trash cans out at the curb for days after the trash had been collected. Lids off, too. Darnedest thing. There was no good reason for the fella to do that; he wasn't old or crippled. I decided to bring it to his attention, nice and polite, just observing how it gave a bad first impression of the street and wasn't quite fair to the property owners, or to me specifically, having to face it every time I sat on my porch. The fella apologized and started pulling up his cans. Good result, right?"

The Math professor nodded, but confusion clouded his face.

"Well, about a week later, I found a stinking mound of dog dirt pushed up against the bottom of our porch steps. You know, like someone had collected the dirt from several enormous mastiffs and put it there, just out of sight, so if I went out early to, say, get the paper, I could step in it. Which, of course, I did."

"The trash fella's vendetta?" asked the Math professor.

Roscoe went on in a leisurely manner. "I will never know. I could have started a little war and done something petty in return, but my wife talked me into taking the high road. The fella moved pretty soon after that, and we got a nice young couple in there who are very responsible. Both teach at the high school. What I'm trying to say is, I'm sure we all have stories about things neighbors do that aggravate us. Ruby told me just the other day that her neighbor reprimands her for not keeping her shades drawn up at the same length. For God's sake! You never know who might take a tiny offense and turn it against you, even if they act polite as pie to your face."

Ruby cast her eyes into her lap to keep from smiling too broadly.

"So, are we ready to take a vote?" Roscoe said after a brief pause. "I, for one, would like to put this to bed so we can get back to the important work of discussing tenure and promotion."

There were willing nods around the table, and Roscoe called for a voice vote on whether to reinstate Gen Rider, effective immediately. To Ruby's surprise, even the Math professor voted "aye." At Frances's suggestion, they voted again, amending their decision to reinstatement with back pay, but that time the Math professor abstained.

When Roscoe gaveled the meeting to an end, Ruby popped out of her chair as if on a spring. "Thank you for maintaining such a clear head, Roscoe," she said, her hand on his sleeve. "You've done this school a great service."

Roscoe didn't acknowledge her thanks. "Doesn't mean I approve, you know," he said. "Gen should—" He held her eyes for a brief moment, then shook his head, picked up his smoking gear, and left without finishing the thought.

From the file of Dr. Virginia Rider

Dr. Lowndes Ramsey
Provost, Baines College
Old Main

Dear Provost Ramsey:

The Committee on Tenure and Privilege met on January 5 to consider the allegations of "unprofessional conduct" against Dr. Virginia Rider.

After careful and prolonged discussion, we found no clear evidence of such conduct. It was the committee's unanimous decision that Dr. Rider should be reinstated immediately and take up her teaching schedule as planned for the spring semester.

The committee also voted to reinstate Dr. Rider with back pay for the three weeks she has been on uncompensated leave.

I enclose the minutes from our meeting.

Sincerely yours,

Roscoe Babcock IV, Ph.D.
Associate Professor of History

Dr. Lowndes Ramsey
Provost, Baines College
Old Main

Dear Dr. Ramsey:

I would like to meet with you soon in private to make an addendum to my previous statement. Over the course of the Baines winter break, I heard disturbing reports from several sources about Professor Virginia Rider's conduct on the Baines campus. One of the reports was from my own daughter, Lee-Anne, who is willing to testify if you so request it. (As you can see if you look at her record, my daughter has maintained a 3.85 GPA for her three semesters at Baines.)

Why I must amend my statement will become apparent when we speak. It is too sensitive a matter to tell you in a letter, but it is very urgent. I am hoping you can see me this week. A group of parents is concerned about our daughters' return to Baines for the spring semester if Professor Rider is still part of the faculty.

I will telephone your office to follow up on this request.

Sincerely yours,

Mrs. Robert (Amanda) Blakeney

Chapter Twenty-Seven

Gen

Every Friday afternoon Gen called Ruby collect from the Lewisburg diner. Even when they talked about nothing more exciting
than a dusting of snow on the mountain roads, Gen liked the
reassurance of her friend's voice and the delighted way she said
"Gen!" each time.

This week, the Faculty Committee on Tenure and Privilege
had met to discuss Gen's fate. Gen had tried not to agonize in
advance. Ruby and Frances were staunch supporters, and Roscoe,
she knew, had voted for her tenure despite a distaste for her
research.

"All that *Negro* business," he said once. "If I didn't know you,
Gen, I'd think you went and changed colors on us!" He had
stopped short of using the phrase "race traitor."

She might have enough support on the committee to survive,
but still Gen slept fitfully.

Although their scheduled call wasn't until five, Gen set out
from the cabin just before four, carefully navigating the sharp
curves, on the lookout for patches of ice. In three weeks, she had
learned to maneuver her way down and back up even in bad
weather, whenever she needed groceries or wanted the company
of strangers at the diner.

The afternoon waitress, Trix, recognized her and greeted her as "Doc." Gen had fabricated a story about being on research leave. It wasn't a total lie. She *was* getting some writing done, finding that her work on Mary White Ovington helped her forget, even temporarily, her troubles back at Baines.

"Jim Cumming's still on the phone," Trix told her. "Medical emergency." She nodded toward the phone booth near the restrooms where Gen made her weekly call.

"I hope his family is all right."

"Sick horse," Trix said, setting her up with a full mug and a bowl of banana pudding. Gen didn't really want the dessert, but the sight of the creamy confection made her mouth water. She took an appreciative spoonful before opening the notebooks she'd brought along.

The pages brimmed with her research on Ovington's early writings on race. Gen had made the notes during a trip to the activist's archive in Detroit the year before. Since coming to Ruby's cabin, she had been making her way systematically through the notebooks, circling and starring important quotes and ideas. Now she tried to focus on her markings, but her eyes kept wandering to her watch and then to the Coca-Cola clock on the wall, wondering which bore the correct time. According to the watch, she had just two minutes left, but the clock read 4:51.

"Your clock slow?" Gen asked as she brought her coffee mug to the counter for a refill.

"As a Sunday afternoon," Trix said. "What time you got?"

"A minute to five."

"I'd put my money on yours."

Gen wandered to the back of the diner, where a man in overalls and a flannel shirt was still monopolizing the phone. She didn't mean to pressure him, but he acknowledged her pacing with a wave, mouthing something that might have been *be right out*. Then he turned his attention back to the phone and took his time tying up his call.

"Apologies, ma'am."

She should have said, "Sorry about your horse" or something else to acknowledge his private trouble, but she didn't like to keep Ruby waiting, so she simply nodded at him and claimed the seat in the booth. Her heart set to beating so loudly in her ears that she nearly missed hearing Ruby accept the collect charges.

"First of all, there's very good news," Ruby said. "The committee voted unanimously to reinstate you. Roscoe delivered our recommendation to the Faculty Senate, and it went from there to the dean. It included that you are entitled to back pay."

"Oh, Ruby, thank you, thank you! That's wonderful! It's been so hard, and I've been so worried. Roscoe seemed like a wild card."

"Yes."

Her friend dragged out the pause. Gen's heart continued to pick up speed as she sensed Ruby withholding something.

"Should I come home?"

"Well, there's this other . . . situation."

Gen clutched the phone cord, her thoughts racing to Juliet. Ruby had admitted that she knew who the woman in the kitchen was and that she agreed that Juliet should remain anonymous.

"Has something happened with Juliet?"

"No, no, she's fine." Ruby paused, her choice of words almost too careful. "The dean honored the committee vote, but when it went to the provost, he—oh Gen, Ramsey overruled it."

Gen struggled to take in Ruby's news. After a long moment of silence, she managed to stammer, "I . . . I don't understand. He can do that? I thought—"

"It's not common," Ruby went on. "It's a faculty matter, and the Senate should have the final say. But he's claiming—" She paused and Gen heard her fumbling with paper, "—'extenuating circumstances that demand a thorough investigation by my office.' That's a quote from his response to the committee. He says a more serious charge has come to light."

She knew the charge against her was "unprofessional conduct"; it was in her suspension notice. That one kiss. How could there be another charge, unless it was a lie?

As Ruby elaborated, white light flashed in front of Gen's eyes. She took a deep breath. She wasn't a fainter, never had been, but the phrase "solicitation of students" jumped out at her and made the blood leave her head.

After that, Gen registered Ruby's news like individual words and phrases without any connection: ". . . the bike . . . Lee-Anne . . . Mrs. Blakeney . . . parents . . . back her up . . . withdraw daughters . . . campus . . ."

Gen cracked open the door of the phone booth for air, but that was all she remembered until Trix's insistent, "Doc, wake up" cut through the haze and brought her back to the reality of the diner. Somehow she had slumped from the booth's seat and landed on the hallway floor, her body curved into a comma. She could see the phone receiver dangling from its cord and hear Ruby's faint voice radiating from it. Gen reached for it but couldn't sit up.

"Take it easy," Trix said. "Not so fast or you could go under again." Then Gen heard the waitress explain to Ruby, "She blacked out for a second is all. Didn't hit her head or nothing. She's coming to. She'll call you back," and click the receiver into its cradle.

A small group of customers gathered behind Gen and Trix, and one man's voice chimed in, "Bad news, huh?" The question brought Ruby's news flooding back, and Gen felt lightheaded all over again.

"None of your beeswax," Trix chided. "How about make yourself useful and help the lady stand up?"

Chapter Twenty-Eight

Lee-Anne

Lee-Anne had watched Dr. Rider being escorted off campus by a security guard, but the news of what had happened to her didn't surface for several days. The early gossip mill cranked out all sorts of wild theories, including that the professor was actually a professional NAACP agitator who had helped organize Negro boycotts and sit-ins.

"All across Virginia!" one girl claimed. "Maybe even all over the South."

"When's she got time for *that*, Lois?" Lee-Anne scoffed. "In between classes?"

More of the story dribbled out. A woman had spent the night at Dr. Rider's house.

Yeah, so what? Lee-Anne thought. She'd stayed over with plenty of friends. When they were up late studying, Susanna sometimes slept in her single at Paxton. They didn't even bother to lie head-to-feet, like girls were supposed to. It was a silly rule anyway, like girls could be tempted into something with each other, sleeping with their heads on the same pillow. Sometimes she and Susanna woke up with their feet touching or their arms entwined, but they jerked apart without mentioning it.

Then the rumors transformed the woman who'd spent the night at Dr. Rider's into a student. Not a senior, but a younger student. In the morning, the girl rode away on a blue bike.

That tidbit made Lee-Anne's mind shoot to the day on the trails when Margaret fell off her bike. Had it been blue? Everyone knew Margaret had a crush on Dr. Rider.

Still, lots of girls used bikes to get around the rambling campus. If you had a class in Waylon and then the next in the art studio or gymnasium, you needed to fly. Even one of the professors pedaled across the quad like lightning. What was the big deal?

Finally, the rumors zeroed in on the big story: Dr. Rider had kissed another woman. Or maybe she had kissed a student who owned a bike. In a window, in full view of everyone. Maybe, possibly, a *bedroom* window. With the curtains open.

Susanna—who should know, because her mother witnessed it—reported that it wasn't a quick, sisterly kiss but an honest-to-God *kiss* kiss. Maybe even a French kiss. They might have been naked.

Lee-Anne had never thought about Dr. Rider kissing anyone, or not having clothes on, but now she could almost imagine her lips, her breasts, her *down there*, likely as raven black as her silky page boy. She shook her head to dispel the picture.

"Did you know she was a . . . lesbian?" Susanna asked. They were still on break but talked on their princess phones many afternoons.

"I heard a rumor," Lee-Anne admitted but didn't say from who. In fact, once Dr. Thoms had called Dr. Rider a dyke under his breath after Lee-Anne finished telling him about her class. "That dyke will be the ruin of this department," he had muttered.

"Mama wants me to transfer to Agnes Scott," Susanna said. "Like there aren't lesbians in Georgia! And, well, you know, wherever girls get together. In fact, who knows Atlanta's not *teeming* with lesbians?"

The repeated mention of lesbians—a word no one said too often—made Lee-Anne's head swim with memories. Dr. Thoms had gotten angry at her one morning during office hours when she'd made a mistake and pushed his hand away. She didn't want his fingers inside her again. "I'm just tired," she'd explained.

"Is that it? Or is this school turning you into a lesbian?" Later, she wished she'd settled for his fingers, which would have been better than what he ended up doing to her.

The echo of that moment made Lee-Anne gasp into the phone.

"Oh, I upset you," Susanna said, her voice punctuated with concern. "I'm not really going to transfer, Lee, don't worry."

Her best friend since ninth grade, Susanna was the only person Lee-Anne had told about Dr. Thoms. She couched what they did during office hours in innocuous terms—kind of like what girls did with boys in the back of movie theaters. Calling it "petting" instead of what it actually was gave it a slightly romantic cast.

"Ooh," Susanna had said. Her eyes widened, and her mouth twitched in a funny way. "With a married man!" Lee-Anne had sworn her to secrecy so Dr. Thoms didn't get into trouble—and bring her along with him.

After the phone call, the L-word hung in the air of Lee-Anne's bedroom like a bewildering fragrance.

Chapter Twenty-Nine

Gen

Gen had been at Ruby's cabin for a month and had run out of clean clothes, so she simply stopped getting dressed. Her flannel nightgown and bathrobe suited her fine, especially on the days she didn't bother to get out of bed. When the morning sun streaked through the curtains and spilled onto the sheets, she curled onto her side and smothered her face with the pillow. She staggered in and out of bad dream sequences, fantasies she'd never entertained—kissing a pretty, nameless student on the lips, fondling her breast—and woke up drenched in sweat, despite the chill in the cabin.

One morning she wondered what would happen if she tucked the sheet around her head so tightly she'd use up all the oxygen and pass out with no one to find her. Would her natural inclination be to fight her way out of the sheet?

Later, she padded into the cabin's bathroom, opened the medicine cabinet, and stared at Darrell's Gillette razor, twisting the bottom of the handle to expose the blade. On the shelf below it sat a prescription with Ruby's name on it—glutethimide, Gen saw when she squinted at the bottle. She didn't know Ruby had suffered from insomnia. Her own medicine cabinet at home contained nothing stronger than Sominex.

Gen replaced the razor and closed the cabinet. She leaned in to the mirror to inspect her haggard reflection—red circles around both eyes, cracked lips, a puckered welt on her left cheek where her pillow had creased her skin. She looked like Halloween. Scowling at her appearance, she ran water, scrubbed her face until it hurt, and plastered her unruly hair into submission. And then, instead of returning to bed, she headed to the kitchen to brew herself a pot of coffee. She needed to wake up.

A mouse had eaten a hole through the bottom of the sugar bag she'd left out, and a line of white granules trailed across the counter. She'd run out of eggs, her staple food. Then the refrigerator light blew with no replacement in sight. The buildup of mishaps led to the conclusion that she'd stayed at the cabin too long.

While she constructed a fire, she noticed her stomach trembling with hunger. Since she had heard the news about the new charges, she'd been neglecting to eat. Gen sat at the table with coffee and a piece of plain toast, which felt like all she could manage. One slice, dry as it was, tasted good, and she quickly made herself another, adding blueberry jam.

On the face of it, it had seemed like a smart idea to disappear from Springboro, but her withdrawal was making her morbid and self-pitying. Soon she'd be talking to herself all the time, a wild mountain woman whom mothers in Lewisburg would point to and warn their children about. That thought was the first thing that made her laugh out loud in weeks, but the laugh made her feel crazy, too.

Her temples ached with the effort of thinking. She couldn't continue hiding here, but what did she have to go back to? A memory shot into mind of Fenton heading to Ruby's car after his uncomfortable visit: "You know how to fight, hon. Don't let them push you around."

Now she pondered that vague advice as she finished her toast. Except for that one handshake with the provost, she didn't know him, and she rarely had contact with Dean Rolfe. She blanked on Mrs. Carr's given name—was it Iris? or maybe Irene?—and couldn't dredge up a picture of Mrs. Blakeney. Yet, taken together, these four strangers seemed bent on ridding the college of her.

Gen washed and dried her plate and glass and arranged them on the shelves. Almost no food remained in the cupboard and the refrigerator. She realized she could throw out the perishables, collect the rest into a single brown bag, and, if she wanted, be on her way by early afternoon.

She packed her suitcases with her dirty clothes and carted them to the trunk of her car. When she popped the hatch, the Belk's box of mementos greeted her from the spot where it had cowered for weeks.

Gen lifted off the box lid and combed through the morass. Envelopes bearing far-off dates, postmarks from a single place— Richmond. The return address changed when Carolyn changed residences. Gen rifled for the earliest ones, written in the tiny third-floor rooms Carolyn occupied at the time they met. She relocated to a more private apartment when Gen's frequent visits drew too much attention from the landlady, who lived down-stairs. Gen could still picture every detail of the first apartment, every eave, the dark, pitted floorboards, the squeaky iron bedstead where they'd first made love.

She stopped herself from reading the letters or releasing pho-tos from the envelopes where they nestled with their negatives. Instead, she replaced the lid and ran a finger idly over the name *Belk's* before arriving at her decision.

The pile made a nice addition to the logs still smoldering in the hearth. From her viewing spot on the sofa, Gen imagined her younger, more innocent self going up in flames.

There was no "For Rent" sign on her front lawn, which Gen took as a good sign. She still had a home to go to, a bed to sleep in. Better yet, the cozy warmth of the living room as she opened the front door surprised her. Ruby, who held her spare set of keys, had laid her mail on the coffee table, cranked up the heat, and filled the refrigerator with rations. On the kitchen counter, a round chocolate cake made her smile, the words *Eat Me* scrolled in shimmering white frosting across the top.

On the telephone bench Gen spied a sealed envelope addressed *Welcome Back, Gen* in swirling penmanship she didn't recognize. She thumbed through the dollars, fives, and bigger bills stuffed inside in neat ascending order. Added up, they must have totaled at least a hundred dollars—enough for three months' rent.

The accompanying note read, *Dear Gen—Some of us took up a collection. Consider this a gift, not a loan. More to come!*

Frances had signed first, and her handwriting matched that on the envelope. Ruby, Vanessa, Juliet, Fenton, and others had added their names below hers. Juliet dotted her *i* with a minuscule heart, tender as a schoolgirl's, and it broke Gen's own heart open. *Please call me,* Juliet had printed in parentheses, the first note she'd ever written her.

Gen sank to the bench and gulped back tears. She badly wanted to obey, but if she called Juliet or even Ruby first thing, she'd dissolve in tears and be a wreck for the rest of the day.

Instead, she unpacked quickly and fortified herself with a ham sandwich from the provisions Ruby had brought. After, she settled in at the telephone with the list of white attorneys Frank Johnson had compiled for her. It seemed like years ago that she had coaxed him to relinquish "five minutes" of his time to address her problem, but it had only been a matter of weeks.

That morning, Frank had consulted his address book and jotted down names and numbers. "I don't know if any of these gentlemen will be familiar with a situation like yours. I've put the most likely candidates first, so I'd start with them."

Gen accepted the short list of names. "This is wonderful. Thank you. But . . . is there a woman you might recommend, too?"

Frank held her eyes for a long minute before paging to the back of his book, under the *W*'s, for another name to add.

"This lady's more than capable and certainly dedicated to justice. She's in Lexington, though."

"That's no problem," Gen added quickly.

"She's a fighter, and you could use that. Plus, she's married to one of the name partners, so she's got some clout with her firm. That said, she sometimes rubs people . . ." Frank pressed his lips together; he didn't have to finish the sentence.

"I'm sure I do, too," Gen replied. That bit of self-deprecation had made Frank's mouth curl into a shy smile.

Now Gen surveyed Frank's list and skipped immediately to the last name. Her finger spun the phone dial until a secretary in Lexington answered with the melodic, "Berry, Briscoe and Werner." Frank Johnson's name got her past the front desk with a couple of "please hold" interjections.

Ursula Werner had an accent that bespoke a Northern pedigree—the Seven Sisters, Yale Law. When she asked, "How *is* Frank?" Gen wasn't sure if the connection was a benefit or a hindrance. Her perfunctory answer was met with polite interest, and she rested easier when Ursula didn't continue probing.

At Ursula's prompting, Gen peeled her story layer by layer. The process of relating the facts to a complete stranger humbled and humiliated her. She was almost unable to say *kiss* or *solicitation*, but she soldiered on with the aid of a few pointed questions.

When she finished, Gen heard a rapping noise from Ursula's end, like the stutter of a pen on a desk.

"And the woman in question—I take it she's not willing to clear you of the solicitation charge?"

Gen's throat dried. "She says she is, but she's more vulnerable than I am. I don't want her to speak up. Besides, wouldn't that actually undercut my defense? I haven't admitted anything."

"Still," Ursula said, "we're talking about the solicitation of students, some still teenagers—"

"Which didn't happen."

"You'd need solid proof. Without it, they could turn everything over to the authorities, who would make it a criminal charge. Your friend's confession would knock that out."

"Criminal" and "confession" hovered in the silence that followed. Gen knew Juliet would step forward at a moment's notice; she had been itching to. But if Gen owned up to the kiss, she and Juliet would likely both be fired on the spot.

"I'd prefer to leave her out of this if we can," she said.

The pencil tapping picked up again, then stopped. "Given *that*, here's my two cents." Ursula's tone dripped annoyance. "Admitting nothing isn't your best defense. Maybe you've watched too much *Perry Mason*, but—"

Gen flinched at the rebuff. "I don't have time for television, Mrs. Werner."

"Yes, well, if I understand your logic, you want someone to negotiate a less humiliating exit? You don't need a civil rights specialist for that. My secretary can give you a few names of attorneys closer to your town, very fine men I can vouch for."

Gen's head spun from the conversation's circular route. "No, wait, please," she pleaded as the lawyer prepared to end the call. Ursula's brusque manner grated on her—Frank had been right about that—but she'd set her heart on a woman to represent her at the hearing. "I'd be more comfortable with a female attorney. And no, I don't want to leave Baines. I want someone to save my job, so this *is* about my rights."

A pause stretched on for a few seconds that felt like minutes. "It's not an easy case," the lawyer said. "It could drag on for months and cost you dearly."

The money needed for a lengthy defense brought Gen's parents to mind. Suspension was sure to erode her savings in no time, and she wondered how to ask her parents for a loan without divulging what it was for. Still, she would cross that bridge later.

"I always pay my bills," she replied.

The lawyer clucked. "I was thinking about the personal cost, Dr. Rider. Especially if the case goes public."

"They want to keep it quiet. That's about the only thing in my favor."

"There's public and then there's *public*." Gen didn't press her to explain the vexing bit of semantics.

Ursula said she would reserve her final decision until they could talk in person and review any documents Gen had to support herself.

"I could drive up tomorrow morning," Gen offered. "I've got nothing else to do."

In the fading afternoon light, the Old Dominion Motor Court outside of Leesville resembled a plantation gone to seed. The white paint flaked from its columned facade, and a handful of lopsided cabins surrounded the main building like slaves' quarters. Probably once a respectable accommodation for families and travelers heading to the Blue Ridge Parkway, it now screamed of quick assignations.

Gen rented a room from a clerk whose graying hair was wound in pin curls. She had planned on signing the register "Virginia Smith," but with a smattering of Smiths already on the ledger, she switched to Virginia Lee.

The clerk considered the signature. "Related to the general?"

"Not that I know."

The woman lifted a key from the peg board behind her but stopped short of handing it to Gen. "We're just a stone's throw from Lexington, you know," she said, nodding toward a row of brochures on the counter. "You won't wanna miss the Lee Chapel or the Stonewall Jackson House."

To feign interest, Gen stuffed two brochures into her handbag and muttered thanks.

"Any bags?" the clerk asked—a funny question for a place that surely didn't employ a bellhop.

"Just one, in the trunk," Gen said. "I can handle it."

"Well, you'll wanna pull around then and use the side door. Closer to your room." The woman finally relinquished the key with a generous smile. A traveler with a suitcase was probably an oddity.

210

"Restaurant's open till nine. There's a special on fried chicken all day. You have a nice evening, now."

In a parking spot near the side entrance, Gen waited with the motor running. She was still ten minutes early, so she turned on the radio, cranking the volume higher when the news reported that a U.S. District judge ruled in favor of two Negro students enrolling at the University of Georgia. The students, the judge said, "would have already been admitted had it not been for their race and color." They could attend classes that very week. The report brought to mind Mae and Frank's daughter and her unsuccessful attempt to integrate Baines.

A quiet tap on the driver's window jolted Gen out of her thoughts. Juliet waved and mouthed *hello* through the pane, her cheeks rosy from the cold.

"Am I late?" she asked when Gen rolled down her window.

"I was early. I got the key."

"Let's go in."

The three little words sent a shiver down Gen's arms. She'd been hesitant about Juliet's suggestion to meet at a motel. Although she wanted to see her and a room outside of town felt safe, the stress of the past few weeks, especially the drive to Lexington that day to consult with Ursula, had drained her of emotion.

Now the sexual feelings she thought were dormant came flooding back. She had no trouble remembering what to do when Juliet drew the curtains and turned on a transistor radio to muffle sounds, when they peeled off their clothes and explored each other's bodies like it was the first time.

Later, they lay on the rumpled sheets with fingers entwined. "Your eyes change color," Gen observed. "I thought they were blue, but now they look green."

"They're sneaky that way."

"What else don't I know about you?" The intimate question popped out of her without thinking about it.

"Lots, I guess." Juliet sat up abruptly and squinted toward the clock on the nightstand. "Wow, it's almost seven."

The observation made Gen bristle. "You have somewhere to go?"

Juliet swung her legs over the side of the bed. "Yeah, to the restaurant. I'm starving."

The attached restaurant was nearly empty, save for a few men eating hot sandwiches at the counter and a young couple seated in a far corner. Gen and Juliet slid into opposite sides of a booth like friends or colleagues, but she imagined what it would be like to press herself up against Juliet on the Naugahyde bench.

After the waitress took their order and poured coffee, Juliet opened up the conversation they'd avoided so far. "So what did the lawyer—shit, I forget her name. What did she say?"

Gen's mind flashed to Ursula. Before they met, Gen had pictured a dowdy matron, hair pulled back in a severe bun, Coke-bottle glasses. Instead, Ursula's hair was coiffed in a stylish bouffant, and her dove-gray suit would have suited Jackie Kennedy. Her nail polish matched her outfit to a *T*.

Ursula was more gracious in person than on the phone, but their thirty-minute meeting had not encouraged Gen. Although they signed a client contract, the lawyer remained skeptical of a win. Gen's adamant protests that she had never solicited a student didn't faze Ursula.

"They'll find students to go on the record and say that you did," Ursula had replied. "The truth is beside the point."

"She *said* that?" Juliet asked, her color and voice rising. The waitress delivered their fried chicken.

"She can try to poke holes in their stories," Gen replied. She omitted the other direction of the consultation—Ursula's recommendation that Gen abandon the idea of not admitting to the kiss and let Juliet come forward.

"I should have gone with you," Juliet said.

Gen's back straightened. "You think I can't speak for myself?"

"Of course, you can, darling, but—"

"Ssh!" Her eyes shot around the space, but if anyone had heard the endearment, they ignored it.

"I just meant, we could have discussed a joint strategy."

"We've been over this. There is no joint strategy." Gen gave her plate a shove, her appetite faded. The chicken breast glistened with grease, and the cole slaw sat in a runny pool of mayonnaise.

"You don't seem to get it, Gen. I'm involved, too—up to my eyeballs. *I'm* the one who put the moves on you. *I'm* the one who came to your house that day. I don't remember who started kissing first, but it hardly matters now." She took a deep breath. "I wasn't going to tell you this because I didn't want to lose my nerve, but I made an appointment with Ted Franklin, our chairman. I'm going to tell him, Gen."

The air in the restaurant had become close and stale, and the sight of the food made Gen's stomach wobble.

"I'm prepared to resign on the spot."

The waitress approached their table, asking if she could freshen their coffee, and Juliet waved her off. "Just the check, please."

Chapter Thirty

Margaret

Spring semester was a day old when Margaret received a mimeographed notice in her dorm mailbox:

> Dear Margaret Sutter:
>
> Over the first week of classes, Dr. Henry Thoms, acting chairman of history, will meet individually with history majors on a most important matter. Your meeting is scheduled for January 11 at 10:15 a.m. Please come to Dr. Thoms's office in Waylon 115 and be prompt. If you cannot make this appointment, please inform Miss Linda Sue Vance immediately.

Margaret had avoided taking classes with Dr. Thoms because something about him made her skittish. Dr. Thoms exuded manners so courtly they almost seemed rehearsed, like he was acting the part of a professor in a play. Dr. Rider had once used the adjective *polished* for him, and Margaret couldn't suss out if her adviser thought that was good or bad.

There were also vague, intermittent rumors about him and students that circulated on campus. Lee-Anne Blakeney, who made Margaret's stomach twist, counted among his favorites. Margaret had also overheard suggestive comments about the size of his office, which could apparently wrap around other professors' spaces several times.

"Lee-Anne says he's got a *couch*," Susanna Carr had told another girl, a little breathlessly, as students waited in line at the dining hall.

"Why's a professor need a couch?" Polly had asked loudly, and Margaret elbowed her. Susanna scowled at both of them and lowered her voice. Because of the eavesdropping, Margaret had been on her wrong side ever since. Still, Margaret considered Polly's question valid and reason enough to approach the professor with trepidation.

When the time for her appointment arrived, Margaret rapped on the door of Waylon 115. Her heart knocked so wildly in her chest, she was afraid it would be audible. Her pulse slowed when the door opened and just past Dr. Thoms's tall frame she spied Miss Vance, the department secretary and a Baines alumna of a few years back, seated at a round table with a steno pad in front of her.

"Miss Sutter, please come in," Dr. Thoms said. "I won't take but a few minutes of your time."

Margaret sank into the chair closest to Miss Vance, while Dr. Thoms arranged his long limbs in the seat across from them.

"You've not been in any of my classes," he remarked with a lazy smile.

"No, sir."

"And Dr. Rider is your adviser."

"Yes, sir."

Dr. Thoms fiddled with a sheet of paper in front of him. "As her advisee, you know Dr. Rider pretty well, wouldn't you say?" He gestured toward Miss Vance, who picked up her pen to begin recording the interview.

Margaret shrugged. "I've had two classes with her, that's all. I'm taking her early nineteenth-century class this term."

In fact, on her way to Dr. Thoms's office that morning, Margaret had passed Dr. Rider's office, intending to pop her head in and say hi. She thought the sight of her favorite teacher might instill courage.

But Waylon 120 sat darkened and neglected-looking, like the office of someone who'd retired. Margaret had pressed her nose to the frosted door but couldn't make out any movement inside. It was unlike Dr. Rider not to be at her desk already.

Now, Dr. Thoms's assertion that "Dr. Rider isn't teaching that class anymore" made Margaret's knee bounce under the table.

Margaret's voice came out as a squeak. "She's not?"

"There's a new professor y'all will like a lot. A fine young fella, single, too. Now, Miss Sutter, I have some specific questions for you, and I want you to consider your answers carefully."

Margaret placed a hand on her knee to steady it. Miss Vance asked if she wanted water, but before she could reply, Dr. Thoms's questions pummeled her like fists.

Has Dr. Rider ever said anything unseemly to you?

Have you ever felt discomfort when you met with Dr. Rider alone in her office?

At these meetings, did the professor ever close the office door?

Has Dr. Rider ever looked at you inappropriately?

Has she ever touched you in an unwanted manner, anywhere on your body, or rubbed against you?

Have you ever been to Dr. Rider's house?

After, in her eagerness to escape Waylon Hall, Margaret nearly tripped off the stoop into the quad. She bolted back to her dorm, where in the hall bathroom she threw up the Cheerios and bananas she'd eaten before the meeting.

216

Testimony of Henry Thoms, Acting Chairman,
History Dept., Baines College for Women,
to the Committee on Values and Moral Standards

Interview conducted by C. Tyler Rolfe, Dean,
Baines College for Women

C. Tyler Rolfe: Thank you for this thorough report and meticulous notes, Henry.

Henry Thoms: You can thank our lovely Miss Vance. She's easy on the eye and takes lightning-fast shorthand, as I'm sure you're aware.

CTR: Miss Vance is a jewel, and we've both been keeping her mighty busy. Now I don't want to take too much of your time. You just conducted interviews with the current roster of Baines history majors, and I was hoping you might quickly summarize your findings for us.

HT: Of course. I was trying to ascertain if any of our majors, who would have more contact with Professor Rider than other students, had anything to report about her behavior. We currently have twenty-one history majors.

CTR: A very healthy number.

HT: I'm quite proud of it, as is Dr. Huston. And I spent roughly twenty minutes with each of them, asking specific questions about Professor Rider. I read all Miss Vance's transcribed notes and came up with a tally of sorts, which is what this top sheet is. I'm sorry to say that nine of them reported having an awkward moment with Professor Rider.

CTR: What did those awkward moments entail?

HT: Most often, a time when she put a hand on their backs or shoulders, something to that effect. One of those also said the professor looked at her in an inappropriate way. You will want to talk more to her about that. Lee-Anne Blakeney is the girl's name. One of my advisees, and a very promising young scholar.

CTR: We'll spend extra time with her. What else, Henry?

HT: Seven additional students said they felt uncomfortable when Virginia—Professor Rider—closed the door of her office to talk to them, but they reported no untoward behavior.

CTR: Did they elaborate on what their discomfort stemmed from?

HT: I assumed the closing of the door, which could establish an unnatural intimacy.

CTR: Yes, but to play devil's advocate, might their discomfort have stemmed from worrying they were in trouble?

HT: Of course, that's an option. Several did mention a certain uneasiness about the content of Professor Rider's courses. Her focus on Negro history, for example. Her denigration of Southern traditions. The syllabus I've seen is troubling, to say the least.

CTR: Yes, I see. Now what about the remaining students?

HT: Three of our majors have not taken classes with Professor Rider. One has not yet returned to campus because she's picked up some sort of bug. Of the twenty girls I made contact with, only one said she never experienced a single uncomfortable moment with the professor. Because she was the only one to make that claim and struck me as a bit guilty-looking, I would tend to discount her statement. My first thought was perhaps she'd been coached.

CTR: That's a serious charge, Henry. Who is the girl?

HT: Margaret Sutter. A sophomore. From what I've gleaned from other students, the girl had a special bond with Professor Rider.

CTR: I don't see how she could have been coached. Professor Rider was escorted off campus in December and has not returned. My understanding is she was out of town part of the time. She wouldn't have direct access to students.

HT: Not on campus, no.

CTR: You think she saw Miss Sutter elsewhere?

HR: I asked the girl if she'd been to Professor Rider's home, and she denied it. But again, I have my doubts.

CTR: Based on?

HT: That same guilty sort of look. Take my word for it, Ty. I can read these girls like a book.

[gap in tape]

CTR: Thank you, Henry. Your analysis has been most helpful. Did you have anything else you wanted to add?

HT: Simply that I have long questioned Professor Rider's teaching materials. Her research agenda, too, is most uncommon and suggests a disturbing leftist bent. My understanding is she is currently doing research on the founding of the National Association for the Advancement of Colored People, of all things, which as you know may have been infiltrated with Communists. I myself did not consider her tenurable, but my esteemed colleagues in the department disagreed.

CTR: Thank you for your generous time, Henry.

Chapter Thirty-One

Fenton

The crop of students at the *Our Town* tryouts included the usual suspects—leftovers from the aborted production of *Charley's Aunt* plus some who hadn't made the cut for that play because the cast was too small. With its ample cast of characters, *Our Town* would accommodate a lot more of them.

Fenton already knew most of the students by name, either from class or past productions, and he called them one by one to deliver their audition monologues while he scribbled notes from the fourth row. Unless there was a surprise bravura performance by someone he hadn't noticed in the fall, the main casting for this play would be a snap.

Fenton nodded encouragingly at each student, but what he wrote down were notes for what he planned to say at his testimony on Gen's behalf at the end of the week. Ruby had asked him to testify, not Gen herself. He and Gen hadn't spoken since his trip to the cabin, and the loss of her from his routine hurt like the devil. As stubborn as she was, though, he had determined to wait for her to come to him.

When he called Margaret Sutter's name, she announced she'd be auditioning as Amanda Wingfield from *The Glass Menagerie*.

Fenton sat up straighter and put down his pen. Everyone before her had chosen tired monologues from Shakespeare, mostly Hamlet or Juliet.

"I think you're doing things you're ashamed of and that's why you act like this," Margaret said. "I don't believe that you go every night to the movies. Nobody goes to the movies night after night."

Her delivery was mature and resonant, suggesting she had worked hard at it and developed an understanding of the character. Students clapped louder at the end than they had for their other peers, and Fenton joined in, forgetting he hadn't applauded anyone else. He wished he'd chosen the Williams play, even with its tiny cast. Margaret's performance could have carried it. But under the dean's scrutiny, he would never be free now to stage something by such a blatant homosexual.

After the other student actors had filtered out of the theater, Margaret hung back and approached him. "Mr. Page? Sorry to bother you."

He stopped in mid-note about Gen's dedication to her students. Could he say that without it coming out the wrong way?

"No bother, Margaret. What can I do for you?"

Margaret's gaze dropped to her hands. The quick motion called Fenton's attention to her nails, so bitten they looked painful.

"I think you're friends with Dr. Rider," she said hesitantly. "So you know about the dean's committee?"

Fenton shifted his focus to her eyes, which had watered over. "Yes, I do."

She paused and drew in a long breath. "They asked me to testify, Mr. Page. No one will tell me why. Do you know?"

"You mean, someone from the dean's office notified you?"

Margaret nodded. "What could *I* tell them?" she burst out. "Maybe they know about that stupid card someone sent her? She thought it might be me, but it wasn't and I—I haven't done anything wrong!"

He couldn't admit Gen had confided in him about the kitten card, so he let it drop. "I know you haven't." He struggled to keep his voice even. "The dean probably just wants to hear from students who admire Dr. Rider. Her advisees."

Margaret's teary eyes met his. "You think that's it?"

"That would be my guess."

"So . . . what should I say?"

He smiled with encouragement he didn't feel. "All the nicest things you can think of. Pretend it's a monologue you're delivering. Let's talk it through."

The note was waiting for him in his mailbox at home:

Dear Fenton,

I know you are set to testify on my behalf and I appreciate your desire to help, but I would rather you *not* appear before the committee. Please do this as a favor to an old friend, and withdraw your name from the schedule.

Gen

He had just spent almost an hour coaching Margaret on her testimony and then another half hour finishing his own notes. It wouldn't look good to back out just days before his hearing. Besides, Gen needed all the support from the faculty she could get. Her request made no sense to him.

Fenton didn't want to think Gen might be embarrassed about him. He was an actor, for God's sake, and had played straight more times than he could count. He could handle the dean's interview.

He was tired from work and needed a cocktail, but he drove to her house immediately. She peeked out the window at him before opening the door. To his surprise, she was fully dressed with her hair styled, as she might be on any school day.

"Are you going somewhere?" he asked without saying hello.

"I have a meeting."

She said it crisply, like they'd never been close. Something splintered inside him and the measured speech he'd rehearsed on the drive over left his mind.

"Well, can I please come in for a second, or do you want me to make a scene on the porch?"

Gen stood aside for him to enter but didn't take his coat, and she made no move to offer him a drink. "You got my note."

"I got your note. Were you *trying* to hurt my feelings?"

She stepped back. "Why would I do that?"

"You don't trust me not to *swish* into the hearing and act like some big old *fag!*" He'd never used the epithet about himself, not even in jest, but now it was his first thought.

"What an awful thing to say about yourself. That never occurred to me."

"Then you're worried because of the police thing? You know that came to nothing."

Gen's lips tightened. "Here's what *did* come to something for me. What you said at the cabin about the bike rumors, and wondering if I'd been with a student. I mean, I tried to forget it, but I can't. Suppose the dean asks a question and you blurt out something you didn't mean to." Her head wagged. "I'm not saying you'd do it on purpose. But what you really think of me—that I might actually have abused my position as a teacher—well, no, I don't trust you."

Fenton reached past her for the doorknob and swept out of the house. In his haste to get away, he missed a porch step and sank onto the brick walkway with a groan. His palm, scraped pink and bloody where it had broken his fall, throbbed with pain. Momentarily shaken, he thought of calling out to Gen for help, but she had already closed the door.

Fenton removed the wooden roller bearing the heavy *New York Times* and set the paper in front of him on the library table. He dedicated time early on Tuesday mornings to dive into the Sunday edition, which took its sweet time wending its way through Springboro. No one but the periodicals librarian had touched it, and the pristine pages crackled pleasingly under his fingers, the fresh ink smudging the tips. As Fenton leafed through the pages, his memories shot back to the previous, glorious summer. Every Sunday morning, if he hadn't stayed out too late or didn't have an overnight guest, he would venture out and bring the *Times*, coffee, and a Danish back to his Village sublet to relish.

This Tuesday, though, he had trouble savoring the paper, even his beloved arts section, book review, and magazine. The cuts from his fall at Gen's house had scabbed over and itched, but Gen's bruising "I don't trust you" still stung.

Years ago, he'd picked her out at a faculty get-together and latched on. Before Baines, he'd bopped from job to job and performed a lot of summer stock. He had charmed his way into stage manager and costume designer jobs to make ends meet. Once a community theater hired him to direct two shows back to back. He developed casual acquaintances but no real friends. The prospect of staying put appealed, so he answered an ad for "Theater Director, Small College in Bucolic Virginia." He wasn't the most qualified for the job in terms of directing, but one summer job in Saratoga Springs had been close enough to New York to satisfy the hiring committee.

The pay had proved steady, though not generous, and he'd enjoyed a certain level of freedom. Summers were always the best. Then this past fall had offered nothing but trouble—the menacing police and mayor, the snoopy provost, his own attempts to straighten up. And since he broke up with Kathy Yost, he kept running into the girl at the bank, the bakery, everywhere. At Darnell's Drug Store, she had loudly accused him of following her.

Now Gen was in distress, and all he'd done was make matters worse. She wouldn't even let him testify on her behalf. What could he do?

His first instinct was to escape, get out of Gen's hair, start over somewhere else. He might have good enough credentials to direct in New York now. The friend who had sublet his apartment to Fenton over the summer suggested his theater company might be hiring. If he actually looked around, maybe other attractive opportunities would offer a way out.

The idea locked onto him. He flicked through all the *Times* sections, picking up speed when he didn't locate the job ads. Then he returned to the front page and started over.

"There's no employment section in the *Times*," he said to the librarian behind the desk.

"Are you sure? Sections might be out of order."

"I checked twice. Did you leave it behind the desk?"

Creases formed at the woman's mouth like parentheses. Last spring at closing convocation, she had received a plaque for twenty-five years of service to the library—an unimaginable amount of time to Fenton.

"That is unlikely," she said with crisp assurance. "A section could have gotten left out when the sorting happened at the printer."

It was a reasonable explanation, but Fenton stared at her with the demand, *And what will you do about it?* ready to pop out. After a long moment, he nodded and said, "Sorry, Mrs. Plunkett."

The librarian relaxed at his apology and softened her tone. "You're not thinking of leaving us now, are you, Mr. Page? I so look forward to your lovely shows."

Fenton forced a smile. "Thank you. No, I'm not going anywhere."

"Oh, good! You know, *Our Town* is probably my favorite play. Such a wholesome, lovely story."

"Why don't I send you some extra tickets? You can bring the family."

She beamed back at him and repeated the word "lovely."

Testimony of Miss Lee-Anne Blakeney, sophomore,
Baines College for Women,
to the College Committee on Values and Moral Standards

Interview conducted by Arthur Burnside, Esq.,
Chief Counsel, Baines College for Women

Arthur Burnside: You look a little shaky, Miss Blakeney. Would you like to put your coat back on? Can we turn up the heat in here?

Lee-Anne Blakeney: I'm okay.

AB: If you become uncomfortable, you let us know. Now, do you understand what this committee is looking into?

LB: I think so. Dr. Rider, right?

AB: Yes, but more specifically, whether Dr. Rider should be teaching here at the college. [pause] You understand?

LB: No one put it that way before, but yeah, I understand.

AB: And do you also know why we asked you to come before the committee?

LB: Because of what I told my mother and Dr. Thoms?

AB: That's right. We'd like to go into more detail about the incident you related to them. So why don't you tell us what happened on Halloween?

LB: Well, everyone was dressed up, all over school. I wore my coming-out gown and went as Cinderella. My mother let me borrow her silver pumps because the ones from my deb ball were worn out. But my mother has a smaller shoe size, and hers pinched. So in the hallway Dr. Rider noticed me hopping on one foot with the other shoe in my hand—

AB: Like Cinderella losing her shoe.

LB: Yeah, right, and she said something like, "Let's hope Cinderella doesn't have far to go."

226

AB: What were you doing in the hallway? Was anyone else around?

LB: Maybe—no, I don't remember.

AB: Are you sure?

LB: I didn't see anyone else.

AB: Here's the thing: Dr. Thoms told the dean privately that he was in the hallway that day and saw the two of you, quote, having words. In your interview with him he said you became very distraught and told him Dr. Rider had made an improper advance.

LB: He did?

AB: Yes. So please think hard. Did she say something else, something that was inappropriate? Because, quote, Let's hope Cinderella doesn't have far to go, seems like good fun to me and not very threatening. How's it sound to you, Miss Yost?

Kathy Yost: Like a joke.

AB: There.

LB: Look, it wasn't anything she said. I had to lift my skirt up to slip my shoe on. Dr. Rider was watching me the whole time, looking at my leg. It made me uncomfortable, I didn't know why at the time. Later, I thought, that's how men look at your legs. And her tone was—I don't know.

AB: There was something sexual about it.

LB: I—I don't know if that's the word.

AB: But you do know, quote, that's how men look at your legs. [pause] Does that shrug mean yes?

LB: I think I meant boys, not men. The boys at D and L might look at your legs.

AB: I see. Were there any other instances that you recall Dr. Rider making you feel uncomfortable?

LB: Not like that. Sometimes she touches your arm when she's talking to you, or maybe she puts a hand on your back. Other girls have mentioned it, too.

AB: When she does, is it different than, say, what a mother or aunt might do?

LB: A little, maybe.

AB: More like what a man—no, a boy—might do?

LB: I guess.

AB: Tell me, did you notice this about the professor before the accusations against her came out? [unintelligible] Could you speak up and stop shrugging?

LB: I may have, I'm not sure. But I did notice she was different. All the girls have. There's just never a man in her life, and she's pretty, you know?

AB: Have you ever personally witnessed her being free with her hands with another girl? Or doing anything inappropriate?

LB: No, but—

AB: Go on. [pause] Are you still thinking about it?

LB: I'm not sure this counts.

AB: Why don't you let us decide that?

LB: My friend, Susanna Carr? Her mother is the one who saw, you know, the kiss in the window.

AB: Dr. Rider has touched her?

LB: No. I mean, maybe. She told me that her mother saw a blue bike parked all night at Dr. Rider's house that day, the day of the kiss, and that nobody knows whose bike it was.

AB: Do you? [pause] Miss Blakeney, do you have information about the bike that you'd like to share?

LB: There's this girl. Margaret Sutter? She's one of Dr. Rider's advisees. Susanna and I always thought she had a crush on her.

AB: Who had the crush, Margaret or Dr. Rider?

LB: Margaret. She always looks so moony over Dr. Rider and she goes to her office a lot. Dr. Rider treats her very friendly. Susanna and I kind of made a joke out of it, it was so blatant. We even—

AB: Yes?

LB: We made a joke out of it, that's all.

AB: And how does your joke relate to the bike?

LB: Margaret's got one. A blue one.

AB: You're sure of that.

LB: Yeah, I saw her riding it on the trails. She fell off it, actually, and when I offered to help her I got a good look at it. A blue Schwinn. When Susanna told me about the bike at Dr. Rider's, I thought—

AB: You can't say for certain.

LB: No. But given how much Margaret idolizes her, how friendly they always seem, it would make sense. If you saw them together, you'd get it. It's more than teacher and advisee. You wonder what goes on in that office. Did someone crank up the heat in here?

AB: We're just about finished, Miss Blakeney. Anything you want to add?

LB: No, that's it. But wait—are you going to tell Margaret what I said about her?

AB: We won't use your name. But the bike is of definite interest. Thank you for that.

Chapter Thirty-Two

Margaret

When the secretary ushered Margaret into the book-lined meeting room adjacent to the dean's office in Old Main, the atmosphere put her at ease. Dean Rolfe, whom she recognized from opening convocation, greeted her warmly and motioned toward a chair across from him at the mahogany table.

The secretary asked if Margaret wanted water, and she accepted. Her throat still smarted from crying out in her sleep the night before. "A bunch of times," Polly had told her. "Blood-curdling. Like someone was killing you."

"We won't keep you long," the dean assured her. "We're just waiting for Mr. Burnside. The college attorney."

Her fear must have shown on her face because the dean continued in a calm voice, "He's just here to ask the right questions, keep us on track. Your testimony could actually help Dr. Rider."

The secretary brought the glass of water then, and Margaret took several large sips.

"They predicted snow today," the secretary said, more to the dean than to Margaret. "I used to love sledding on Rebel Hill when I was a student."

Dean Rolfe turned to Margaret to include her. "You have a sled, Miss Sutter?"

She cleared her throat and took another drink. "Not here. It's home, in the garage."

The dean inquired where "home" was when Mr. Burnside, the college's attorney, strode into the room carrying a legal pad. Margaret's stomach pitched at the sight of the inordinately tall man with a hunch to his shoulders, wearing a black suit that reminded her of an undertaker's. His thick eyebrows met in one wriggling line.

"Sorry to keep y'all waiting," Burnside said as he fished in his jacket pocket for a pen.

"Just chatting about snow," the dean said. "I'll let you take it from here, Arthur."

At that, the secretary opened her steno pad and began writing in the swirls and flourishes of shorthand.

Burnside flipped over the sheets of his pad until he came to one with a lot of writing on it. Margaret thought she read her name at the top in block letters.

"Good morning, Miss Sutter. Thank you for agreeing to come in today."

When the summons came from the dean's office, Margaret didn't think she had a choice. "Sure," she said.

"You understand we're here to talk about Dr. Rider."

Margaret gripped her glass. "I told Dr. Thoms everything already."

Burnside assessed her with a long, skeptical look. "We're not in any rush, Miss Sutter. Give this some thought. Another student suggested you might have more to say than what you told Dr. Thoms."

"I don't have anything to say except she's a great teacher."

The lawyer's pen scratched something onto his pad. "Nothing related to her conduct?"

Margaret shifted her attention from Burnside to the dean to the secretary. They were all regarding her in the same measured way, as if they knew the answer to a quiz she hadn't studied for. She only had two good guesses about who might have implicated her.

"Look, if Lee-Anne Blakeney gave you my name, she doesn't like me. She and Susanna Carr may be setting me up."

He chuckled. "I'm afraid I don't follow."

"They want to make it look like I do creepy stuff."

Burnside shot a look at the dean, who pursed his lips in a way that might have been code—but for what? "Well," the lawyer continued, "let's get to the root of this and try to figure out why your name came up. I'll ask you some specific questions to spark your memory. Now I understand that you are fond of Dr. Rider."

"A lot of girls are."

"Yes, she's a popular teacher. But we also have testimony from a few girls who say Dr. Rider has—on occasion, mind—looked at them or touched them in a way that made them uncomfortable. Has Dr. Rider ever done that to you?"

Annoyance mounted in Margaret as the interview played like a rerun of a show she'd already watched. "I already told Dr. Thoms no."

"This is a different interview, Miss Sutter. Please just answer the question." The lawyer set his pen down and folded his hands over the legal pad.

"No, she has not done that to me."

"Has she ever said anything *inappropriate* to you?"

Once or twice, her adviser had made comments about Dr. Thoms, remarks that bordered on sarcastic and indicated the two teachers didn't get along. The jabs had seemed unusual to Margaret, given Dr. Rider's reliably professional demeanor. But that's not what the lawyer was going for.

"No," she said, hoping she hadn't paused too long.

"And what about touching? Some of our girls say that the professor feels free to touch them on their arms, backs, and shoulders."

Margaret took the smallest sip of water. The level in the glass had gone down quickly, and she should conserve the rest. "She's kind, is all."

"So she *has* touched you?"

"I never saw anything wrong with it."

Burnside leaned toward her. "*Where* did she touch you? On the arm?"

Margaret nodded.

"On the back or shoulders?"

The warmth of Dr. Rider's hand on her back flooded into memory. Her touch made Margaret feel special, cared for. "Maybe."

"You can't recall."

"It didn't bother me."

The lawyer sat back again and made a long notation on his pad. His face gave nothing away, and the dean and the secretary studied the table as if bored. How many of these interviews had they sat through? Could this be the end of hers?

Then Burnside regrouped, his new question throwing her. "Why do you think it might bother other girls but not you?"

Dr. Thoms had never asked her anything personal, a question that didn't center on Dr. Rider but on her own feelings. Margaret floundered to find the right answer. "Because . . . because there was nothing wrong with it?"

The dean cleared his throat as if he intended to jump into the interview. But maybe that was just another signal, because the lawyer shifted gears and accelerated the interview.

"Miss Sutter," he said, "a few girls have told us you have a crush on Dr. Rider."

Margaret drained her glass. Could she ask for more water? The secretary's eyes focused on her again, her pen poised for Margaret's response.

"Could I have more?" Margaret's voice sounded scratchy in her own ears. She inched the glass toward the secretary, who refilled it from a crystal pitcher on a credenza.

The pause gave Margaret time to breathe. Mr. Page had counseled her about pivoting—taking a question she didn't like and answering another. But there was no question, just a statement about a crush.

What else had Mr. Page said? She struggled to remember, but then his words surfaced in her memory: "Stop and take breaths whenever you need them. Imagine you're on stage, panicking that you've lost your line. Take your time, breathe, repeat the cue in your head, and you'll be back on track in no time."

Margaret thanked the secretary and drank slowly. *A few girls have told us you have a crush on Dr. Rider.*

"If you're referring to the card and ring," she began, "I didn't do it. I swear. I told you, Lee-Anne and Susanna may be trying to set me up."

"What card and ring are you talking about?" There was only one card and one ring that she was aware of. Either Burnside really didn't know about the card, or he was bluffing.

Across the table, the dean took several loud breaths, his eyes boring into her. "Miss Sutter?" he said.

Mr. Page's advice came back to mind: "You don't have to answer. It's not like a courtroom and you're under oath."

"I'm starting to think I need a lawyer or something," Margaret said, and Burnside huffed.

"I *am* a lawyer, Miss Sutter," he snapped. "I represent the college and everyone affiliated with it."

"You aren't in any trouble," the dean cut in. "Mr. Burnside is trying to help."

"So," the lawyer said, "forget the mysterious card. Let's get back to your crush on Dr. Rider."

Margaret opened her mouth to object but wasn't fast enough.

"Girls in school do that, don't they, and then outgrow the crushes later. You see this all the time at girls' schools. But what I'm trying to determine is if you've been swayed in an unsuitable direction by someone you admire and trust. An authority figure. Like Dr. Rider."

"No." Margaret's cheeks lit with anger. "Never."

"She hasn't suggested a different relationship?"

"Than what?"

"Than teacher and student."

"No!" The room seemed smaller than it had at the start of the ordeal. Margaret squirmed in her seat. What if she just stood up and said she'd had enough? Could they expel her?

"Now, I apologize for having to use this word in your company, I am simply quoting someone else. Last spring, did you tell a boy at a dance that you and another girl are, quote, *lezzies*?"

She popped out of her seat. "I have to go"—but she had no idea where.

"We aren't finished, Miss Sutter. It won't be much—"

"Look, he was bothering us. I was joking!" She didn't often attend dances. Either the richest, most attractive boys snubbed her for girls like Susanna Carr, or Margaret had to fend off guys with acne and bad posture. That night, a boy had leered at her and Polly from across the room before sidling up beside her and insisting she dance with him. He smelled like a liquor cabinet. When she refused politely, he persisted until he finally spat out, "What, are you two lezzies?" and she agreed just to get rid of him. She and Polly had laughed it off. Someone must have overheard and told.

Margaret shook her head to dispel the memory. She lobbed her next comment at the secretary. "Have *you* ever tried to get rid of a creepy guy who was bothering you?"

The secretary nodded, and Dean Rolfe tapped the table. "Let's move on, Mr. Burnside. If you could just sit back down for a minute, Miss Sutter."

Margaret grabbed the arms of her chair and lowered herself back down.

Burnside consulted his legal pad. "Miss Sutter, do you own a blue bicycle?"

Where was he headed now? She shook her head furiously.

"Are you sure?"

235

"Yes, I'm sure. My roommate does."

"Do you ever ride hers?"

Margaret breathed as evenly as she could, but her reply still came out snappish and disrespectful. "Sometimes, sure. I'm allowed to."

The lawyer examined the nails on his left hand, rubbing them with his thumb. The gesture struck Margaret as menacing, and she stared down at her own bitten nails in her lap. Had he seen them?

"What I'd like to know is, have you ever ridden this bike over to Dr. Rider's house?"

Her heart picked up a beat. "No! I don't even know where she lives."

"Are you sure you've never visited Dr. Rider? You weren't, say, at her house the Friday after Thanksgiving."

"I was home all day. Ask my mom. While you're at it, maybe she'd like to know what's going on here."

"No need for threats, Miss Sutter," the dean said. "We believe you."

"It doesn't sound like it."

Burnside returned her glare. "Someone on a blue bicycle was at Dr. Rider's that day."

"It wasn't me. Other girls have blue bikes. There's even a professor who rides a bike. I forget her name." Margaret stood, her hands clenched at her sides. "Why are you picking on me like this?"

"No one's picking on you. We are just trying to figure out what happened between you and Dr. Rider."

"Miss Sutter," the dean interrupted, "do you need a short break? We could take a few minutes, then come back and try again."

"I don't want to talk to him anymore. I want my own lawyer, or I won't say anything else."

The dean nodded slowly. "Would it help if I ask the questions?"

"I don't feel well."

A lightheaded feeling overwhelmed her, like the time she broke her arm as a kid and temporarily tumbled into shock. Suddenly, the secretary was at her side, helping her out into the hallway.

The secretary halted at the door to the ladies' room, and Margaret broke away from her suddenly. As she burst through the double doors of Old Main, she heard "Miss Sutter! Miss Sutter! Come back!" behind her.

Fat flakes of snow melted on her upturned face and her tongue and revived her. She'd left her peacoat in the meeting room, but there was no going back now.

Chapter Thirty-Three

Gen

Gen pressed the receiver to her ear, listening to Juliet's account of her meeting with the head of Modern Languages. As a "courtesy," the chairman had offered resignation instead of the ignominy of suspension or firing. In her office, Juliet had typed up a letter and delivered it to him within the hour. He had instructed her to vacate Cavendish House by the next day but gave her until the end of the week to dismantle her office.

"A generous guy, right?" Juliet's laugh came out as a snort.

A stew of fury and despair simmered inside Gen, leaving her with no response. After a pause, she cleared her throat and said, "What did your letter say?" Then she silently cursed her selfish, thoughtless question.

Juliet didn't skip a beat or chide her for it. "Just a basic, I resign my position as Assistant Professor effective immediately, blah, blah, blah, blah."

Her voice tripped on the word *resign*, and Gen reasoned all the tacked-on *blahs* were to avoid a cascade of tears. The tactic worked, because Juliet proceeded without stopping. "Honestly, I wasn't sure he'd go through with it. Who's going to take over my classes on such short notice?"

Gen marveled at the naïveté but held her thought. "Where will you go?" she asked instead.

"I called Ruby a few minutes ago and she offered their guest room until I have everything sorted. I won't get in anyone's way in such a big house."

Dependable Ruby—she could never be compromised by association with Juliet.

"Could I, I don't know, help you pack?" Cavendish sat on the eastern fringe of Baines, and going there might technically not be an incursion for someone who'd been escorted off campus.

"Too risky. Anyway, you've seen my rooms. All the furniture and kitchen stuff belongs to the school. There's just my books and clothes, and I actually packed up the books last night in case the meeting didn't go well. I got some very curious looks from a couple of girls who spotted the boxes. I said I was tidying up."

Her tone was too light, too casual for someone who'd recently relinquished her job, future, and home. Gen still trembled at the memory of her suspension and banishment from campus.

"I don't understand why you're so calm. You just—" She couldn't finish the thought without blubbering herself.

Juliet drew in a long, audible breath. "Darling, you don't know me well enough, but this is me about to burst. My motto is, keep moving."

After the call, Gen filled her gas tank and drove out of town. She intended to wander aimlessly, but once behind the wheel, with the well-worn Virginia atlas propped open on the passenger seat, she realized she always planned her routes. Before she knew it, her car took her to Lexington, to deliver the news to Ursula.

For days, Gen expected a call from her attorney, telling her that Juliet's admission of the kiss had ended the speculation about who had been with her the day after Thanksgiving and had brought the provost's investigation to a close. The best-case scenario, Ursula had theorized, was that Gen would get the chance to resign, like Juliet, and maybe garner some severance, given her long years of exemplary service to the college. "We'll work on that," she promised the day Gen showed up at her office without an appointment.

What Ursula related when she *did* call hit like a flattening punch.

"The school's attorney has dropped his inquiry into who was in your kitchen on November 25," Ursula informed her. "He knows it wasn't a student, what with Juliet's testimony, and your friend Ruby corroborating it." Ursula's laugh was edged with derision. "Hard to believe so much of their case comes down to a bike. Anyway, that's the good news."

Gen's pulse continued to race. "Why do I think you've held back the bad news?"

Ursula was quiet except for the pencil-tapping Gen had come to expect—the only ghost of nerves her attorney ever showed.

"Please, Ursula."

"The bike wasn't their only card to play; we knew that," the lawyer said. "There are still all the history majors who testified that you made them uncomfortable, either with looks or inappropriate touches."

"Unprovable, right?"

"Yes, it strikes me, like the Salem witch hunts. Do you cover that in your classes?"

"Wrong period for me. But of course I know about them." In her anxiety, Gen struggled to dig back into what she'd learned in a colonial history class in grad school. The Salem trials had sparked mass hysteria on flimsy grounds. From Fenton she also knew about *The Crucible*, a Broadway play that addressed the Salem trials and, as he put it, "scarred" him.

"As in Salem," Ursula went on, "we have a situation where one girl is particularly vocal about your purported guilt. She's given testimony twice. The second time expanded her story considerably. She says that because of your quote, attempted solicitation, her grades have slipped and she can't focus. There's was something about your hand on her—I'm sorry, Gen, on her breast—"

240

"That is a complete lie!"

"I have no doubt. But now, just this week, her parents brought her home. Seems she's too distraught to continue at Baines because the school can't ensure her safety."

Gen exploded. "Safety? If they want to keep girls safe, they shouldn't be looking at the *female* faculty."

The tapping from Ursula's end stopped. "Tell me more."

Gen shrugged, even though Ursula couldn't see her. She had no evidence against any male professors, only the gossip that drifted around.

"Never mind," Gen said. "Who's the girl, anyway?" She tried to toughen her voice, but the effort to sound strong proved impossible when her whole body was trembling.

"Confidential," Ursula said. "But maybe you can mull it over and see what candidates you come up with. Parents appear to be big donors, if that helps."

"Wealthy parents at Baines are more the rule than the exception," Gen said. Her mind, though, was already sorting through the possibilities and landing squarely on one girl.

The idea first materialized when she was inspecting her dwindling savings account. She'd had the same savings book from Bank of Botetourt throughout her years at Baines. On the lines for credits and debits, she'd inscribed the regular birthday and Christmas checks from her parents, the five or six dollars a paycheck that she tried to put aside (not always successfully), the $100 she withdrew to buy her sofa bed, the rental deposit for the cottage she shared in Rehoboth with Carolyn, and most recently the hundreds that had gone to Ursula's law firm.

Thank God for the generous kitty from her female colleagues, which would ward off eviction for several months. She hadn't yet deposited the assortment of raggedy bills, and they were tucked between the last page of the savings book and the back cover.

Since that first collection, Frances Palmer had delivered a second, smaller installment from the faculty with an apology.

"People are still recovering from Christmas shopping. I reckon it'll be more next month."

"In my book, y'all are angels," Gen had replied, giving the woman a hug.

Now, as Gen unfolded the bills to count them again, a piece of paper fluttered to the carpet—Fenton's folded check for five hundred dollars, which he'd asked her to hold in case he needed to make bail. He hadn't requested it back, probably out of embarrassment. She stared at it for a moment, her fingers leaving sweaty marks on the edges. How easy it would be to write her own name on the blank line, to literally make him pay. But for what? For disappointing her? *As friends so often do,* she thought.

And that made her reconsider what he'd asked of her, and hatch a plan for what she needed of him now.

When she appeared unannounced at his door, Fenton's face clocked surprise for a split second before he clutched her hand and drew her into his rooms. At just past 7 p.m., he was already wearing his flannel bathrobe, a Black Watch tartan that looked new. She resisted the urge to test the softness of the sleeve.

"Want a drink?" he asked, nodding toward the table where he'd set down a glass of honey-hued liquid next to a bottle of Jim Beam.

She shook her head and unclasped her pocketbook without speaking. The check lay loosely among the bag's sparse contents—her Parker pen, comb, hanky, car keys, compact. When she held the slip of folded paper out to him, Fenton's lips formed a small *O*.

"I forgot about this," he said.

"You didn't for a minute, don't pretend. *I'm* the one who forgot."

He winced at her growling tone. "Well, you've had other things on your mind. But you could have dropped it in the mail, you know, or just voided it. I'm probably the last person you wanted to see."

"No, that would be the provost."

Fenton smiled at the dark joke. Gen's eyes drifted back to his table and the glass he'd abandoned there. "I've changed my mind. I'll take that drink."

He splashed a generous amount into her glass and topped off his own. Although he invited her to sit with him on the couch, Gen said she preferred to stand.

"You came to me with the check, and that was a big favor to ask," she began.

He examined his drink before taking a slow, refined sip, the way debonair men drank in old movies. "And I'm guessing you have a favor to ask me?" He paused. "The answer is yes."

"You haven't heard it yet."

"The answer is still yes. I—lately I've been so angry at myself for the way I hurt you that . . . well, I can't even tell you what I've been planning."

A chill ran up her arms. She'd never pictured him as the suicidal type, but she knew some gay people chose that path when they lost hope. Gen assessed him over her own drink, which she had yet to sample. "Nothing stupid, I hope."

Laughter rippled out of him, and she relaxed. "Oh, not *that*, hon. I ain't done with this world yet." He paused. "Actually, I've been thinking about getting another job."

"Where?"

"New York. For the breathing room." His head tilted to observe her better. "You might like New York."

Her laugh was more of a sputter. "Where I'd do . . . what?"

Fenton shrugged. "Last I saw, New York had schools, archives. Places where history people go." The conversation had reached a bizarre intersection that reminded her of past talks with Carolyn. She needed to end this conversation and show her hand.

"Look, never mind with that. I need your help." The bourbon burned her throat on its way down. "Susanna Carr is one of your students, isn't she?"

Chapter Thirty-Four

Fenton

"Anyone seen Margaret?"

Fenton scanned the table twice, but Margaret was missing. Her stellar audition had gained her the choice role of Emily Webb.

"She wasn't in my lit class today either," one girl offered.

A bug was sweeping across campus, and cast members had clear instructions to stay away if they were ill and to notify Joan, the secretary.

Fenton shuffled his papers, searching for a note from the secretary. Nothing. He'd selected Susanna Carr as the understudy for Emily. Her acting chops didn't compare to Margaret's, but he hoped Margaret had simply neglected to send word.

"Susanna, you'll have to read for both Mrs. Webb and Emily until we can locate our leading lady."

Susanna straightened in her chair. The girl had not hidden her desire to play Emily, rather than Emily's mother, and she did a passable job as they progressed through the acts.

After the table read, he asked Susanna if she could stop into his office.

"It's getting pretty late, Mr. Page," she said, after a nervous peek at her wristwatch. "I have reading for your class tomorrow."

"I'll excuse you from that. We'll mostly be doing improv anyway. This is important."

Instead of closing his office door or leaving it cracked a few inches for privacy, he flung it open. The students had departed quickly, and the only person left in the building was the janitor, who was tidying the stage upstairs and unlikely to overhear.

"I hope my reading was okay." The girl's voice wobbled.

Fenton searched for an adjective that would respect her effort. "It was solid, Susanna. I'm grateful to you for pinch hitting. Hopefully, you won't have to do it again." Her pleased expression faded, and he added, "Only because I hope Margaret's okay. Anyway, that's not what I wanted to talk to you about."

"Oh, I can't stage manage again," she said before he could explain. "That was more work than I thought."

"It looks like we're all set with that, as long as no one else takes sick. No, this is actually about one of your friends."

Susanna's face clouded. "You mean Lee-Anne?"

Word had spread that Lee-Anne had withdrawn from Baines. Fenton's thoughts shot back to Margaret, who'd also been interviewed. Had her parents taken her out of school, too?

"I do." He leaned forward in his chair, mustering his concerned professor affect. "I'm worried about her. And you."

"How do you know Lee-Anne?" Her eyes narrowed.

He didn't. The Blakeney girl had never enrolled in one of his classes or auditioned for anything. When he ran into Susanna on the quad or the library, she was often accompanied by a blond girl, but he couldn't summon up a clear visual.

"I'm worried in general," he hurried to say, "about all you girls."

Susanna stared with her mouth slightly open, but she didn't speak.

He delved further, as gently as he could. "Is there anything, well, going on that you wish you could tell someone?"

Her forehead creased. "You know what's going on, Mr. Page. Nobody likes it."

"The interviews?"

Susanna nodded, her gaze falling to her lap. "Thank God they haven't called me. Seems like it's just history majors. I don't know what I'd say."

After a pause, he pressed on, "You mean about Dr. Rider?"

The girl fidgeted. "I've only had her for the one class," she said. "I was amazed I got an A. She's tough."

He leaned in closer. "Did Lee-Anne tell you her concerns about Dr. Rider?"

Susanna blinked rapidly. "It was news to me. And we used to tell each other everything." She cast her glance toward the open door. Her voice turned soft and urgent. "Promise you won't say anything to anyone?"

Fenton zipped his lips.

"It's just—well, she's been my best friend forever, and now she won't even talk to me. When I call her house, her mother says she's 'indisposed.' Like she's sick or something, but she isn't. It's weird."

He'd been hoping for a more substantial revelation. "Is she angry with you, maybe?"

"I don't think so. I mean, no. The interviews got her all worked up. And Dr.—" Susanna bit her top lip. "Let's just say I'm not sure this is about Dr. Rider."

Fenton scratched his cheek. "What's the 'this'?"

"Her going through whatever it is she's going through . . . like a nervous breakdown or something. My aunt had one of those, but she's at least fifty." The girl jerked at a noise in the hallway.

"It's fine. Old buildings creak," Fenton reassured her. "Susanna, nerves can hit you at any age. Maybe it's schoolwork, or pressure to do something you don't want to. Or having to keep a secret."

Susanna stood abruptly. "I should go."

"Of course." Fenton's mind raced to keep her in place. She had crumpled on the verge of divulging something.

"Susanna, I just want to say, if you have a secret that's weighing you down, you can tell me. I might be able to help."

Susanna grabbed her bag from the floor and was gone before he had even stood up.

Fenton sank back into his chair and propped his chin in his hands. He despaired about telling Gen he hadn't gleaned any information from Susanna—the one request she'd made of him, and he'd failed. He postponed calling her.

And then, after class the following morning, Susanna tapped on the glass of his office door.

"I do sort of have a secret," she said slowly.

Chapter Thirty-Five

Margaret

Margaret ignored the knocking until it grew more insistent and rhythmic, like a woodpecker's drumming. She dragged herself to the door and undid the lock her parents had agreed to with reluctance when she was fifteen. In the frame, Margaret's mother swept a long, critical look from her fuzzy slippers to her uncombed hair.

"You can't stay in there forever." She crossed her arms in front of her.

"I won't."

"It's been almost two days, Margie. Are you ready to tell me what's going on?"

"I told you."

"But you said the professor they're investigating is gone."

"There could be more." Margaret bit at a ragged fingernail until her mother lightly pushed her hand away from her mouth.

"I thought you broke that habit."

"This whole terrible thing has brought it back!" Margaret said. "I'm a nervous wreck, Mama." Tears stung her eyes, remembering the humiliation of her interview by the attorney, how he'd implied she was a lesbian.

The tears made her mother's face soften, and she wrapped an arm around her. Margaret let her head fall to her mother's shoulder, trying to ignore the sharpness of the bone.

After a silence, Margaret ventured, "I'd like to transfer."

Her mother's posture stiffened, and she dropped her comforting arm. "Baines is a prestigious school and connected to Davis and Lee. You could meet a nice boy—"

"But this changes everything," Margaret insisted. "I heard other girls are leaving, too. The place is tainted, Mama."

Her mother raised her eyebrows. "Maybe there are a few rotten apples," she said. "It's not the entire college."

Margaret erupted in sobs. She had thought even a whiff of scandal would be enough to sway her parents to let her leave. The idea that her mother might drive her back so soon, that she might have to face Dean Rolfe and the horrible Mr. Burnside once more made her gulp for air.

"Now what is all this?" Her mother slipped her arm around her shoulders again, and the gesture soothed her. Margaret blew her nose into a clean hanky her mother offered.

"Don't make me go back!" She turned the lace-trimmed square over and over in her hands. Her tears were real, but her mama didn't need to know what caused them.

"You'll lose the credits for this semester if you drop out now," her mother said. "We already paid—"

"I'll get a job. I'll pay you back! I know Daddy will be mad, but you can talk him into it, Mama, I know you can. He didn't even want me to go to college until you convinced him."

She remembered the closed-door arguments between her parents, her mother's measured tone, her father's bellowing. Her mother had married two years out of high school, when Margaret's father finished college, but neither Margaret nor her sister showed prospects of an early wedding. While at Baines, their mother had reasoned, the girls would have their pick of boys at Davis and Lee. "Damned expensive way to find a husband," her father had complained before giving in.

249

In desperation now, Margaret suggested, "I could transfer to a state school. That would be so much cheaper." Her mind skipped through the possibilities. "How about William and Mary?"

Her mother didn't reject the idea out of hand, even though Williamsburg was clear across the state. William and Mary could compete with the best of private schools, and it was her father's alma mater. Nearly thirty years after his graduation, he still made the trip to Williamsburg most Octobers for Homecoming.

Mrs. Sutter patted her leg and rose to leave. "We'll talk about this more when your father gets home," she said—a good sign that she was weighing the plan's merits. "Nobody wants you scared to go to school."

"Thank you, Mama!"

"Nothing's settled. Your father's still the head of this family, and don't you forget it."

Her mother clicked the door closed behind her. Margaret collapsed back onto her bed, hope recharging her body.

At an early hour when she knew Polly would be in biology lab, Margaret drove her mother's station wagon to campus to pick up her belongings. She avoided the front door of Freeman Hall, opting for the back entrance and stairwell that led almost directly to Room 314. Aside from one girl heading to the showers, she sneaked in without seeing anyone she knew.

When she unlocked the door, her room was uncharacteristically dark, with blinds drawn like on Saturday mornings when she and Polly both slept in. She switched on the overhead, and Polly whimpered from her narrow bed.

Margaret flipped the light off. "Polly, you slept through lab!" A sliver of light peeked through a cracked slat in one of the blinds, and she inched cautiously toward her own half of the room. Polly was somewhere under a lump of scratchy-looking army blankets.

"Until you woke me up." Polly groaned. "I'm sick. Bet it's that awful bug going around."

Polly sat up in bed and turned on her nightstand lamp, also army issue. When Margaret had first seen Polly's furnishings at the beginning of the school year, she had asked if her father was in the service because so much of what the girl owned was olive green. Polly had admitted to buying everything cheap and last minute at the Army-Navy store in her hometown. With Margaret's bright quilt, framed Monet prints, and brass desk lamp, an invisible curtain of color and taste separated the two sides of their room.

"Where have you been the past three days anyway?" Polly asked as Margaret shoved notebooks and pens into a box.

"Home," Margaret said. She hoped that would shut the questions down; she didn't want to get into anything with Polly.

Polly was upright now and watching her closely. She had lifted the blind on her window to admit more light. "So . . . what? You're moving out?"

Margaret couldn't face her roommate. Her lashes felt wet, and crying would only slow her down. "Damn," she said under her breath when a box's lid wouldn't close.

The honk of Polly blowing her nose filled the room. "You got way too much stuff. There's an empty box at the bottom of my closet you can have. I'd get it for you, but with germs and all . . ."

Margaret fetched the box from Polly's closet with trepidation. She had never looked inside the closet and expected lab equipment to fall out on top of her. The inside, however, was as orderly as an army private's. An empty box was folded up, like it was waiting for her.

"Don't tell me you're dropping out." Polly's voice was hoarse. When Margaret didn't reply, her roommate added, "Good God, you're dropping out."

"Transferring."

"At the beginning of the semester?"

Margaret sighed. "You sure have gotten nosy."

"Nobody transfers in February, Sutter." Only Polly called her by her last name, as if they were prep school boys.

"So I'll be the first."

"Christ, you're stubborn." Polly pulled her blankets up around her chin.

Margaret had lugged her mother's biggest suitcase with her, the one purchased for an anniversary trip to London, and now she proceeded to fold and stack her clothes neatly onto the creamy satin lining. She had intended to be quick with her packing, but now some part of her wanted to linger and hear her roommate's voice one last time.

A long silence followed, punctuated only by a raspy cough from Polly's side of the room. "You know, it doesn't matter to me," Polly said.

Margaret lifted her eyes. "That I'm leaving?"

Polly coughed again, but this time it sounded forced. "What people say about you."

Margaret's cheeks burned with shame. She didn't want to know what anyone said about her.

"They're not worth your time."

"I don't know what you mean." Margaret's eyes were filling again, and she turned away. She busied herself with removing Monet's water lilies from the wall and wrapping the framed print in a pillowcase.

"You're a smart girl. You shouldn't let them ruin your life."

She could have hugged Polly. "They haven't, don't worry," Margaret said. "I'm going to William and Mary." It wasn't a sure thing, she had to be admitted, but her father had approved the planned transfer.

Polly nodded. "Oh, wow. Good place for history, I bet."

Margaret snapped the suitcase closed. "You should go back to sleep," she said. "I'll be out of your hair in no time, and then you'll have a single for the rest of the year."

Her roommate continued to watch her until she lifted the last box and said she was leaving. Polly gave her a little wave from her bed, almost a salute, and then Margaret closed the door behind her and was gone.

Chapter Thirty-Six

Ruby

When Amanda Blakeney answered Ruby's knock, she didn't have her face on. Her hands flew to her cheeks as if she could powder and rouge them by sheer will.

"Ruby! Oh, I must look a fright." She peered around Ruby to her house across the street. "What's wrong? Is Darrell all right? The boys?"

Ruby noted the rapid progression of Amanda's thoughts, from agitation about her appearance to genuine concern for Ruby's family. It confirmed that somewhere in Amanda's body resided a human being.

"Everyone's fine, Amanda. I didn't mean to startle you." Ruby drew in a breath. She'd decided to extend the invitation in person, at a time when Darrell would be having coffee (drinks, she suspected) with his former law partner. But on the Blakeneys' front porch, the words she planned caught in her throat.

"I simply . . . well, I wanted to invite you to tea this afternoon."

Amanda cocked her head to the left. "Why?"

Ruby had prepared for the question. She had never invited her neighbor to tea before, and Amanda knew that Ruby and Gen were friends.

"Just wanting to be neighborly," Ruby said as casually as she could manage. "I know you're going through a lot. Your family."

"You heard."

"I thought you might like to talk about it."

Ruby's neighbor wiped her hands on her calico apron, drawing attention to the frayed edge of the patch pocket. Amanda quickly untied the strings from around her waist and balled up the apron.

"Will your *guest* be joining us?" she asked.

For a second, Ruby worried that she meant Gen, but then realized Amanda had likely seen Juliet coming and going. "Dr. May just left. She stayed with us a few days."

"I heard she was asked to leave Baines."

"No, she resigned. Family matters in Wilmington."

Amanda blinked several times, as if she almost believed Ruby's explanation. "I'm not sure there's anything to talk about, Ruby," she said after a long pause. "I've about talked myself silly, what with the provost and the dean and my husband and Lee-Anne."

Ruby noted that she didn't mention Mrs. Carr or an attorney. "I understand. Maybe we could just relax then, enjoy some cookies and talk about the books we're reading."

Amanda smirked. "Oh, I don't have time to read, what with the children and everything." Ruby wasn't sure what constituted "and everything." Amanda's offspring were all in school, and she employed a Negro housekeeper who came daily for cooking and cleaning.

Ruby was about to accept defeat with a cheery *rain check, then,* when she noticed Amanda's shoulders sag, as if the effort of holding them back and straight had finally overpowered her.

"It would be nice, though," Amanda said, "to just sit and have tea like a normal person."

When Ruby suggested four o'clock, she inwardly reproached herself for planning to ambush a woman who was so despondent and tired-looking. She considered calling Gen to cancel, but her guilt passed quickly. Amanda Blakeney had set everything in motion. She'd ruined two good women's lives, and she needed to be held to account.

Darrell put a glitch in Ruby's plan by sauntering into the kitchen as she set out her china tea cups and arranged snickerdoodles on a plate.

"Shouldn't you have left already? Did you forget your coffee with Jack?"

Darrell examined her evenly. They'd been married too long not to pick up on each other's tricks. "He's got to be in court today. We postponed till next week." He nabbed a cookie and polished off half of it in a single bite.

"What's going on here?" he asked through a mouthful.

Ruby held onto the counter while considering her options. None of her possible lies were strong, and besides Darrell would see right through anything she picked.

"I invited Amanda for tea," she said, hoping that simple truth would satisfy his curiosity.

"Amanda Blakeney?"

"I don't know any other Amandas."

Darrell watched in silence while she bustled around him. As she poured milk into the creamer, he said, "I count four cups."

"You missed your calling, darling. You would have been a terrific prosecutor."

Neither the endearment nor the quip distracted him. Her husband followed her into the living room, where she set the silver tea tray on the table in front of the sofa.

"What are you up to, Rube? Amanda Blakeney has come to tea, let's see . . . I'd say never. Who else will be here?"

She made a show of taking her time to lay everything out neatly. "Frances Palmer, from biology. About my age, plump with salt-and-pepper—"

"I know who Frances is. Who's the fourth?" He stilled her hand, which was fussing with the cups, and turned her to meet his gaze. "Tell me it's not who I think it is."

Ruby drew a long sigh.

"My God, Ruby," Darrell said. "I know you probably think

255

you're helping, but you could hurt Gen more by putting those two in the same room. Amanda's attorney—"

"I don't think she has one."

"Then Gen's. Gen's attorney would advise against it. Hell, *any* attorney would. *I* would, and all I did was taxes."

"No one's on trial," Ruby noted. "It's not like witness ... tin-kering."

"Tampering."

"Tampering. Thank you." She reached out to stroke his cheek, dark with afternoon stubble, but he deflected her touch. His brow creased with a mix of worry and vexation.

"Don't do this."

"You don't even know what 'this' is."

"I have a fair idea."

"Go somewhere, Darrell," she said, returning to the tea cups. "Please. They'll be here soon."

The front door slammed, rattling the cups. Her husband didn't take his hat or gloves, which he needed on such a cold day. Ruby glanced out the window, relieved to see the street had been salted after the recent snow. Maybe Darrell would drive around playing the radio, as he did years back when they fought and the boys still lived at home. She hadn't meant to upset him, but his disapproval didn't figure into her plans.

Chapter Thirty-Seven

Gen

Gen spotted the green and white Roadmaster parked at the curb in front of Ruby's, and the tightness in her chest loosened. The women in Ruby's faculty group all teased Frances about owning such a classy car.

"Not my idea." Frances had blushed, leaving unspoken whose idea it actually was. Frances rarely mentioned her companion, Ellen, by name, and out of discretion no one asked about her. "If it were up to me," Frances had joked, "I'd drive a twenty-year-old station wagon."

Ruby had instructed Gen to slip in through the unlocked front door without ringing the bell. "Give us a fifteen-minute lead," she'd suggested.

On the threshold, Gen glanced at her watch, which read 4:17. She took a deep breath of frosty air, which burned her lungs, then twisted the knob and strode in unannounced. In the foyer, she decided to keep her coat on, in case she needed to make a hasty exit.

"That must have been a very hard decision," she heard Frances say. Tea cups clinked against saucers.

"Oh, yes. The women in my family have always attended Baines." The lilting voice reminded Gen of Vivien Leigh in *Streetcar Named Desire*. "I did have one aunt who broke with tradition and enrolled at Wellesley. She never came back. We get a Christmas card from Boston every year from Aunt Mabel and her assortment of beagles."

Cued by the round of laughter, Gen entered the living room, and the women's heads swiveled toward her. Ruby and Frances smiled encouragingly, while Mrs. Blakeney's mouth flopped open.

"Amanda, I hope you don't mind," Ruby said. "I invited Gen Rider to join us. You haven't formally met, but you've heard quite a bit about each other."

Amanda shifted her cup and saucer to the table and rose to leave. She tugged at the sweater slung around her shoulders and held in place with a silver clasp.

"Ruby, you surprise me. I wouldn't have thought you capable of such a low trick. May I have my wrap?"

Ruby and Frances stood, too, but all of them remained frozen in place and speechless. Gen's gaze circled from one to another but rested for the longest time on Amanda. She was a dead ringer for her daughter, a trim blonde with nails freshly painted a rich shade of cherry.

"I'm sorry I upset you, Mrs. Blakeney," Gen said. "Please don't blame Ruby or Frances. The surprise meeting was my idea."

Amanda shot a glance toward the foyer, as if weighing how to make her escape. Yet she remained rooted in place like a trapped animal.

"If you could hear me out," Gen continued. "I have some information that might help your family."

Amanda thrust her chin forward. "You've given quite enough *help* to my family, thank you."

"Mrs. Blakeney—" Frances tried to intercede but was cut off.

"And you two, Professor Palmer, Ruby—I'm amazed you associate with someone of such low character. This woman—who knows how many girls she's scarred? She sets her cap for *children!*"

"That is just not true," Gen said.

"You're calling my daughter a liar? I didn't raise a liar!"

Gen's hands curled into fists, and her breathing picked up speed. She wanted a drink of water but had to press on and not lose momentum.

"Let's say I think Lee-Anne has made up some stories. Not to be vicious, but because she's scared and doesn't know how to get out of the mess she's in. I have reason to believe she—"

Amanda raised a hand to stop her. "I don't care what you have reason to believe. It's clear you will say anything."

While Ruby accompanied Amanda to the door, Gen was left facing Frances, who didn't seem to know where to look so she focused on the Persian rug. Gen heard murmurs in the foyer that she couldn't make out and then the soft click of the front door.

Ruby returned to the living room, her hands balled into fists.

"It could have been worse," Frances said. "She might come around and want to hear Gen's side."

Ruby sighed. "She mentioned a restraining order."

Gen's stomach twisted. Her naive idea that she might make things right if she could just *talk* to Mrs. Blakeney and lay out the facts had compounded the trouble. There was nothing to do now but call Ursula and put an end to the circus, follow Juliet's lead, and get the hell out of town.

The hang-ups started again that night, right after she had heated the leftover chicken and dumplings Ruby offered her and set the meal on a plate. Eating felt like the only thing she could control.

Gen struggled to chew a mouthful before answering. She expected Ursula's voice on the other end. After the debacle at Ruby's, she had called the attorney, who had registered shock at her decision to fold.

"That doesn't sound like you," Ursula had said. "What's happened?"

Gen had ignored the question, not wanting to divulge the harebrained scheme to talk to her accuser's mother.

"I'll check in later and see if you've changed your mind."

"I won't."

But it wasn't Ursula. A dial tone greeted Gen, and she returned to her meal. Her eyes drifted to the Carrs' house, so dark and still except for a light in an upstairs window facing her bungalow.

Within minutes, the ringing resumed, five, six, seven insistent counts. In mid-bite, Gen eyed the phone but let it whine until it stopped.

While she was washing her dinner plate, the phone started again, droning on until she picked up the receiver.

Gen didn't bother with a greeting. "Who *is* this?"

This time the mystery caller didn't hang up, and through the wire Gen distinctly heard sniffling. She tried again in a more patient tone. "Why are you crying?"

The female voice that replied was young, tremulous, unidentifiable. "I can't stop."

Gen shut down her urge to play a guessing game, deciding it might only irritate the caller. Someone needed to talk to her, and she reasoned that her identity would soon come to light.

The caller's next words were so hushed, Gen couldn't grab on to them. "I'm sorry, I missed what you just said." She pressed the receiver to her ear until it hurt, wishing for a way to turn up the volume.

"My mother—" The girl trailed off, but now Gen knew for sure.

She kept her tone calm, although what she really wanted was to throttle the girl, demand to know why she was lying. "I'm sorry if I made things worse for you with your mother. I didn't mean to."

Lee-Anne's whispered question threw her. "Could you— could I talk to you . . . somewhere?"

Heat rushed to Gen's face. What kind of new game was she playing? "You can talk now, Lee-Anne. I'm listening."

More sniffles traveled through the line. "Someone could pick up downstairs."

In her head Gen heard Ursula's stern warning: *Do not engage with the girl. She lies through her teeth.*

"Given the situation, that's not a good idea," Gen replied. "I don't want anyone to get the wrong idea."

"I can't . . . I don't . . ." Lee-Anne's crying turned into sobs and gulps. "*Please*."

Gen imagined the worst scenario: Mrs. Blakeney there in the room with her daughter, egging her on, setting a trap for Gen. She shook away the paranoid idea, something from a movie or novel and not real life.

"I won't meet with you unless you tell me what it's about," she said.

Susanna Carr had already told Fenton, but Gen needed to hear it from the girl's own mouth.

The name sounded like the hiss of a snake.

Chapter Thirty-Eight

Gen

The frigid wind bit at Gen's face as she trudged to Ruby's house. Ruby had instructed her to walk, not drive, and to take the circuitous route through a copse of loblolly pines to the backyard. Gen had chuckled at the elaborate instructions, reminiscent of a spy thriller.

Neighborhood children had worn a trail through the woods, and with the recent snowfall and the dappled light through the pines the route to Ruby's rear door was magical. Gen so rarely walked anywhere. The only noise came from the crunch of her boots on frozen leaves and the trill of a solitary finch that apparently hadn't flown farther south.

As she approached Ruby's house, Gen dove deeper into her knitted wool scarf, steeling herself for seeing Lee-Anne. In normal circumstances, meetings with students were routine, but so much rested on what Lee-Anne was willing to admit in front of Ruby.

Behind her someone else's feet crunched through the snow. Lee-Anne was bundled into a fur-trimmed white parka, the hood obscuring her face, and her hands were stuffed into the slash pockets. In leggings and red boots, she looked like a schoolkid dressed for a snow day.

"My mother's taking a bath," she said. "I've got about thirty minutes."

In the mudroom, they peeled off their layers of winter wear. "The family room's nice and toasty," Ruby said, motioning to a dark, narrow hallway Gen had never seen before—at one time, a passage for servants, she guessed. In fact, as long as she'd known Ruby, which seemed like forever, Gen had never entered through this part of the house.

Lee-Anne plopped onto the sofa, and Ruby handed her a crocheted afghan as she took a seat next to her. Gen faced them in a separate chair, the distance making her feel like an interrogator.

With a reddened hand, the girl reached for the cocoa Ruby had set out and cradled it in her hands. Without makeup or barrettes, without a flouncy skirt and matching sweater set, Lee-Anne seemed much younger than her nineteen years.

Minutes ticked by in silence. Gen reminded herself that Lee-Anne had requested this meeting, and she should let the girl lead. Still, the matter of time pressed in on her.

"Why don't you start, Lee-Anne?" Gen said. "You wanted to speak to me about something."

Lee-Anne sipped noisily at her cocoa. "I didn't know *you'd* be here, too, Dr. Woods. I thought we were just meeting in your house."

Gen cast a wide-eyed glance at Ruby, a frantic signal of *Don't leave me!*

"I didn't think you'd mind," Ruby said, her focus shifting to Lee-Anne. "Why, we're old friends. I've known you since you were tiny."

Lee-Anne's face relaxed into a smile. She tucked her stockinged feet up under her on the sofa.

"Now, you've been saying some things about Dr. Rider," Ruby said to urge her on.

The girl nodded in a choppy way. "I didn't mean for it to go this far." Her blue eyes misted over. "I told . . . him about that one time, and he blew it out of proportion. He pressed and pressed—" Her fists tightened around her mug of cocoa.

"You mean Dr. Thoms?"

Her head jerked again.

"And what was the one time?" Gen probed. "I seem to have made you uncomfortable without even realizing it."

Lee-Anne shrugged but then offered the answer. "Halloween." The word came out with a burble. "I was putting my shoe on, and I saw you looked—"

Gen sifted through her memories to the day when she saw Lee-Anne emerging from Thoms's office, disheveled and flummoxed. She thought she recalled asking if the girl was all right and remarking on her costume. But what had she done other than that?

"—at my leg!" Lee-Anne finished with a sob, and Gen let out a loud breath.

Ruby leaned away from Lee-Anne and crossed her arms across her chest. "*That's* what this is about? My God—"

Gen caught Ruby's eye and wagged her head once. *Please don't antagonize her,* she hoped the gesture said.

Lee-Anne sniffled and went on in her piecemeal style. "We all heard you might be, you know. I always said no, you're too pretty, but there's no men . . . and Margaret—"

Gen flinched. "Lee-Anne, do you know anything about some gifts I got this fall?"

Sobs erupted out of the girl. "I didn't think things would—"

Ruby pried the mug from Lee-Anne's shaking hands and passed her the tissue box from the coffee table. The girl crushed it against her like a teddy bear.

"I don't feel well," she announced. "Can I use the bathroom?"

Ruby escorted Lee-Anne to the powder room. Through the stillness, Gen heard the distinct sound of retching followed by Ruby's comforting, motherly tone. She pictured her friend holding back the girl's long hair as she vomited into the commode.

Gen crossed to the window for something to distract her, but her mind worried over the fact that time was slipping away and Lee-Anne had set a thirty-minute limit.

When Lee-Anne and Ruby returned to their seats, the girl's face had drained of color, and she dabbed at her mouth with a dampened washcloth.

What would Ursula do? The lawyer would have disapproved of this clandestine meeting to begin with, but if she *were* in charge, she would firmly steer the witness to the point.

"Lee-Anne, Dr. Woods and I would like to help you." Gen propped herself at the edge of her chair. "But we can't until you tell us more. Like why you've been making up stories about . . . how I've acted with you."

Lee-Anne's chin jutted out as if she were poised to object and carry on the charade. But then her bottom lip quivered and the tears flowed again.

"You have, haven't you?" Gen continued. "Been making things up."

When Lee-Anne's head dipped up and down reluctantly, Ruby reached over and patted her hand. "It's all right, dear," she said. "No one's angry."

"I—I needed them to get me out!"

"Of school?"

Lee-Anne nodded again, and tears dropped off her chin onto her cardigan. "I wanted to just leave, but they wouldn't let me. I couldn't stay."

Gen inclined farther toward the sofa, willing the truth out of her.

"And I . . . I couldn't tell them the real reason," Lee-Anne sputtered.

Ruby shot a worried glance at Gen as she stroked the girl's hand gently, but Gen couldn't decipher what the look meant. Was she going too far? How could she stop now? She sucked in a determined breath and posed the question she already knew the answer to.

"Lee-Anne—you're . . . expecting, is that right?" She'd almost chosen *pregnant* but settled on the more muted phrase.

Pain and panic crossed Lee-Anne's face. "I told Susanna not to tell!"

"Susanna did the right thing," Ruby said. "You haven't told your parents?"

"They're gonna find out pretty soon," Lee-Anne muttered, rubbing her stomach.

The girl wasn't showing yet and she had morning sickness, so she was likely only a few months along. Susanna had refused to tell Fenton who the father was, but she did disclose that Lee-Anne had become "involved" with a male professor in the fall. On the phone with Gen, Lee-Anne gave Thoms's name as the reason for wanting to talk but wouldn't go into detail until they met in person.

Gen thought back to Halloween: Lee-Anne flustered, hopping around in one shoe, Thoms stealing off down the hall. Now it was too late to make it right—for Lee-Anne, anyway. Her parents would likely send her away in disgrace when she got too big to hide her condition.

But maybe there could be one final jab at Thoms to keep him from hurting the girls yet to come.

Chapter Thirty-Nine

Gen

Men's laughter undulated from behind the closed door. Henry Thoms emerged from the chairman's office as if he belonged there, and the sight made Gen shudder.

Thoms slapped a younger man on the back jovially. With the other hand he rattled a set of car keys. "My boy, you have made my day."

The other man resembled Thoms, lanky with high cheekbones. His hair held no traces of gray, though, and was plastered down with a Brylcreem shine.

"You enjoy that car now, Uncle Henry. You picked a beaut."

Gen placed him immediately by his voice. He was the thug who had bashed her car door in Slocum Point at the Grace AME Church.

Thoms and his companion spotted Gen at the same time and smiled.

"Virginia, so sorry to keep you waiting," Thoms said. "My nephew dropped in early with a nice surprise. Spence, this is my colleague, Professor Rider."

"Pleased to meet you, ma'am. You ever need new wheels, you come visit me and I'll fix you right up." The nephew winked and flashed a business card that read, "Spencer J. Thoms, Manager—Big Beau Motors, New & Used Cars."

Gen couldn't resist a taunt as she returned the card. "You already fixed me right up, Mr. Thoms. Back in October?"

Spence's grin faded, and she suspected her face may have finally registered in his memory. "Don't rightly recall that," he said, turning away.

Spence shook his uncle's hand and left in a rush.

"Isn't it a small world, you buying a car from my nephew?" Thoms gestured toward the chair Gen had occupied when Huston informed her of Mrs. Blakeney's accusation. The chair looked the same but felt different, less stiff.

"Actually, I didn't buy anything. Your nephew bashed my car door with a baseball bat when he saw me coming out of a meeting at the Negro church. Used some choice language, too. The dent's starting to rust, what with the snow." She hadn't meant to divulge so much, but her days at Baines were numbered anyway and he might as well face the low caliber of his kin.

Thoms's brow furrowed as he settled into the chair next to her. "I apologize for my nephew's crude behavior. He's a good boy, but he's gotten into some scrapes. I thought we were past it." He laced his hands together in his lap. "Let me take care of that repair for you, Virginia. I don't like the sound of that rust."

Gen examined Thoms curiously. For the first time in her long acquaintance with him, his tone didn't reek of condescension or sarcasm. The show of humanity fit him as poorly as a cheap suit, and she wondered how often he tucked away the Henry Thoms she was accustomed to—someone only a few notches above his nephew.

"Feeling guilty, Henry?"

Thoms snapped to attention. "Whatever for? *I* didn't bash your car." He moved to the chair behind Huston's desk. "Well, the offer stands. I like to make things right. Now, on to business."

Gen glanced down at her right hand, fastened on the chair arm. Before she left for Wilmington, Juliet had slid her grandmother's sapphire onto it. "For luck," she had said. When Gen resisted, Juliet added, "It's just on loan, mind, so you'll have to come find me to return it."

The ring was a size too large, and Gen hadn't worn it for fear of losing a precious heirloom. Today, it shimmered on her middle finger and made her loosen her grip on the chair.

When she looked up, Thoms had folded his arms, his face unreadable. "I assume you have a letter for me."

Gen drew back. "Oh, I'm not here to resign. The school will have to fire me to get rid of me. And you don't have that authority, Henry, so it will have to come from the provost or dean."

Thoms's frown brought back her familiar adversary. "Then what is this about? I don't have time to play games with you."

"Yet," she began, considering her words with care, "you seem to play them with your students."

Thoms rose from his seat, glaring at her. "To think, I offered to help you and all you do is try to intimidate me about ... well, God knows what. If you aren't here to resign, I'll ask you to leave."

Gen scowled back at him, trying to make herself look fierce even though her heart hammered against her chest. "I have some information about Lee-Anne Blakeney you might want to hear."

His Adam's apple jerked. "I'm sure I know Miss Blakeney better than you."

"Why don't you sit down and we'll see?"

He remained standing, but clutched the edge of his desk. His hands were as slender as a pianist's. "I will stand, thank you. I'm not in the habit of discussing advisees with other professors, and besides, you are on suspension and under investigation. I've asked you to leave, but if you won't, you'll force me to call security to escort you off campus. Why, they might even press charges for trespassing." His hand hovered over the phone.

Gen held his eyes. "No need for that. I'll leave on my own in a minute. But I wanted to give *you* the chance to consider resigning before I take the information I have to the provost. You've been having an inappropriate sexual relationship with Lee-Anne and she's pregnant."

Thoms fiddled with a black striated fountain pen lying on the

269

blotter. It looked expensive, like a Mont Blanc. He removed the cap from the pen and clicked it back into place several times.

"I won't deny we've been intimate, but she wasn't in my class in the fall. She's a flirtatious thing, as you yourself have seen—"

"I've seen no such thing."

"So you say. Anyway, we had a handful of enjoyable times that she initiated. It was all very tender and satisfying, and she got what she wanted."

Gen stared at him in disbelief. "To be pregnant?"

"I know nothing about that. I'm sure she's been with numerous Davis and Lee boys. If she claims I'm the father . . . well, I broke it off with her at the start of the semester, and she got angry. She actually thought I'd leave my wife and boys for her." He snickered. "I couldn't keep it going, what with her taking my seminar this term. I made the ethical choice."

Thoms's affect never changed, and Gen realized with a jolt of disgust that he actually believed his version.

"So, no, Virginia, I have no intention of resigning. I reckon there's not a professor on this campus who hasn't had a girl make up a fanciful story about him."

Gen took her time standing up. "Yet you were so quick to believe a girl's story about me as the God's honest truth."

Thoms sniffed. "Apples and oranges," he said. "You're jealous, admit it. When push comes to shove, you're just an unhappy lesbian."

Gen reached over and slapped him, a crack so forceful his head twisted. She had never struck anyone before and didn't know she was capable of it.

"I've wanted to do that for such a long time."

His fingers grazed his cheek where her smack left pink marks. "Get out of here."

At the door to his office, she glanced over her shoulder and caught him leaning forward onto his desk, breathing heavily.

Chapter Forty

Gen

The Great Hall occupied a wing of Old Main. The elongated, second-story reception room boasted a polished parquet floor, two elaborately carved mantelpieces, two chandeliers, more sconces than Gen could count, and a wall of French doors that opened onto a balcony. The space was not unfamiliar to Gen; she had attended a formal reception there for newly tenured faculty just last May. The evening of the event she and Ruby had clinked champagne glasses while marveling at the mountains on the horizon, swirled with peach and purple in the dusky light. "You did it, my girl," Ruby had said, triumph and joy filling her voice.

Such a grand place was hardly needed for a meeting of Gen, Ursula, the provost, the dean, and a few minions. "They're trying to intimidate us," Gen whispered to Ursula as they entered.

Ursula squeezed her arm lightly. "They're welcome to try," she said.

Their heels clacked against the parquet as they traversed the room to the table and chairs set up at the far end. Dean Rolfe was already present and stood for them.

"I apologize for the space," Rolfe said. "The provost's reception room is being prepped for a luncheon today, and my meeting room just won't hold us all."

"It's lovely. All we need is a string quartet." Ursula's sense of humor charmed the dean, whose face lit as he hastened to Ursula's place to hold her chair.

A butler in a crisp white coat offered them coffee, which Gen declined. She wanted to be alert, not shaky. Ursula, however, wrapped her elegant fingers around her cup and sipped with apparent rapture.

"That truly is delicious coffee," she said directly to the butler. He looked surprised, maybe that one of the white people in the room was speaking to him without barking out orders. "Could I trouble you for a splash more before you leave, Mr.—?"

"Just Harvey, ma'am."

"Thank you so much, Harvey."

Kathy Yost appeared next, carrying a steno pad and an armful of folders. Ursula had informed Gen there would be no recording device at this meeting. The secretary nodded toward her in recognition, then quickly set about passing a slim folder to each person at the table except Gen.

"My client needs a folder, too," Ursula noted.

Kathy's face blanched. Gen watched her counting the bodies at the table. "I was told to make four. You, the dean, the provost, and Mr. Burnside."

Ursula's lips tightened, but her tone remained calm and polite. "That is quite all right. I'm happy to share with Dr. Rider."

Five minutes, maybe six, passed in which Ursula exchanged chitchat with the dean about her trip from Lexington, the mild weather, the architecture of Old Main. "These old schools are like traveling back in time," Ursula remarked, without adding whether the effect was positive or negative. Having thumbed through the documents in her file folder, she passed it to Gen, who spotted Henry Thoms's name on the top document and closed the folder without looking any further.

Finally, the provost entered with another man. Ramsey introduced Arthur Burnside, the college counsel, then offered an extensive apology that called attention to itself—something about a report his office was rushing to finish for the college president.

He paired his regrets with a light touch to Gen's shoulder. His words echoed in her ears, a reminder that the recommendation to the president about her status would come from him.

"No problem at all," Ursula said. "We've been enjoying some wonderful coffee while the dean regaled us with the history of this building." She favored Provost Ramsey with one of her gracious smiles. "You're a fortunate man to work in a place with such a rich past."

He acknowledged the smile with a brisk nod before glancing at his watch, a flashy gold timepiece that demanded notice. "Sadly, I have to leave you good people in twenty, twenty-five minutes. Hopefully, we can wrap this up quickly."

Someone had lit a fire, and despite the room's size the air thickened. Beads of sweat trickled down Gen's torso to the waistband of her suit's skirt. She missed the provost's opening comments as she reached over to pour herself a glass of water from the silver pitcher positioned near her.

"... of course, a very difficult situation with conflicting views," the provost was saying. "We have the Tenure and Privilege Committee and the Faculty Senate that recommend reinstating Dr. Rider, and we have faculty who have provided strong statements in a similar vein. On the other side, we have a former faculty member who told her chairman that she and Dr. Rider did indeed kiss—"

"Dr. May's letter of resignation doesn't mention any such thing," Ursula pointed out.

Burnside rifled through the documents in his folder and lifted out a sheet of paper that Gen assumed was Juliet's resignation letter.

"Point taken," he said. "We're not relying on that anyway. Far more compelling are the statements from students who say they felt uncomfortable around Dr. Rider, and one student who recounts an incident where Dr. Rider fondled her . . . private parts." He poked his pen at a mimeographed sheet, and the rest of them leafed through their folders to find it.

The phrase made Gen lightheaded, and she clutched her glass

of water for support. Ursula inched her copy of Lee-Anne's interview toward Gen, and they scanned it together. The girl's "revised" testimony to the committee was far beyond anything she could have imagined her concocting. Gen's fingers left damp spots on the paper as she pushed it back toward Ursula.

Gen slid her reading glasses down her nose and cast her attention toward Burnside. The unblinking intensity of the counsel's stare almost made her avert her eyes—as if he wanted to hypnotize a confession out of her. She forced herself to hold his gaze until he himself broke the spell and looked away.

The provost continued, "The girl's parents have already withdrawn their daughter solely because of Dr. Rider's behavior, and there is some concern that others are prepared to follow suit."

"Yet," Ursula said, "you've shown us no proof that what the girl alleges ever took place. Or *if* it did, that it happened with Dr. Rider."

"How would anyone prove something like that?" the dean asked, more of Burnside than of Ursula.

"As Mr. Burnside is aware," Ursula said, "a court of law would dismiss this so-called evidence. Dr. Rider is prepared to present some other information that should help this proceeding."

Burnside frowned. "This is the first I've heard of your new information."

"And this is the first time we've seen the revised testimony from the student witness, so I guess that makes us even." Ursula leaned back in her chair. "Dr. Rider, would you like to take over?"

They'd planned for this moment, and if she'd been in a classroom setting, Gen would have easily assumed control. But in this grand hall, facing men convinced she was a danger to students, the ground she and Ursula had covered so carefully shuddered beneath her. The voice that came out of her belonged to the scared little girl she always urged her students to overcome. "This is . . . this is a bit delicate. I don't know—"

Ursula cut in with a tentative, "Shall I?"

Gen took another gulp of water, waving her lawyer off more abruptly than she intended. She stood and flattened her palms against the table for support. "Thank you, I'm fine," she began. "I'll come directly to the point. The student in question is lying. I know who she is because she asked to meet with me, and we don't need to continue concealing her name. I'm very familiar with Lee-Anne Blakeney."

She removed her glasses, wanting to see more clearly who among the blurry faces at the table showed surprise.

"But not because of this filthy thing she alleged about me. I have never crossed a line with any student, and the incident simply never happened, not on campus and not at my house. In fact, Lee-Anne has admitted to me that she lied."

Burnside guffawed. "Oh, please. You want us to believe a girl would make up a story that could actually damage *her* reputation."

Gen glanced toward Ursula, whose head bobbed to urge her on.

"Lee-Anne saw an opportunity to get out of some trouble," Gen continued. "She needed her parents to pull her out of school—" She stopped and took a deep breath. "She's pregnant."

The provost sat up straighter at that bit of news, and Burnside tapped his pen against his legal pad. "This is preposterous," the lawyer said. "I don't believe a word. Counselor, you should be ashamed to let your client spread idle gossip."

"My client got it from the girl herself," Ursula said, "and they had a witness."

"And who was *that*?"

"Dr. Ruby Woods," Ursula explained. "The highest-ranking female faculty member at Baines. You already interviewed her, Dean Rolfe, but she says she's happy to testify again."

The provost steepled his hands in front of his mouth before speaking. "Why would the girl have to concoct such an elaborate ruse for leaving school?"

"She panicked." Gen caught a glimpse of Juliet's ring, shimmering on her finger. "She needed to get away from campus, and that was the surest way she could see. The baby's father is a professor at Baines, her adviser, and she needed to stop what was going on. I—"

"Enough," the provost said, popping out of his chair. "Mrs. Werner, Dr. Rider, I don't know what game you're playing here."

Gen's lips tightened at the irony of his words, almost identical to what Henry Thoms had said when confronted about Lee-Anne.

"The professor is Henry Thoms," Gen said. "He's admitted a sexual relationship with Lee-Anne, although he claims it was consensual. That she started it. Lee-Anne remembers it differently." She paused to pace herself, as she and Ursula had discussed. "I'm sure Baines parents would love to read in the morning paper about the perils awaiting their daughters here from the male faculty."

The provost's face reddened. "I don't like threats."

"No more than I like being suspended, my name dragged through the mud, and my livelihood taken away when it was in fact another professor who molested a student and left her to face the consequences."

The provost's mouth twisted into a grimace. "*Molest* is a harsh word. These students are young women, not children. Some of them are, shall we say, flirtatious. Students have dalliances with the faculty all the time—the men, I mean—almost like a rite of passage. Do I approve? Of course not. Can I stop it?" He shrugged.

"Henry Thoms is up for J. Montgomery Cash Distinguished Professor," the dean added.

"There, you see," the provost said, as if the dean had proven something. He checked his watch again. Gen held her breath, waiting for him to end the meeting by firing her. Instead, he swatted his hand toward Burnside.

"Mr. Burnside will be in touch with you, Mrs. Werner, to discuss your terms. In the meantime, I would like your assurance that you won't discuss the matter with the press."

Ursula deferred to Gen, who nodded numbly. "Your terms" meant the plan had worked, or so it seemed. Distinguished professor candidate Henry Thoms might be as good as gone.

Ramsey exited quickly, with Kathy trailing behind him.

As the rest of them gathered up their folders to leave, Burnside said, "Well played, Mrs. Werner, Dr. Rider."

Gen escaped the meeting first. She waited for Ursula on the porch of Old Main, settling into one of the white rocking chairs lined up there. The melodic *crick-crack* of the chair worked like magic to slow her heartbeat.

Ursula emerged from Old Main a few minutes behind her, brandishing Burnside's business card. "Well, I'd say that went well," the lawyer said with a lavish grin. "Treat yourself to a cocktail tonight and draw up a list of what you're looking for. We can go over it tomorrow. Obviously you want your life back, and as soon as possible."

Your life back echoed in the empty quad. What would that life look like?

Chapter Forty-One

Gen

Gen clicked on the TV. She'd first tuned in to *To Tell the Truth* on Fenton's recommendation, and now watching had become habit, a perfect distraction. Four celebrity panelists made wry observations as they tried to guess which of three "challengers" was telling the truth about an occupation or life experience.

It turned out that Juliet loved the show, too, and before she left for Wilmington they had several times called each other to view it together. Juliet had watched it for years, and even had a favorite contestant—the scratchy-voiced Peggy Cass with her delightful Boston accent.

"Wouldn't it be a hoot if sometime they invited the person who wrote *Girls' Dormitory* to be a challenger?" Juliet had said. "I bet the author's a housewife in Peoria."

"Or a professor moonlighting," Gen said, and Juliet liked that hunch even better.

Some weeks the challengers were more interesting, like when Wilma Rudolph, the Negro runner, appeared. Even though Rudolph had won three gold medals at the 1960 Olympics, the white panel had no idea what she looked like.

This week the challengers were all white. The show's host read the affidavit for three women all claiming to be a cat breeder. The breeder's fluffy, medal-winning angora served as a prop but kept trying to jump out of the host's lap. Gen wondered if the cat would accidentally reveal the woman's identity and ruin the game.

When she heard the rat-a-tat at the door, her heart skipped. Juliet's beaming smile met hers in the doorframe, and Gen hugged her without considering which neighbors might see them. Then she drew Juliet inside and kissed her, warming her cold lips.

"You're just in time for round two," Gen said when they pried their lips apart. "A cat breeder."

"I prefer dogs, but cats it is."

She took Juliet's suitcase and helped her strip off her coat and scarf. "How was the bus? You know I would've driven to Richmond to get you. You must be hungry. I've got pot pies in the oven. Do you like beef? I wasn't sure."

"Take it easy, darling." Juliet took her face between her hands and surveyed it. "The bus was fine, and I liked having the chance to stop overnight with my cousin. And beef pot pie sounds divine."

The gentle action and words slowed Gen down. They sat side by side on the sofa, holding hands.

"Granny's ring looks right on you," Juliet commented, examining the hand entwined with hers. "I don't think I'll take it back."

"You'll have to stay close, then. You might need its magic powers."

The shrill oven timer interrupted their kiss, and Gen popped up to get their meal, which she set out on TV trays.

As they ate, their eyes wandered to the screen but neither paid attention to the cat breeder for long. After a few bites, Juliet addressed the obvious.

"So, tomorrow," she said. "How are you?"

"Nervous. Ursula seems confident, though." Gen sat back, her pot pie only partially eaten. "It isn't fair that I might get to keep my job and you lost yours."

Juliet waved her fork over her plate. "It had to be done," she said. "I couldn't keep quiet while you were raked over the coals."

"But you hurt yourself, and it didn't even help my case."

Juliet examined a forkful of pot pie, then set it back on her plate. Her brow creased. "It *did* help," she said. "It got rid of that business about kissing a student, didn't it? And as far as hurting myself?" She shrugged. "Looking back, I think I was ready to be done with all of it."

Gen searched Juliet's eyes for clues that she was holding something back, not being truthful, but she couldn't find any. She remembered that even before they became lovers, Juliet expressed dissatisfaction with academia and a willingness to try something different if she didn't get tenure.

"So, you'll try to teach in Wilmington?"

Juliet shook her head with force. "I'm just at my folks' to regroup until I find something totally new. I read Spanish and Italian, too, and my Russian's passable. A grad school friend gave me a lead on translation work." She paused, her eyes on her tray. "It'd mean another move."

Wilmington was already so far from Springboro—five or six hours by car and, without the inevitable delays, twelve hours with two transfers on the bus. "Where to?"

The question hung between them for a moment before Juliet sighed and answered, "New York."

Gen deflated. She had just settled into the idea of having a new relationship, and it was being ripped away. "Oh," she said, making swift calculations in her head—a longer trip than from Wilmington, although there might be train service.

"I know it's not ideal," Juliet said. "We wouldn't see each other very often. I'd totally understand if it wasn't something you wanted to do."

Juliet had worn her hair loose and as she dipped her head blond waves fell over her right cheek and eye like a mask. Gen brushed them behind her ear with a couple of strokes. She needed to see if Juliet was trying to tell her something—that she herself didn't see a way forward for them or, worse, that she didn't want one. Memories of Carolyn resurfaced, the way she'd sprung her move to Maryland on Gen with no warning. But now Gen didn't read duplicity in Juliet, just sadness.

"It might not even happen, you know."

Gen's next words were hard to get out, but she managed. "And if it does, you should absolutely snap it up. Sounds like a real opportunity."

Juliet's eyes brimmed over, and she refocused on her tray, repeatedly poking her fork into the pot pie. "You let go of me awfully fast," she said as she stabbed at the crust. "Thanks for telling me where I stand."

Gen reached over and gently stopped the pot pie massacre. "Juliet, you gave up everything to help me. What am I supposed to say? Give up more? Don't go?" She paused before adding the question she hadn't dared to ask. "Come back?"

Tears spilled onto Juliet's tray. "You know that's impossible. Even if you get your job back, they're going to watch you like a hawk."

Gen returned her hand to her lap and twisted Juliet's sapphire ring. "Obviously, you want your life back," Ursula had said, and Gen had agreed that regaining her position at Baines was of utmost importance in the negotiation. She wanted everything she deserved—her job, her reputation, her standing in the department, her dignity— that had been taken from her.

But even if she could regain her old life, that meant she'd continue to sacrifice privacy. Juliet was right: The administration was sure to watch her even more closely than before, waiting for her to fumble. Ursula had already warned her of the unlikelihood that Henry Thoms would be punished in any way. "They can't afford to look at any of the male faculty too closely."

The fabric of Gen's professional life had frayed, the threads loosening like in the old Persian carpet in her office, so worn in spots she could almost see the floorboards. Now, she coaxed Juliet's head onto her shoulder and they sat coiled together as the TV screen flickered.

In the lobby of the law firm, Ursula folded her arms in front of her and glanced from Gen to Juliet and back again.

"Dr. May, I assume," she said, extending a hand slowly toward Juliet. "I'll try not to keep Dr. Rider long, if you'd like to wait out here. I can have my secretary bring you some coffee—"

"Juliet's with me," Gen interrupted.

Ursula's lips stiffened, but she didn't demur. She led them back to her office, clicking the door behind them.

"It's not what we wanted," the attorney said when she was seated behind her desk. "They're worried that parents think women like you are waiting to prey on their daughters."

The phrase "women like you" jolted Gen. Ursula had never treated her like a freak, but now she appeared to view her differently because she was part of a couple.

The attorney jotted notes onto a legal pad, ripped off the top sheet, and handed it across the desk to Gen. "So the administration wants you to go away."

The college was offering to pay her to leave—two years' salary, paid monthly, and an expunging of the investigation's records, as long as she left town and didn't talk to the *Gazette*.

Gen's palms felt slick, and she passed the sheet to Juliet.

"Now they're not going to budge on your job," Ursula pointed out when Gen didn't respond. "What we *can* do—what I'd recommend—is threaten a defamation suit and try to get that figure up. Given there's no hard evidence and Lee-Anne Blakeney's willing to retract her testimony, we'd try to boost the offer to more years. But it could take time."

282

Gen threw a sideways glance at Juliet. Like Ursula, she was staring at her, waiting for a reaction. "You've got time," Juliet pointed out.

"If you can manage financially a while longer," Ursula added.

After three months without pay, cash was tight. She'd run through most of her savings paying Ursula, and the contributions from the female faculty covered rent but not much more. Both Ruby and Fenton had offered her small loans, but she hadn't accepted them yet. Another month or two and she'd be forced to move in with her parents in Charlotte—although she hadn't figured out what reason she'd give them for leaving her job.

Gen's stomach burned. If she said yes to either plan, it was like accepting that women could be ruined because of rumors, but the proven misconduct of men would be swept under the carpet. Henry Thoms would remain in his job without even a slap on the wrist; in fact, he'd likely be rewarded with an advance to Distinguished Professor.

But then, that wasn't news. Gen knew about inequality. She'd spent her career studying how Negroes fared in a white-majority society. Her experience at Baines didn't even approach what Negroes had endured, but the offer still stank.

An idea hit her, but she didn't voice it. Instead, after a long pause, Gen said, "I'll take the offer, but I want the money in a lump sum. I don't want to keep in touch with them for two years. I'll resign when I get a check, and I won't talk to the *Gazette*. They'll destroy any evidence that I was ever under investigation. And they'll give me an apology in writing."

Ursula shook her head slowly. "I doubt we'll get any apology. That's an admission."

"Doesn't hurt to put it out there."

Ursula advised her to think on it more, to sleep on the idea of a defamation suit, but Gen refused to consider it. "I'm done," she said.

Juliet was quiet as they left the firm and approached Gen's car. She surveyed the quaint street, the red-brick buildings from another era, as if she wanted to stay awhile.

"We could have lunch," Gen said, nodding across the street to a diner.

Juliet took a deep breath. "I don't want lunch," she said. "Why didn't you fight? Ursula wanted you to. *I* wanted you to. You gave them everything, even the part about talking to the press."

Gen unlocked the passenger door. "You know how you said you wanted something totally new? It turns out I do, too," she said. "And they only said I couldn't talk to the *Gazette*. Nobody reads that little rag anyway."

Juliet smiled, slid the keys from her hand, and relocked the door. "Let's get lunch."

Chapter Forty-Two

Lee-Anne

Lee-Anne's parents outlined her only option; it wasn't a choice. She would remain at home until May, covering her bulging stomach with big sweaters and smocks and staying out of the public eye. In her final trimester, her father would transport her to the Florence Crittenton Home in Brighton, Massachusetts, just outside of Boston. She would remain there until she delivered the baby, which she would give up for an adoption that the home arranged.

"A child needs two parents," her father said.

Her mother expanded on the plan, which they'd fleshed out in detail. "We'll tell everyone you're spending a year with your aunt in Boston, maybe dabbling in classes at Wellesley," she said. "It's only a partial lie, since Aunt Mabel's offered to be on your visitor list."

Lee-Anne wondered if one could "dabble" at a school as elite as Wellesley, but if *she* didn't know, maybe no one else would either.

The distance between Springboro and Boston both scared and thrilled her. She'd never been further from home than Atlanta or

DC, and that was back in high school. In her freshman year at Baines, she had approached her parents about spending junior year abroad in London. Susanna Carr was considering it, too, and they could travel together.

Her father swiftly burst her bubble. "You're in college to find yourself a Davis and Lee boy," he said.

Susanna had a cousin who'd been sent to a Crittenton home in Norfolk. Despite her being seven months pregnant, the staff put her to work scrubbing bathrooms. "Right out of Dickens or something," Susanna said. "Plus, she had to go by a fake name. Nobody knew anybody's real one, not even her friends."

After hearing this dismal information, Lee-Anne asked her mother why she couldn't move in with Aunt Mabel instead.

"Because you're a handful and she can't manage it," her mother said. "She's an old lady, and who knows what trouble you'd get into. I trusted you, Lee, but you went and broke my heart." This last sentence came out with a little sob.

Clearly, it didn't matter to her parents that she hadn't asked for trouble, that she'd never been past first base until Dr. Thoms took her to second, then third.

"We had the talk when you were twelve," her mother pointed out. "You've got no one to blame but yourself."

While packing for her trip, Lee-Anne found a beat-up paperback at the bottom of her nightgown drawer. She and Susanna had each bought a pulp novel in the Roanoke bus station one day when they played hooky. They had tittered over the titles—*Girls' Dormitory* and *Women's Barracks*. "Lezzie stuff," Susanna had said. The back covers hinted at what "lezzie" meant, but Lee-Anne wasn't completely sure of the subject matter until she read the novels herself.

What had happened to Dr. Rider's copy? Lee-Anne didn't remember how she'd come up with the idea of the pranks or even why, except that she felt a stab of jealousy every time she saw Margaret Sutter accompanying Dr. Rider to her office. The fake gifts seemed funny at the time. Susanna had laughed, too, even though she was nervous when they actually delivered the items.

Now, Lee-Anne rifled through the pages of *Women's Barracks*, stopping here and there to glance at pages she and Susanna had dog-eared and giggled over. Afterward, she sneaked it downstairs and buried it below food scraps in the garbage, where the housekeeper wouldn't find it.

Chapter Forty-Three

Ruby

Ruby called out for Darrell twice when she got home, but his name echoed in the stillness of the foyer. Had he mentioned something about a racquetball game with one of the boys? She made a hurried tour of the second floor to see if he had fallen asleep or worse—he'd had two heart scares that had hastened his retirement—but she realized she was alone in the house.

She sank onto the edge of their bed. Her body juddered, and she wrapped her arms across her chest to steady herself. Rage filled her body like a fiery cascade, starting in her throat and spilling down to her toes. She let out a low moan that crescendoed until she was screaming, trying to release the fire inside.

When she couldn't maintain the intensity of the scream anymore, when her throat ached with the effort, she found she was crying—and for herself, which seemed ridiculous on the face of it. If she tallied her blessings, which she rarely did, she'd been a lucky woman—finding Darrell, building a life together, enjoying a rich career, having sons who were making their way in the world and giving her grandchildren. Friends had weathered blows from children who flunked out of college, couldn't hold a job, or divorced after a year or two. So why did she feel so sorry for herself?

Fat tears dripped onto the front of her coat, which she had unbuttoned but not removed. In her protracted fit, she did not hear Darrell's light steps on the stairs and in the hall, and she jumped when he appeared in the bedroom doorframe.

"Rube?" He took a place next to her on the bed and slid an arm around her shoulders. Darrell was not a demonstrative man given to hugs or squeezes, and hearty handshakes with his sons were about as expressive as he got. Their intimate life, robust in the first decades of their marriage, had dwindled in their middle age to a peck on the lips before bed. Now as he pulled her in close, Ruby buried her head in his chest and remembered the comfort of physical contact.

Darrell fished in his pocket for the handkerchief he always kept there and handed it to her. Ruby blew her nose ferociously, like that might expel her pain. When she was done, she related Gen's settlement with the college in detail.

Darrell nodded as she spoke. "Well, it's probably the best she could have hoped for."

She waved her hands dramatically. "It isn't! Her lawyer wanted her to press on and file for defamation, but she's just throwing in the towel."

Darrell squinted at her, clearly puzzled. "Well, it hardly sounds like that. Gen put up quite a fight, didn't she?"

"But it's such a waste! It shouldn't have been like this. All that education and experience. All the years I spent nurturing her—just to lose her. And Juliet's gone, too. Is Frances safe? Fenton? Who's next? I might as well leave, too, retire early. They'd like that. They'll hire some young fella to replace me in a heartbeat, just watch."

The rant left drops of spittle on her lips. Her words sounded pathetic in her own ears, but she didn't care. She needed to unpack all her years at Baines, all the women who hadn't gotten tenure or been promoted, all the mediocre men who'd prospered and advanced.

Her husband leaned back as if to get a better view of her face. "Well, I understand the despair, sweetheart, I do. It's not a happy situation. And you know I'd like nothing better than for you to retire and me to whisk you off to the cabin." He paused for a breath, as if preparing to rest his case. "But right now, it's not about you, is it? Gen's the one who's lost so much, and she could use her good friend Ruby."

The rational attorney wasn't the Darrell whose company she craved right now. She wanted him to comfort her as she focused on her own pain.

"And when you think about it, what you've lost is your idea of Gen—not Gen herself."

She flinched, ready to demand an explanation for the perplexing statement, but he was already off the bed and leaving the room.

"I'm going to warm up the leftover stew," he called over his shoulder. "You come down when you're ready."

The February day was crisp and bright, the first sign of a spring thaw, although winter in southwestern Virginia would hang on for at least six weeks. Ruby looked forward to the drive at the same time she dreaded it—her last time with Gen before she left Springboro for good.

Much like Juliet's, Gen's resignation letter claimed she was leaving to take care of family matters, which Ruby assumed was a ruse. No one resigned in the middle of a semester. As it turned out, though, Gen told Ruby and Frances she intended to spend a few weeks at her parents' house in Charlotte while she planned her next steps.

"But the family part was an inside joke, too," Gen had admitted. "I wanted to get the last laugh." Frances smiled knowingly, but the humor was lost on Ruby.

"'Family' is a code word," Gen explained. "For gay people."

Ruby had blushed, although she wasn't sure why. It was just one more thing she didn't know about Gen, Juliet, Fenton, and likely others.

Now, with Ruby behind the wheel, Gen admired the Bel Air's pristine interior. "You know, I've never been in your car."

"Sure you have," Ruby objected.

"Nope. I would have remembered." She stroked the smooth upholstery that Darrell kept shiny and spotless.

"Well, I don't guess I've ever been in yours either," Ruby said after a pause. "And while we're confessing things . . . I've never been to Barrington."

"It's ten miles away! How is that even possible?"

"I never go anywhere, too busy with school and such. You know how it is."

Gen's face clouded, and she turned it briefly toward the passenger window.

"I'm sorry, Gen."

"Don't be. I'm looking forward to whatever it is I'm going to do." Her smile was faint. "I've talked to my grad school adviser. I've mentioned her to you before."

"Muriel . . . sorry, I've forgotten." Ruby's mouth tightened at the second faux pas she had to apologize for.

"Whitbread. She's working on some possibilities for me. In New York." She set the news down between them, and Ruby didn't pick it up. Her throat constricted, trapping what she wanted to say: *As far away as that! Please don't!*

Gen pointed out the window toward a bright red awning. "There, that's the place. You can park right in front."

When they stepped through the door of the quaint tea shop, Ruby felt lighter. "Oh, we're in an Edith Wharton novel!"

"I knew you would love it here," Gen said.

While they waited for their tea, Gen related how she had found the shop on one of her trips from Richmond and returned every chance she got. Sometimes, she said, she had met Carolyn there. "You remember her? You met that one time. My friend in Richmond?"

Ruby ran a hand over the crisp white tablecloth. Gen had talked about Carolyn over the years, but Ruby had never questioned their relationship. Now Gen was finally easing open the door, and Ruby wasn't sure how far into her privacy she wanted to go.

"We were actually more than friends. That was just the safest word."

291

Heat rushed to Ruby's cheeks, unwelcome, and she brushed a hand over them as if the action could take it away. "Like 'family.' You didn't—" Ruby stopped for a moment as the waitress delivered their order. "You couldn't trust me."

Gen sniffled. "I didn't want to lose your respect. Your love."

Ruby tried to pour tea into both their cups, but her hand trembled and she set the pot down again. "I wasn't a good friend to you. I seem to be saying I'm sorry a lot, but I am. Truly." Her voice splintered. "My dear, no matter where life takes you, you will always have my respect. And my love."

Chapter Forty-Four

Fenton

Gen's possessions were packed up in boxes, which now occupied most of the living room. Her furnishings had already been given away or sold.

The emptiness and disarray filled Fenton with sadness. He watched as his friend searched for two glasses. With all but one chair gone, they sat on the rug and toasted.

Fenton had a new adventure planned, too, but it wouldn't be as thrilling or as daunting as Gen's. He was only moving twelve miles away to Roanoke. It was no New York—hell, with its solitary gay bar, it wasn't even Richmond. But its size offered him breathing room, something Springboro lacked. And with Gen leaving soon for Charlotte and then probably New York, the sleepy college town held no attraction for him at all. It was just a place to make a living.

He'd continue scanning employment ads, for sure. But if he didn't find anything, well, he reasoned it was better to grow old in something that resembled a city. Maybe at Roanoke's one gay bar he'd find a guy like him, not too young, not married, and on the lookout for love.

"I so wish that for you," Gen said, as he related his hopes.

"Someone to watch over me," he sang, but his tenor voice shook with emotion.

"Now don't go all maudlin on me," she said. "We'll see each other again." After a couple of shots, they were both a little tipsy. He curled up next to her and rested his head on her leg. "And I plan to check on you regularly."

He sat up suddenly, almost spilling the remainder of his drink. From his shirt pocket he withdrew a check made out to Gen. Her mouth flopped open as she read the five-hundred-dollar amount once, then a second time.

"What is this, Fen?"

"A check. When you said you were going to check on me, I remembered it. Thank God I didn't drive off with it still in my pocket!"

"I can see it's a check, but what's it for?"

He shrugged, as if he gave her hundreds of dollars every day.

"I got a settlement. I'll be okay. Is this your granddad's railroad stock?"

"Doesn't matter."

"I can't take your inheritance." When Gen tried to hand it back, he stowed his hands behind his back. She slid it into his breast pocket, but Fenton dug it out immediately.

"You have hurt me to the quick," he said. "I try to give you something to remember me by, and—" He let go of the paper, and it fluttered into her lap.

Gen stared at it, then at him. "I don't know what to say."

"A 'thanks, old chap' would do."

"I don't say things like old chap."

"Yes, but I'd love to hear it from you just once."

She gave in to a smile. "Thanks, old chap."

His head down, he murmured something about leaving; he dreaded the actual moment of good-bye. But then Gen popped up from the floor, he assumed to fetch the bourbon bottle for a refill that would keep him for another round. Instead, though, she rifled through a folder lying on top of a closed box and removed a letter-sized envelope, addressed and stamped but not sealed. The front read *George Kilwin, Editor, The Roanoke Times*.

"Read it for me?" she asked. "Juliet approved, but these days she seems to think everything I do is gold."

He slipped the folded letter from its envelope. His vision blurred from the bourbon, but he managed to focus enough to read the single typed sheet. Cagily written, the missive named no one but hinted that at least one male professor was taking advantage of students at Baines and the administration had purposely ignored the matter. Written down, the story read salaciously, even though he was sure Gen didn't mean it that way. It took Fenton back to the pulp novels boys bought at the drugstore when he was a kid, where a busty girl in a bra served as the front cover illustration. The fact that the pictures had never tantalized him had been the first hint of his difference.

Fenton returned the letter to its sheath and handed it back to Gen. "I thought your deal came with a gag order."

"They said no *Gazette*."

"Sneaky." He scratched his chin. "I don't suppose the paper has a female reporter?"

"I called, but the *female* receptionist acted surprised by the question." Gen sighed as her hands gripped the letter, as if poised to rip it in half. "Hopeless, right?"

It was indeed a long shot for a Roanoke paper to care about one teacher and a pregnant student in another town. And the story was as old as time. Still, Fenton didn't want to discourage Gen, so he replied with a vague, "Maybe not, hon. Don't give up."

She set it aside on the carpet, saying she'd reserve the decision for when she was driving out of town. "Who knows? I might just toss it in the mail and let fate decide."

"What's past is prologue," he recited without hesitation, "what to come, in yours and my discharge."

When confusion clouded her face, he added, "*The Tempest*. I always have a line from Shakespeare handy."

When she smiled again, he memorized it.

❖ ❖ ❖

Fenton's car bulged with boxes, suitcases, and bags. His scanty furniture had already left town in a truck that morning, along with a few choice items from Gen's house—including her almost-new sofa bed and the phone bench he had helped her pick out and had admired for years.

"You sure you got everything?" his landlady asked, hands on her hips. She looked like a mother sending her boy off to first grade.

"If I forgot something, you keep it, Mrs. R.," he said with a wink. "You get inside now before you catch your death."

On the kitchen counter next to the keys, Fenton had left behind a couple of full matchbooks from Maroni's, a bar in Richmond that catered to guys like him. He imagined Mrs. Rash offering a match to a guest someday, completely unaware of what it signified. "Where did you get this?" the guest, who was savvier than Mrs. R., would ask in disbelief. And then his landlady would find out who had lived above her for years.

Or maybe she'd toss the matches into a junk drawer filled with twine and scissors and loose batteries and forget they existed. Her son would find them when she died and wonder aghast how his mother had come to have them.

The reverie went on and on, shooting a ripple of pleasure through Fenton. He gave the passenger door a satisfying slam.

Epilogue

May 1961

Juliet's letter directed her to take the A train to her apartment building in Greenwich Village, and every time Gen glanced at the instructions the Duke Ellington song played in her mind. She had traveled to cities like Chicago, Detroit, and Washington, DC, but never to New York, and the prospect of riding such an iconic subway line both thrilled and terrified her.

Once she disembarked in Penn Station and made her way through the vaulted concourse, the vastness of the city hit her like the fast-moving train she'd taken from Richmond. Although it wasn't in her budget, she tucked away the instructions about the subway and hailed a cab, hoping the driver wouldn't take her on a scenic route to West Twelfth Street.

She tried not to seem like too much of a rube, staring out the window open-mouthed at the buildings, the busy crowds, the crabapple trees in full bloom. Luckily for her, the driver turned out to be a polite young man who called her ma'am and volunteered to carry her suitcase to the front stoop of Juliet's apartment building.

The label on the buzzer read "Dr. J. May." Gen ran a finger over it before pressing the button.

Juliet's voice crackled through the speaker. "Who is it?"

"Dr. Rider to see Dr. May."

Gen had barely managed to lug her suitcase through the building's two massive oak doors when Juliet appeared, flying down the stairs from the second floor. Juliet enveloped her in a hug that pulled her off balance, and her warm breath tickled Gen's ear.

"You're early!" Juliet leaned out of the hug to examine her. "What did the esteemed Dr. Rider think of the New York subway?"

Gen's cheeks warmed. "Truth? I splurged on a taxi."

Juliet erupted in a hearty laugh. "First thing, we'll have to put you on a budget." She grasped Gen's hand, then held it out with a questioning look at the bare ring finger.

"Never fear," Gen said. "Packed away for safety."

"God, I'd like to ravish you right here, but I'll wait."

The grand tour of the apartment took less than a minute. Juliet's rooms at Cavendish House would have swallowed this space with room to spare. The kitchen accommodated only one person at a time, and the toilet was located in the hallway, separate from the sink and tub. Juliet's bedroom held a double bed, a tall dresser, and a nightstand, and her clothes hung from wooden pegs in the wall. "No closets in these old places," she explained.

She led Gen by the hand back into the front room. One window was partially obscured by the woven bars of a fire escape, but the other looked out onto a charming pocket of old New York ablaze with colorful tulips. "How lovely."

"A view of Abingdon Square is not to be sniffed at." Juliet coaxed her toward another doorway, separated from the rest of the apartment by a sheer curtain. "And here's the *pièce de résistance*," she said, throwing back the fabric. "*Your study, Mademoiselle Docteur.*"

The room was no more than a cell, even more cramped than her office at Baines. Juliet had outfitted it with a maple desk and chair, a three-shelf bookcase, and a dented green filing cabinet that someone else had likely discarded. The desk faced a tiny window that looked out onto the bricks of a neighboring building. On the desk she had set a Royal typewriter Gen recognized as Juliet's own and a cut-glass vase filled with daisies.

Without warning, Gen's bungalow in Springboro flashed into memory, with its spacious rooms and sprawling backyard, the homey study lined with bookshelves, the stocked liquor cabinet. A fierce shake of her head dispelled the image, bringing the kitchen window into view. This apartment might be cramped, but the life she'd left behind had smothered her.

Juliet must have misread Gen's momentary hesitation as disappointment because she added quickly, "We'll hang some of your pretty photographs and it will be better, I promise."

Gen drew her in for a kiss. "It couldn't *be* any better, Juliet. Thank you so much."

In truth, she might not even need a study. Muriel had helped her secure a private space at the New York Public Library. "Office sounds too grand. It's more of a carrel," her former mentor had hastened to explain. There she could complete her book on Mary White Ovington, the white woman who had cofounded the NAACP.

"This is a good neighborhood for people like us, too," Juliet said, still on the defense. "There's actually a bar over on Eighth Avenue for gay gals called the Sea Colony. I've been nervous to go alone, but we'll try it together."

"Do they have food?"

Juliet thought they only served drinks, so instead they headed a short two blocks away to the White Horse Tavern, which she said was a favorite hangout for writers and other bohemians. The scruffy façade needed a coat of paint, but the dark wooden interior welcomed Gen like a hug.

"That was Dylan Thomas's booth," Juliet said, expressing amazement when Gen admitted her ignorance about the Welsh poet. "Jeez. Even I know who Dylan Thomas is and I'm not a *writer*," she teased.

"I'm not a writer yet," Gen hastened to point out.

It was an identity she was just going to try on for size, she had told herself. Muriel's publisher had contracted with Gen for her book on Ovington. The tide was turning in the United States, the editor said, and he envisioned a series of biographies of white and Negro champions for civil rights. He tossed out the word *bestseller* like a promise.

Gen didn't trust that she could actually make a living from such work, but maybe she could write articles, too, or even teach a class. When she presented Frank Johnson with a hefty check for the NAACP chapter, he had offered her a contact at The New School, a college that apparently welcomed progressive thinkers and political outcasts as teachers.

"I busied myself on the train trying to come up with my pseudonym," Gen said when their wine and burgers arrived. "I've settled on L.V. Ryder, with a *y*. What do you think?"

"Where'd the *L* come from?"

"I can't say."

Juliet put down her burger. "You're blushing! You have a first name you're ashamed of? Were you named for Aunt Loretta or Lavinia?"

"Worse. Great Aunt Lula."

"I love it! I'm about to live in sin with Dr. Lula Virginia Rider." Juliet fiddled with one of her French fries. "Well, L.V. does suggest a scholar. But Gen, I love the name Virginia."

Gen struggled for the words to explain. It was more than a desire for a new beginning, and she wasn't afraid of being haunted by her past at Baines. Ursula had more than earned her fee by making sure the college scrubbed Gen's record squeaky clean.

"I feel protective of her," Gen said after a considered pause. When Juliet scrunched her forehead in confusion, Gen added, "Of Gen Rider. She deserves a chance to be herself."

A smile lit Juliet's face, and they tapped wineglasses. "To Gen."

"To Gen," she echoed.

Acknowledgments

In 1952, Martha Deane, a respected full professor at UCLA, was suspended without pay after a neighbor reported to the dean that he had seen her kissing another woman through the window of her home. Female faculty banded together to help support her financially during a lengthy hearing process. Eventually, Deane settled with the university and left teaching. The administration buried her case deep in its records, but a historian unearthed it by accident fifty years later while writing about the Cold War loyalty oath on the UCLA campus.

Testimony took its inspiration from Deane's story, although I transported my novel to another location and year. Deane's experience resonated with me for two reasons. On the negative side, it underscored how the insidious nature of homophobia has repeatedly ruined people's lives. On the positive side, Deane's story spoke to the power of the support networks that queer people and women create.

Cases similar to Deane's are plentiful. During the 1950s and early 1960s, many queer teachers lost their jobs in a wave of right-wing fanaticism. From 1955 to

1965, for example, legislators in Florida systematically purged gay faculty, students, and staff from that state's colleges and universities. In the 1960s, esteemed literature professor and scholar Newton Arvin lost his position at Smith College.

I wrote and revised this novel during a new flood of anti-LGBTQ sentiment, wanting to give a human face to the individuals who experienced the chilling effects of antigay activism. Happily, as I was revising in June 2020, the U.S. Supreme Court delivered its historic ruling in *Bostock v. Clayton County*, stating that anti-LGBTQ discrimination in employment violates Title VII of the Civil Rights Act of 1964.

I'm indebted to numerous research sources. The article that sparked this novel was "The Case of Martha Deane: Sexuality and Power at Cold War UCLA," by Kathleen Weiler, but also invaluable was *The Scarlet Professor: Newton Arvin: A Literary Life Shattered by Scandal*, by Barry Werth. Other helpful books and articles included: *Communists and Perverts Under the Palms*, by Stacy Braukman; *The Deviant's War*, by Eric Cervini; *Cures: A Gay Man's Odyssey*, by Martin Duberman; "Doing the Public's Business: Florida's Purge of Gay and Lesbian Teachers, 1959–1964," by Karen Graves; *The Lavender Scare*, by David K. Johnson; "Homophobia in Mississippi, 1958" by Jonathan Ned Katz on OutHistory.org; and *My Butch Career*, by Esther Newton.

This project was supported by the North Carolina Arts Council, a division of the Department of Natural and Cultural Resources, with funding from the National Endowment for the Arts. Time is a gift to a writer, and the fellowship allowed me time away from teaching to make this novel what I wanted it to be.

For reading partial or complete drafts of *Testimony* at various stages, I thank writer-friends Selene dePackh, Debra Efird, Paul Reali, Rachel Stein, and Lucy Turner; and especially my wife, Katie Hogan— my alpha reader and most cherished writing buddy.

As always, big thanks and hugs to the women of Bywater Books, who have dedicated themselves to publishing lesbian literature. The community and I owe you a debt of gratitude for bringing these stories to light.

About the Author

Paula Martinac is the author of a book of short stories and six novels. Her debut novel, *Out of Time,* won the Lambda Literary Award for Lesbian Fiction (Seal Press, 1990; e-book Bywater, 2012). Her novel-in-stories, *The Ada Decades* (Bywater, 2017), was shortlisted for the 2017 Ferro-Grumley Award for LGBTQ Fiction, the Foreword Indie Award for LGBT Fiction, and the Golden Crown Literary Society Goldie Award for Historical Fiction, and her novel *Clio Rising* (Bywater, 2019) received the Gold Medal for Best Regional Fiction (Northeast) from the 2020 Independent Book Publishers Awards. She has also published three nonfiction books on LGBT themes, including *The Queerest Places: A Guide to Gay and Lesbian Historic Sites.* In 2019, she received both a Creative Writing Fellowship from the Arts & Science Council of Charlotte/Mecklenburg County and a Literature Fellowship from the North Carolina Arts Council. She is a lecturer in the creative writing program at UNC Charlotte.

Read more at paulamartinac.com.

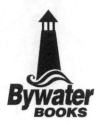

At Bywater Books we love good books about lesbians just like you do, and we're committed to bringing the best of contemporary lesbian writing to our avid readers. Our editorial team is dedicated to finding and developing outstanding writers who create books you won't want to put down.

For more information about Bywater Books and the annual Bywater Prize for Fiction, please visit our website.

www.bywaterbooks.com

CPSIA information can be obtained
at www.ICGtesting.com
Printed in the USA
JSHW031502071220
10048JS00003B/14